Bite Me

BETH BOLDEN

Chapter One

The crash woke Miles up, the sharp metallic clang of stainless steel against the deeper, resonating thud of the wood floor.

Almost certain dents in his favorite copper pot—*check.*

Scratches in the hardwood floor their landlord would definitely freak about—*check.*

Bruises his roommates would inevitably punish him for? Still in question, though if Xander's exaggerated howl of pain was any indication, Miles Costa thought those were inevitable.

"Goddamn it, Miles," Xander exclaimed loudly, as Miles dragged his head up from where it had landed in a slump of exhaustion only a few hours before on his marble pastry slab. If he was a betting man, he'd definitely bet that the fine grain of the marble was imprinted on his cheek.

He probably shouldn't have fallen asleep in the kitchen after filming the video, and he definitely shouldn't have piled those pans in such a precarious pile to dry after washing them. Inspiration had struck midway through the dinner service last night, and he'd been in too much of a rush to work out the intricacies of the recipe in his head to care much about the consequences of yet another late-night/early-morning filming marathon.

"At least I washed the pans out?" Through his tired squint, Miles could just make out Xander's disgruntled expression. He was annoyed, not pissed off, which boded well for Miles. He was also pretty sure that Xander had a few crumbs clinging to his chin, which meant that he'd already sampled some of last night's experiments.

Having eaten one over the sink just past 4 a.m., Miles knew just how fantastic those tarts were. Xander's forgiveness was no longer an uncertainty, but an inevitability.

"Good, huh?" Miles asked with a grin. After culinary school, working in many good kitchens, before finally moving to the *great* kitchen at Terroir, and then ending up with three chefs as roommates, he knew all about the culinary ego. Sure, he had one, but constantly crowing about how talented he was got exhausting. He normally preferred the food to do the talking for him—but in this case, distracting Xander from the fact that he'd used the kitchen until 4 a.m. *again*, was way more important.

"You film these too?" Xander asked ruefully. He reached for another tart, not even trying to be subtle.

Miles remembered when they'd first met, and Xander, all that ego barely restrained, had looked down his nose at pastry. He'd claimed to not even like sweets, but now he was chowing down on Miles' tarts like there weren't about a hundred more packed away in neatly stacked Tupperware.

It was particularly sweet to convert someone who didn't appreciate his craft, just like he enjoyed bringing the skill of his craft to the masses. Even the masses who didn't necessarily appreciate it, but watched his videos anyway.

"Of course I did."

Xander might have been converted to liking Miles' tarts, but Miles knew he probably wasn't ever going to understand why he filmed himself making them, and posted them to social media. For Xander, it felt too much like a magician giving away his secrets for free.

Xander might want the cultured and erudite to enjoy his food, but he didn't want to teach them how to make it.

He shook his head. "You're wasting your time," he said.

Miles was tired. It couldn't be any later than 8 a.m.—because that was when Xander took his run every day—and that meant he'd gotten only a handful of hours of sleep on a marble slab that wasn't quite the same as his feather pillow. He had a fierce crick in his neck, and he had to be at work in two hours for prep.

Which was why he nicked the tart from Xander's fingers, and popped the remains in his own mouth. "But it's my time," Miles said, and made a shooing motion. "Now go jog like a good boy."

Xander made a face, shrugged, and then turned away, shutting the door behind him a little louder than normal. Miles might be worried things would be weird between them, but they worked fourteen-hour days at one of the most exacting restaurants in the world, and after going through Chef's bullshit each shift, nothing ever seemed weird for long.

Miles bent down and started gathering his pots. Yes, there was definitely a dent in his favorite copper sugar pan. Damnit. He'd just got the sink filled with soapy water so he could wash them again when his other roommate wandered in.

Wyatt was rubbing the sleep out of his eyes, but they lit up when they saw the Tupperware containers. "You filmed last night?" he asked, popping the lid off. "Oh, these are pretty. Raspberry and strawberry?"

Wyatt's nose was legendary. He could sometimes tell the separate ingredients in a dish just from the aroma, and always by taste. Sometimes Miles enjoyed trying to stump him, but today, he just nodded, then turned back to his sink full of pots.

"Delicious," Wyatt pronounced through a mouthful of pastry cream and flaky tart shell. "I never would have dreamt of doing just raspberry and strawberry. Mixed berry is so middle-class housewife. But you elevated it."

Since he had his back to his roommate, Wyatt couldn't see Miles roll his eyes. Every chef he knew believed they were as high class as the restaurant they worked with. He would be the first to tell anybody that Terroir was special, because it was. Chef Bastian Aquino had built something one of a kind deep in the heart of the Napa Valley, and then maintained it—which, Miles knew, was most of the struggle. But most of the chefs he knew also came from decidedly low or middle-class origins. And they wanted to forget them as quickly as possible.

But Miles had lots of good memories of his childhood, and the dreaded "mixed berry" had shown up lots of times in bundt cakes and muffins and as far as he was concerned, it was a classic. He'd just used a little of the technique he'd spent so many years perfecting to make it even better.

"Wish we could get marionberries here," Miles said, because he wasn't going to tell Wyatt, who was one of his best friends, that he was full of shit. He'd already antagonized Xander this morning, and he tried to only piss off one of his roommates per day.

"Chef could," Wyatt said. Miles rolled his eyes again. Chef could get *anything*, because he was Bastian Aquino, and a god of American cuisine. Pans washed, he started drying them one at a time, because he wasn't letting them air dry in a precarious pile again. His precious copper sugar pot might not survive another tumble.

"At the farmer's market," Miles clarified, which Wyatt must have known he meant. Chef was only vaguely aware of Miles' "little internet experiment," as his boss had termed it, and as far as Miles was concerned, it was going to stay that way. He wasn't going to go around name-dropping Bastian Aquino to get some marionberries.

Wyatt might, but then Wyatt was a fucking idiot.

"They're good just as they are," Wyatt said complacently, which as far as Miles was concerned was Wyatt's biggest drawback as a chef. He rested on his laurels. He made the vision in his head, and if it matched, declared it done and perfect.

Miles knew his own personal drawback was that no recipe was ever truly done. The tarts *would* be better with a single marionberry resting on the glossy surface of the pink pastry cream. They'd not only look better, they'd taste better too.

Putting the last pan away, Miles turned back to Wyatt. "I'm going in at eleven. What about you?"

"Just got a text. Bunch of artichokes came in. Lots of prep today. So I'm going in early." Wyatt flashed him a carefree smile that belied the fact that he'd be spending approximately the next sixteen hours at the restaurant, deep in the bowels of the kitchen. "But your tarts were a great start. Breakfast of champions."

"You're welcome," Miles said, wiping his hands on a towel.

"Go get some sleep. You look like the walking dead. And not that hot one with the bow and arrows either."

Miles didn't look in the mirror when he walked back to his room, but he considered it for a brief moment. He probably did look like hell, nothing like that admittedly very hot man from *The Walking Dead*. He *should* go take another catnap, but he wanted to get the tart video posted before his shift started.

He spent the next two hours editing his footage, and without even watching it all the way through, posted it to his page, *Pastry by Miles*. He took a lightning-quick shower, jumped on his bike, and was walking through the back door to the kitchens at Terroir right on time for his prep shift to start.

Part of the beauty of posting a video before a shift began was that there was no time to check hits or views or comments or anything at all. He was deep in prep, waist-high in white chocolate lemon mousse pyramids when René, the head pastry chef, stopped in front of his station.

René was sort of a dick, but almost all the chefs that reached his level were, so Miles mostly didn't hold it against him.

"Did you put the rosemary in the cream while it steeped?" René asked, like Miles hadn't been making these all summer. Terroir was considered one of the best restaurants in the world, and René wasn't a terrible innovator—it wasn't like they were making hot fudge lava cake or anything—but sometimes his desserts were a little obvious. Miles had also discovered the hard way that René wasn't a huge fan of anyone having an idea other than him. If this wasn't Terroir and the best job anyone at his level could hope to have, Miles would have left long ago, but here he still was, fielding René's stupid questions and creating white chocolate lemon mousse pyramids.

And it should have been thyme, not rosemary, as far as he was concerned. But nobody had ever asked Miles and that wasn't about to change.

"Yes, Chef," Miles answered respectfully, but didn't glance up from his work.

"Good," René said, and then lingered in front of his station, which made Miles nervous. René lingering didn't usually mean good things; it usually meant a great deal of unexpected work, and Miles was already tired.

"Your new video," René said, and Miles couldn't help but tense. René knew about the videos but he'd never imagined René might watch one.

He'd had to tell René, and René's boss, Chef Aquino, what he was doing with *Pastry by Miles*, because he figured it was better to beg permission now than to be fired later. Chef Aquino hadn't cared, because it wasn't about him, and René had only insisted that the desserts he created be Miles' ideas and Miles' ideas alone.

That was perfectly fine by him, because the site had originally been created because he'd been creatively stymied at work, so he had zero intention of ever posting a white chocolate lemon mousse pyramid to *Pastry by Miles*.

"Yes, Chef?" Miles said, glancing up when René didn't spit it out right away. His dark beady eyes seemed to grow even beadier. Or maybe Miles had just been up three quarters of the night baking. It was hard to say exactly.

"It was good." René's voice was gruff, like he could barely bring himself to say anything positive. "An innovative concept."

So much of his job was biting his tongue, and Miles kept right on biting it. "Thank you."

"I might mention to Chef Aquino that we could use it as a special next weekend."

Miles had to tamp down his excitement so it wouldn't show. It wouldn't be a surprise to see Chef taking some poor *sous* apart for not cooking the scallops to perfection, but celebrating in the Terroir kitchen? Out of the question.

"That would be good," Miles said, and because he was too tired not to, took a risk. "I didn't even realize you watched the videos, sir."

René had turned to move on, but looked back at Miles' question. "I don't," he said. "Chef Aquino recommended I watch it. Apparently he really enjoyed it. He said he was seeing it all over his Twitter feed."

Miles couldn't hold back his smile at that. He might not enjoy the reign of Chef René but he very much respected Chef Aquino. And all over Chef's Twitter feed? He knew his videos were popular, but he'd never heard of them spreading that quickly before. He wished he could put his pastry bag down and look at his phone, but he still had a good hour left and these pyramids needed to chill before the dinner service started.

He'd check his phone on his break.

When he finally finished the white chocolate lemon mousse pyramids, and they were nestled in the blast chiller, the crick in his neck was much worse than it had been that morning. Trying to stretch it out, he detoured into the tiny locker room next to the dishwashers. Grabbing his phone out of his locker, he was floored by how many notifications he had—and he'd anticipated having a ton.

Chef Aquino hearing about his video and seeing it on his timeline had been a pretty good hint that his video had gone viral. The avalanche of notifications he was trying to sort through proved it.

After fifteen minutes, Miles felt overwhelmed and for the first time ever, he was relieved his break was over. It felt like he'd barely touched the growing mountain of comments and shares and likes.

He couldn't put his finger on why the sudden flash of white hot popularity bothered him, but as he was dusting the mousse pyramids with edible gold, it hit him.

Pastry by Miles had never been about becoming popular. It had been an expression of his creative side that had been stifled at Terroir—a necessary outlet that he paid attention to in fits and starts. He didn't post videos weekly, or even regularly, but he must have hit a nerve because each video he posted seemed to exponentially increase his social media reach.

It was, Miles decided, a serendipitous symptom of something he enjoyed doing. He'd still record the videos if nobody but his little sister watched them.

"Costa," a voice bellowed across the kitchen. Miles glanced up and tensed. It was Xander, his short brown hair covered by a bandana festooned with chili peppers, and he had his phone in his hand.

"What do you want?" he asked shortly, and far more quietly than Xander. It was just like Xander to believe that even in another chef's kitchen—even in *Chef Aquino's* kitchen—he could do whatever the fuck he wanted.

Sometimes Xander pushed his buttons, and all Miles wanted to do was push them back. But Miles always remembered he was a roommate and a friend, and even worse a co-worker, before he punched Xander in the face.

"You didn't tell me you were famous," he said, coming to stand over by the tray of pyramids. Miles set his brush on the lid of the gold dust with a steady hand.

"I'm not famous," Miles said, even though the notifications blowing up his phone might argue otherwise.

"I don't know," Xander said skeptically, "when my aunt in New Jersey texts me to say she thinks our kitchen is a pit, I sorta feel like you are."

Miles stared at his friend. "You don't have an aunt in New Jersey."

"But I *could*," Xander said blithely.

"You're an asshole," Miles said, scowling as he picked his brush back up. "Now go away, I have to finish these. Don't you have about a thousand artichokes to break down?"

"Roughly two thousand," Xander announced cheerfully.

Miles shook his head in disbelief. Not at the artichokes—that didn't surprise him at all because Chef Aquino was a famous perfectionist and a closet sadist—but at how happy Xander seemed to be about them.

"Did you have sex?" Miles demanded quietly. "Is that what this obnoxious cheerfulness is about?"

Xander just laughed. "You look tired. You should get some sleep, Costa." He sauntered away without ever answering Miles' question.

"You shouldn't let him get to you," Kian said. Kian was Miles' third roommate—Napa was insanely expensive and the only way Miles could afford a halfway decent kitchen with halfway decent light was to split the rent four ways.

"Easy for you to say," Miles retorted.

"I had a tart. Actually two," Kian confessed. "They were awesome."

Miles had a soft spot for Kian. He reminded him a lot of his little sister, Gina. Except that Kian was male and tough as nails because he was the bottom of the food chain in Terroir's kitchen. Miles had no idea how Kian even survived the diabolical tasks Chef Aquino put on his plate. Miles usually thought women were usually way tougher than men, but what Kian put up with put Gina to shame regularly. And Gina was a freshman in college.

"Thank you," Miles acknowledged. Kian was way more respectful than Xander, and had kept his distance so Miles could pick his brush up and get back to his careful, artful dusting of the pyramids. Chef René might not make crazily innovative desserts, but he was a stickler for presentation. Every single one of his desserts was a work of art.

"Xander's just jealous, you know. He has a secret, desperate yearning to be famous."

"It's not so secret," Miles said darkly. "In fact, it's hard to miss."

Kian burst out laughing. "True."

"You're too nice to him."

"I'm too nice to everyone," Kian said, which was also true. "I'll leave you alone to your geometric wonders."

When Miles finally finished the dinner service, he had gold dust under his fingernails and a shit ton of sleepy grit in his eyes. He tossed his bike into the back of Kian's little hatchback, and barely remembered his head hitting the pillow.

⁕ ⁕ ⁕

His phone blared shrilly, interrupting Miles' deep dreamless sleep.

His hand shot out of the covers and grabbed what he thought might be the shape of his phone. Not bothering to look at the screen, he blindly pressed the answer button.

"What," he barked. It better not be Xander, waking him up to go for a jog. Or Kian, trying to be cute and failing.

"You're famous!" his little sister Gina sang into the speaker, sounding even brighter than she normally did.

Miles groaned and fell back to his pillow. "What time is it?"

"I waited until nine, at least," Gina said. "I've got a class in five, I just wanted to tell you that you're famous, in case you missed it somehow."

"You'd be surprised," Miles told her wryly, because he'd pulled an extra-long shift and then fallen asleep. He hadn't exactly had time in the last twenty-four hours to wrap his head around his sudden, inexplicable fame.

"What class?" he asked before she could tell him the breadth of what he'd neglected by choosing sleep. He didn't get a lot of time to talk to Gina since she'd started at Cal in the fall, and he'd missed their chats.

"Philosophy 101," Gina said, and he could hear her eye roll.

"Not enjoying it?" he asked. He'd chosen to go to culinary school instead of college, and it had absolutely been the right choice for him, but he was thrilled at the brave step Gina was taking. She was one of his favorite people—smart and funny and bright as the sun—and she was the first of his family to go to college. He couldn't think of anyone better suited to fight for what she deserved.

"Oh, it's plenty dumb at points," Gina said. "Like whether we're actually not here, but figments of someone's imagination. Of *course* we're actually here. It's just . . ."

Miles heard her pause, and he was still wiping the sleepy cobwebs from his brain so it took him a long second to catch up to why she was hesitating. "What is it?" he finally asked. "What happened?" He was still, and would always be, a big brother.

"There's this guy," she said, frustration evident in her voice. "He argues with *everything* I say. I'm not sure he even agrees with what he's saying, but it doesn't seem to matter."

"He sounds like an ass." What he sounded like was a guy with a crush on Miles' baby sister, and no idea how to go about getting her attention like an adult. Miles wanted to punch him in the face.

"He definitely is," Gina said, and though she didn't say it, Miles could hear the hesitation in her tone. She didn't think he was an ass at all. And just like that, Miles realized that she probably wouldn't be his baby sister for much longer. At least not in her mind. She was eighteen and in college and discovering the world.

"I've got to go," Gina continued, "but don't think I didn't notice you changed the subject. We still need to talk about *you*, big bro."

"Someday," Miles said.

"Sooner rather than later," Gina insisted.

After she hung up, Miles hesitated before unlocking his phone again. Did he even want to look? When he finally did, he grimaced. If the avalanche of notifications yesterday had been daunting, the pile this morning was insurmountable.

He wasn't sure if it was a good or a bad thing that René had told him he wouldn't need to be in until four today.

He debated whether he wanted coffee or not—not a real debate, more like whether Miles wanted to pull on pants and stumble into the kitchen—and he'd just about made up his mind that coffee was required if he was going to slog through his phone when there was a knock on the door.

Miles pushed his hair back and grabbed a pair of loose sweats on the floor by the bed. Pulling them on, he opened the door to Kian's way too bright smile.

It was hard to scowl at all that cheerfulness, but Miles was a pro and managed it just fine.

"I brought you coffee," Kian said, extending a cup filled to the brim. "Two sugars, dark as sludge."

Miles eyed his roommate suspiciously. "Why are you being so nice to me?"

"I'm always nice." This was partly true. Kian was definitely the nicest of his roommates. Xander and Wyatt could be assholes on a good day. But Kian had a sort of apprehensive puppy dog thing going on this morning, and Miles was naturally suspicious, but he wasn't usually wrong.

"Have you looked at your phone?" Kian asked, sounding way too much like Gina for Miles' peace of mind. If Kian hadn't emphatically expressed his preference for the male sex, Miles might have thought about introducing them.

"Sort of."

Kian shot him a frank look. "Take a closer look," was all he said. "Last I saw, Martha Stewart retweeted it, and then Snoop Dogg picked it up too."

Miles' jaw dropped open. "Snoop Dogg retweeted my video?"

"I mean, have you even watched that cooking show he hosts with Martha?" Kian rambled, as Miles clumsily unlocked his phone after three tries and sat down on the bed, coffee abandoned to the bedside table as he scrolled through some of his notifications.

"I don't get it," Miles finally said, looking up and realizing that Kian was still expectantly standing in the doorway. "Most viral stuff has a good hook. This was a video of me . . . baking tarts."

"But you've never showed yourself as much as you did in this one," Kian pointed out. "And, honestly, you looked pretty cute and intense, hair falling in your face, and I think at one point you might've had some raspberry puree smeared across your cheek."

Miles stared at his friend.

"You did watch it before you posted it, didn't you?" Kian asked awkwardly. He was so young—okay, not that much younger than Miles, but in your twenties, sometimes three years felt like an eternity—and sort of naïve. Very naïve, depending on the moment.

"Technically yes." Miles thought back to the morning two days ago when he'd gotten approximately three hours of sleep on a marble slab and decided he might not have been entirely coherent enough to do the editing justice. "But I was a little tired at the time. I probably thought the raspberry puree gave me a sort of rakish charm."

"It totally did," Kian said, very loyally. Kian was much nicer than Xander. Since Xander had yet to give him shit over the puree that must mean he hadn't seen it yet. Miles hoped that state continued for a long time, though considering the way the video was spreading, he probably wouldn't get that lucky.

"So I looked . . . funny?" Miles asked, unable to keep the desperation out of his tone.

"No, no," Kian corrected quickly. "You just look really intense and cute and driven. It's a good video, and people like it for the right reasons, I promise. Plus, the tarts look delicious—and they tasted even better, by the way."

"Okay." Miles took a deep breath. "Is it totally weird if I didn't want this to happen?"

Kian's gaze grew sympathetic. "Uh, no. It's a lot of scrutiny. I'm not sure Chef Aquino will like it, if I'm being totally honest."

That was something Miles had not even considered. Chef Aquino was notoriously driven by his gigantic ego. Where Terroir was concerned, he didn't like anybody else stealing the spotlight. Especially a lowly pastry assistant.

"He seemed okay with it two days ago," Miles said.

"Miles," Kian said, "*Snoop Dogg* retweeted it. He's probably not okay with it now."

Miles had difficulty wrapping his head around Chef Aquino even knowing who Snoop Dogg was, never mind caring what he thought of the video, but Kian was almost always right when it came to Chef Aquino. Chef had handpicked Kian from his culinary school's graduating class and had taken him on as a special assistant. From what Miles could figure out, that mostly meant that Kian got to bear the brunt of their overbearing boss. But no matter how many times Chef yelled at Kian, or generally embarrassed him in front of the rest of the staff, Kian still worshipped him.

Personally, Miles thought there might be a little more than hero worship going on there, but he wasn't going to open that bag of worms anytime soon. If Kian was smart, he'd get over it and move on. If Kian wasn't smart, he'd eventually get chewed up and spit out by their illustrious leader. Miles liked Kian a lot, and hoped the kid could keep his head on straight.

"Well, I'll find out tonight," Miles said. "I don't have to go in 'til four though." He already knew what he'd be doing the rest of the day, and even though he knew he should be celebrating his success, all he felt was a mild dread. He hadn't set out to become popular or famous, and he wasn't sure how this video would ultimately impact his fairly simple life. A life he liked *because* it was simple.

"Drink your coffee," Kian ordered. "I'll see you tonight."

⁂

Miles slunk into the staff entrance at Terroir at fifteen minutes to four. He'd drunk three cups of Kian's excellent coffee, almost fully cleared out his notifications, and had even had a little time to start wrapping his head around what had just happened to him.

With a decent night's sleep and some high-quality caffeine in him, Miles found he could actually enjoy the really positive comments to the video. Especially flattering, though bordering on creepy in some moments, were the many people who seemed to want to pick him up. Men and women both, and Miles realized that he'd never outright stated on his *Pastry by Miles* page that he was gay. Oh well, it wasn't like he was taking anybody up on any of the offers—even the ones that seemed particularly attractive. And there had been more than a few of those.

His only real concern remained Chef Aquino's developing reaction to the video's unexpected success. Kian hadn't texted him any red alerts during the afternoon, so Miles could only pray that Chef Aquino was still okay with it. He was even harboring a secret hope that the popularity of the video had only made Chef more determined to feature the tart as a special dessert.

"Costa," Chef René barked out as he caught sight of him slinking into the break room to put his bag in his locker.

"Yes, Chef?" Miles asked.

"There's someone to see you," he said.

"Chef Aquino?" Miles began to sweat a little under his whites.

Chef René shook his head. "No, someone else. They're on the terrace, waiting for you."

Miles definitely was sweating now. Was he going to be fired? He'd done good work here—nothing innovative, because Chef René wasn't that kind of chef—but he'd created solid and consistent product. He'd never even explicitly stated in his videos that he worked at Terroir, though a few commenters had voiced their suspicions that he did when he'd mentioned working at a famous restaurant. He'd never confirmed anything, but even though there were a lot of top-notch restaurants in Napa, there was only one with Michelin stars, and that was Terroir.

He walked through the empty restaurant, the tables already sparkling with glassware and silver, out the side door, and onto the terrace. Terroir overlooked some of the vineyards Napa was famous for, and the terrace was one of the most prized dining areas in California—probably in the whole United States. Trellised ivy and grapevines wound around the brick stonework of the building, and even though the terrace was technically outside, every inch was swept and pristine. Miles thought Chef Aquino probably even frightened the bugs away.

There was a man on the end of the terrace, sampling a cheese platter, with a glass of sparkling wine at his elbow. He had dark hair, shaved close, and a broad set of muscular shoulders that his white t-shirt only seemed to emphasize. He looked up with dark, intense eyes as Miles approached.

"You're Reed Ryan," Miles said, before the man could introduce himself. He couldn't believe he hadn't recognized him the second he'd spotted him. Xander worshipped the man something fierce, both for his incredible culinary expertise and also because he was seriously hot. Miles had teased Xander more times than he could count about hanging a poster of Reed Ryan above his bed, and now he was here, in the flesh.

Xander was going to eat his heart out when he discovered who'd come to see Miles. He'd never mock *Pastry by Miles* ever again, not if the site drew Reed Ryan up to Napa.

"And you're Miles." Reed stood and offered a firm handshake. "Sit down." He gestured to the glass. "Would you like some wine?"

Miles shook his head. "Sorry, but no, I'm on shift tonight."

"Right, of course," Reed said. "Well, I'm sure you're wondering why I asked to meet with you."

Miles was desperately curious. He knew Reed had closed his famous Chicago restaurant, Garnet, and had disappeared for a year or so, reappearing on the West Coast, but he couldn't remember what it was that Reed was doing now. Xander had certainly told him, probably more than once, but Miles blocked out most of the shit Xander said.

"I didn't realize you'd opened another restaurant," Miles said as Reed selected a chunk of brie and popped it in his mouth.

"I haven't," Reed said. "I'm the culinary producer at *Five Points*." *Five Points* was a pop culture and sports website that had been recently branching into short culinary video series.

Miles now remembered all those rants Xander had subjected him to about Reed Ryan wasting all his talent by selling out.

"I've been following *Pastry by Miles* for awhile," Reed continued, picking through the thinly sliced meats on the tray. "I had always planned to offer you a show on our site, but after the last forty-eight hours, I decided I'd better get up here and do it before someone else beat me to the punch."

"A show on *Five Points*?" Miles asked skeptically. "You teach people how to bake bread out of melted ice cream. How to make edible cookie dough out of garbanzo beans. *Pastry by Miles* is a serious pastry blog."

Reed shot Miles a very frank look. "I'm a serious chef, Mr. Costa. I want to make a serious pastry show. Believe it or not, I have higher ambitions than teaching the masses how to make a dessert with three ingredients or less. I want to teach them what good pastry is about. And I think you're exactly the person to do that."

Garnet had been legendary in the food scene. It was hard to picture a Reed Ryan who didn't take the culinary arts very seriously. But there was still a whisper in the back of his head that *he'd* be selling out if he quit to film a show for *Five Points*. He wouldn't be able to come back to Terroir. His job wouldn't be waiting for him. Chef Aquino might let him go, but he'd never forgive Miles for moving on, no matter how unfair that might be.

"How much input would I have into the show?" Miles asked, because that, more than anything else, felt very important. He wasn't going to dumb down his ideas for anybody. He wasn't going to be subject to someone else's vision, not if he was going to take the drastic step of walking away from employment at one of the very best restaurants in the world.

"There would be a producer. Me, maybe, or someone else. Maybe my assistant, Evan. I've been looking to promote him, and your show would be a great fit. But the process at *Five Points* is collaborative." He paused. "I said it before, but I'll say it again. I don't have any intention of dumbing down your skill. I want something accessible, but elevated. I want you to teach people about pastry."

When he'd begun *Pastry by Miles*, he'd wanted to share his creativity with people who weren't just his roommates or his family. He'd wanted a way to express his vision without being constantly shut down.

"How long do I have to think about it?" Miles asked.

"As long as you need," Reed said. "But I guarantee there will be others after me. That video was *very* good, Mr. Costa. I'll email you over a sample contract with compensation attached. But everything is negotiable."

"Thanks, I'll be in touch," Miles said, getting to his feet, his fingers already itching to check his email and see how much Reed was offering him to leave Terroir and everything familiar. "I've got to get back to my prep."

If he detoured through the locker room and grabbed his phone to check his email, who could blame him? He scrolled through Reed's email, and his jaw dropped open at the offering bid for fifteen episodes. That was two years of salary at Terroir, plus there were stipulations about housing and moving costs *and* additional bonuses if certain benchmarks were met.

Miles hadn't gotten into the culinary business to make money—most chefs weren't rich, or even close to rich, but he couldn't deny the money held an attractive appeal.

Later, as he was making yet another tray of white chocolate lemon mousse pyramids, sure he would be dreaming about gold dust, Miles thought that the money paled in comparison to the opportunity to do whatever he wanted, whenever he wanted. True creative vision. And extra bonus: no more white chocolate lemon mousse pyramids and no more gold dust.

Miles biked home because it was a gorgeous night—clear and with just the right amount of briskness in the air. He couldn't deny he was avoiding his friends because they'd try to talk him out of leaving. Especially Xander, because he was the most vocal of the three—though Miles knew he'd get arguments from all of them. They knew just how special finding a place at Terroir was, and then how much work and determination and thick skin went into staying there.

It wouldn't be something they'd want him to give up lightly, but Miles realized as he pulled into the drive that he'd been ready to move on for awhile now. Why else feel compelled to start *Pastry by Miles* at all? He shouldn't need to come home from a long, exhausting shift, and bake. As far as Miles was concerned, he should feel creatively fulfilled at the position he'd worked his ass off for.

And if that wasn't the case anymore, then he *should* move on. It was the right thing to do, Miles knew as he walked into the house, but it didn't make telling his friends any easier.

It was after midnight, and they'd all worked at least ten hours today, but when he walked into the living room, Xander and Wyatt were on the couch, and Kian was sprawled next to them on the floor. The TV was tuned to ESPN, which meant Wyatt had picked the channel, but when Miles walked in, he muted it.

Three sets of eyes swiveled his direction.

"So Reed Ryan came to see you today?" Xander's statement was phrased like a question, but it wasn't like Miles could deny it. He slumped into an old chair and let his bag fall to the floor.

"Yeah, he came to see me."

Xander scooted to the edge of the couch. "And you didn't come get me?"

"It wasn't that kind of visit." Miles hesitated and then continued before Xander could reload again. "Listen, I know you're all going to try to talk me out of it, and that's fine, but I've made up my mind. I'm giving my two weeks tomorrow."

Xander and Wyatt didn't look all that surprised, but Kian turned to him, accusation and dismay all over his delicate features. "You're really going to quit? I heard people talking, saying you might, and that's why Reed Ryan came by, but I didn't believe them. I couldn't believe them. Miles, you've more than earned your place at Terroir."

"I've earned it yeah, but that doesn't mean I enjoy it."

Sacrilege, to admit he didn't love every chef's dream job, but it felt so good to finally say it out loud.

"You really mean that," Wyatt said with disbelief. "It's not the money? I was sure Ryan threw a bunch of money at you."

He had, and maybe Miles should have used that reason, instead of the truth. But the more he thought about it, the more he realized how all of them had been restricted and restrained by Chef Aquino's iron-clad rule. Every single one of them had their own point of view as a chef, and none of them were expressing it.

And Miles couldn't help but think that was just sad.

"Someday, you're going to understand, I promise," he said.

Kian made a scoffing noise, and Wyatt rolled his eyes.

Xander didn't say a word. Miles supposed he should be relieved that Xander was so unusually quiet, but Xander was also one of his best friends. And for someone who loved to argue and express all his opinions, all the time, the silence was sort of galling. Like Xander had already given up on him.

"I'm sorry I'm going to leave you without a fourth roommate," Miles added, though he knew with the addition of Kian eight months ago, it wouldn't be as tough of a financial hardship.

"We'll manage," Wyatt said.

Xander scowled, and Miles just couldn't help himself. "Aren't you even going to attempt to change my mind?" he asked, but Xander just shrugged.

"You've already made up your mind. It would be a waste of breath."

Miles got to his feet. "I'll see you guys tomorrow, I'm wiped." And he realized as he headed towards his room, that he'd only have two more weeks of waking up and heading into the restaurant with his friends.

On the flip side, he only had two more weeks of Chef René's insultingly obvious questions and only two more weeks of white chocolate lemon mousse pyramids.

Chapter Two

Evan Patterson was used to people not understanding his choices.

When his boss had asked if he wanted to come with him to a world-famous restaurant, renowned throughout the globe for its food and its ambiance, to meet with the man whose show he would very likely be producing, it had been easy to turn Reed down.

It wasn't Evan's pitch that was going to win Miles Costa over to the idea of leaving Terroir and everything he knew behind; it was Reed Ryan, culinary star a little dented and tarnished but still present and still glowing.

"But you'll be working with him. Closely. Don't you want to meet him?" Reed had protested. A token protest. He was great in the kitchen, and also great at inspiring his underlings to follow in his culinary footsteps, but he was not good at business.

Evan was and they both knew it, so it usually wasn't very tough to convince Reed that Evan was right.

"I've already met him," Evan had said, pointing to his laptop screen, where he'd been compiling a dossier on Miles Costa. A dossier he'd started long before the latest *Pastry by Miles'* video had gone viral.

So Reed had gone to Terroir alone, and come back to a signed contract, and an assistant who was now officially a producer.

Evan's decisions might be considered strange, but nobody could ever argue with the results.

Reed recognized this and also Evan's value, which was why Evan had already decided not to usurp his job eventually. Evan needed Reed to be the esteemed figurehead, and while everyone was oohing and aahing over Reed's big muscles and all his culinary credibility, Evan would be behind the scenes, getting shit done.

The promotion was nice though, and Evan had every intention of paying back his boss and mentor's faith in him in spades.

Evan straightened his shirt and glanced over at his boss, who was scribbling on a piece of paper as he leaned over the receptionist's desk. Either a new idea for *Dream Team*, the one show Reed still produced, or a new recipe he'd just thought of. Evan returned his attention to the elevator and its closed doors.

He'd planned very carefully for this day. Not just after he'd been hired for the *Five Points* internship. Not just after he'd gotten into college. Not just after he'd won valedictorian at high school graduation. He'd known much earlier than that, that one day he'd be someone people looked to, that people followed, at a place where he would be taken seriously.

All those other days had been stepping stones to *this* day.

The elevator doors dinged open, depositing Miles Costa on the carpet in front of him.

Evan had been studying Miles for months. He didn't vet dates with as much scrutiny as he had Miles Costa—which probably explained his extensive date-less drought—and he'd expected very little surprise facing him for the first time.

But Miles did surprise him. Shocked him, in fact. He walked up, his cloudy gray eyes lazy but direct, dark wavy hair a tousled mass on his head, and Evan felt a thrill in a place he'd never felt a thrill before.

He'd known Miles was handsome and very possibly charismatic. That was one of the reasons he'd been an easy selection as a candidate. He had a way of making you like him that was subtle and easy—you just slid right in.

Evan didn't just slide, he catapulted.

"Miles Costa," the man in front of him said, extending a hand. Evan was dimly aware of Reed straightening next to him, and shoving the paper in his pocket.

Evan reached out and shook Miles' hand, and even though his brain felt sluggish and distracted by the way Miles' lips tilted up in a half smirk, managed to introduce himself. "Evan Patterson."

Miles turned to Reed, and they shook hands "How badly did Aquino take it?" Reed asked. "I didn't hear from him so he must not have been too pissed off."

The gray eyes turned thoughtful, and Evan swore he saw a little worry there, but before he could look closer, it was gone. He told himself he was watching so carefully not because Miles was so carelessly handsome, but because he needed to figure out how Miles Costa ticked so he could control him.

"Actually," Miles said, "he wasn't all that pissed."

"Well, we're really happy you're at *Five Points*," Reed said warmly. He could be socially awkward; in fact, Evan was almost certain he had social anxiety, but he had gotten better at hiding it. Evan also recognized when Reed was passing the torch onto him, and he stepped in, smoothly, like they'd discussed it ahead of time even though they hadn't.

"I've been watching *Pastry by Miles* almost since the very beginning," Evan said. "What Reed told you is true. You've been on our radar for a long time."

"I'm honestly excited to be here. I'm looking forward to something different, if I'm being honest."

Reed chuckled. "Well, you and Evan will get along like a house on fire then. He's sort of unapologetically blunt."

It was true, but Reed didn't need to go around sharing all of Evan's secrets during the first five minutes. "Don't you have that meeting?" he asked his boss pointedly. He didn't have a meeting, but Evan knew how happy Reed would be to escape. This was the part of his job that he didn't love.

"Right, well, I just wanted to stop by and say welcome, and we're so happy you're here," Reed said. "Evan will take good care of you. He'll give you a tour and show you your office and the kitchen. And then you two can get started."

Evan was watching closely, or he might not have noticed Miles' eyes grow cloudier. "Thanks again," Miles said, voice normal. Except that Evan didn't think he'd imagined any of the undercurrents running through his new partner.

Miles might have a laid-back, casual attitude, but Evan had a feeling that there was a lot more to him than met the eye.

"Let's start with a tour," Evan said, trying to tone down his own tendency to take control over everything. "I'm sure you're dying to see the kitchen."

"Sounds good to me," Miles said casually.

They went on a quick tour of the office, with Evan pointing out the bathrooms, the conference rooms, Evan's cubicle, and Miles', which was right next door. Miles looked around the tiny box, setting his messenger bag on the small desk, and Evan wished he could read minds as his new partner took in his surroundings.

He was exceptionally difficult to read, and Evan didn't like that at all. He wanted to know where he stood. The unknown was a scary place, full of pitfalls and potential failure lingering at the end like a bad smell.

"We film at a local studio," Evan said as they entered the kitchens. "We don't have the room or the resources here, but eventually we're going to move to a bigger space and we'll build our own soundstage. So we do all our prep here, practicing and perfecting the rundown of the show, and then we film the final product at the other studio."

The other man glanced around the kitchen, his eyes not missing a thing, from the commercial appliances to the long stainless steel counters.

"I filmed with way less than this at my house," Miles pointed out. "Maybe we could figure out how to do small stuff here."

Evan didn't want to tell him that it had *looked* like Miles filmed in an unprofessional environment and that part of the bonus of signing with *Five Points* was his production value was going to undergo a significant upgrade.

"We'll see," was all Evan said. He wasn't willing to promise anything more. They had certain standards at *Five Points*, and Evan not only intended to honor them, but to exceed them. And there was no way they could do that with some sort of cobbled-together video they did in the test kitchens.

"Reed runs the kitchens, then?" Miles asked. Evan wasn't sure he liked the hopeful note in Miles' voice, because he needed Miles to like him—for purely professional reasons, of course. But even as he insisted on this to himself, Evan knew he was lying.

Evan could admit that complicated an already potentially complex business partnership, but Evan was also willing to be flexible if it meant great results. *Dream Team*, the first show *Five Points* had done, had paired together two people already in a relationship, and even though the culinary side was well-developed, the reason it had such a high viewership was how charming Landon Patton and Quentin Maxwell were together. *Dream Team* had changed Evan's perspective about what could and what could not work in a TV environment.

"Reed is the executive producer and the director of the test kitchens, yes," Evan said. "But the day-to-day manager of the kitchens is Lucy. If you need anything specific, you ask her."

Miles glanced over, and Evan's skin burned as his gaze skimmed over him. "And you?"

"Me?" Evan clarified, proud that his voice hadn't come out squeaking, like he'd regressed about a dozen years. He'd won his confidence with a shit ton of hard work, and he didn't like how this man dismantled it so easily. It was infuriating.

"Your position here," Miles clarified.

Evan was not thrilled. Reed was supposed to have covered all this stuff in the contract and Miles was already supposed to know they were going to be working together closely. Evan wasn't supposed to have to break it to him.

"I'm the producer of your show. We're going to be working together. A lot."

One discernible emotion out of the man in the last fifteen minutes, and it had to be dismay at being paired with Evan.

"Reed didn't tell me that you had any culinary experience. I assumed he'd be my producer, since he has the background," Miles said, and Evan realized that this was the laid-back Miles' way of issuing a protest at who he'd been stuck with.

Evan liked this even less. His ego was smarting more than he wanted to admit. He hadn't ever anticipated that *Miles Costa*, that super cute guy who he'd been admiring for months, would be such a jerk.

"I have a degree in business, with an emphasis on marketing," Evan said, trying to tamp down the testy edge to his voice. "I've also been Reed's assistant for almost two years. I know how to produce a successful program."

Miles shot him an almost pitying look. As if the degree Evan had worked his ass off for meant nothing. "But do you know anything about pastry?"

"You do," Evan said, and the confidence he felt was genuine. The way Miles had always been able to pare down difficult concepts and explain them was brilliant. He'd be great at showing a brand-new audience how to bake in a way they hadn't experienced before. And Evan's job was to provide that audience.

On paper, they were a great team, something that Reed had unhesitatingly stated more than once. But now that he and Miles were standing in front of each other, Evan wondered if he and Reed had made a miscalculation.

They hadn't taken into consideration that Miles Costa was quite possibly a culinary snob who didn't like to bother with anyone lacking his training.

"Right," Miles said, and he did not look convinced.

Evan decided this wasn't the right moment to argue the point and definitely not the right place—right in the middle of a kitchen that he'd never used, so he changed the subject. "Let's swing by IT and get your laptop."

Miles followed and didn't argue so Evan took that as a success, then dropped him at his cubicle, with a promise to get him for their first brainstorming session in a few hours. Reed had already promised to take Miles by the cafeteria for lunch. Maybe after spending time with a chef of Reed's culinary pedigree, and realizing how committed *Five Points* was to authenticity, Miles would soften his stance.

After a quick lunch at his desk, Evan went to the bathroom to wash his hands and to give himself a pep talk in the mirror.

Opportunities like this didn't come around very often and he wasn't going to blow the first big one he'd ever been handed. Once they started working on Miles' show, he would see that Evan was just as committed as he was to making it a success.

When he returned to his cubicle to grab his laptop and to fetch Miles next door, for a split second, Evan considered leaving behind all the prep work he'd been doing on his vision of *Pastry by Miles*.

But all of it was important market research and branding. Stuff that Miles needed, whether he admitted it or not. Stuff he needed to develop if he wanted to expand beyond retweets by Snoop Dogg.

It had been very clear to Evan from the beginning of *Pastry by Miles* that Miles had no real marketing plan, and that's all this was, Evan justified to himself. He took the folder and hated that Miles had made him question his motives.

"What did you think of the cafeteria?" Evan asked as they set up in one of the smaller meeting rooms.

Miles wrinkled his nose. "It was okay, I guess."

Reed had been appalled when he'd first started at *Five Points* at the quality of the building's cafeteria, and had worked hard to improve the quality of the food they served. They still didn't do everything well, but they'd made huge strides. It was definitely better than anything that Evan could cook himself. Which, he realized, was the root of Miles' problem.

It wasn't too hard to imagine him feeling regret at taking this step, but Evan still believed they could make this work. There was a reason they'd been spending months looking over the market and the talent available, and had ultimately decided on Miles.

"Maybe you can give Reed some suggestions on how to improve," Evan said. "He doesn't technically run the food service, but he has a lot of influence and works with them frequently."

"We already discussed it," Miles said, making it very clear that he was done discussing food-related topics with someone who apparently couldn't understand them. Which was going to make the next two hours rather difficult.

Evan decided there was no point in further procrastinating. "I thought it might be helpful to start with a rundown of the videos you've produced so far, and talk about where we might make improvements, and what facets we would want to keep for your show here."

But instead of just *agreeing*, Miles shoved his long, tapered fingers through dark curls and pinned Evan with an adversarial look that Evan knew he should have found entirely obnoxious, but instead of simply being annoying, it was intense and left Evan feeling unsettled. Exposed. Warmer than he liked.

"So you bring me in here," Miles said, "and claim you want me so badly to sign with you, so badly you send a famous chef to meet with me, then when I agree to film videos for you, you stick me with some marketing guru who doesn't know anything about pastry who wants to change everything." He leaned back and folded his arms. "Why?"

"I didn't send anyone," Evan argued. "Reed wanted to go, and he's the boss." Technically true, but also partly a lie.

"I think you'd understand, being some marketing expert, what false advertising is. You lured me here with Reed, because you knew I'd never agree to work with you."

"You're working with me because your show needs to improve its marketing angle and develop some polish," Evan said through gritted teeth. "And I bet you that's what Reed told you when you complained to him at lunch."

Miles gave a short bark of laughter. "Sort of, yeah." For the first time, Evan felt the spark of Miles' natural charm. He wanted to pettily reject it, but also bask in the novelty of experiencing it for the first time in person.

"You want things to be perfect, even if they're unstudied in their perfection," Evan said, pulling out every persuasive technique he'd learned in a lifetime of bad living situations. "I can help you with that."

Miles looked intrigued, but not completely convinced, but Evan decided that maybe it would be better to show, not tell. "For example," he said, pulling out his notes from the folder he'd brought in, "you experimented with a lot of different camera angles and placements while you were filming. Every episode is slightly different. I can help figure out the best one and then standardize it. Do you want to be featured on camera? Not on camera? Just a pair of hands?"

"Someone told me my last video was so successful because I was on it more," Miles said, but he sounded skeptical.

Evan did not want to say that *yes*, everyone ate up that footage because there was nothing hotter than a good-looking person absorbed in what they were creating. Even to the point of missing a smear of pink pastry cream across one chiseled cheekbone.

"There were definitely factors that helped that video spread virally," Evan said. "I can help you recreate them."

Miles nodded. It wasn't exactly enthusiastic, but it was something, and even Evan couldn't work with nothing.

"I didn't think I'd care if people watched my videos or not," Miles admitted, and Evan barely restrained from doing a little cheer at the man *finally* revealing something about what he was looking for from this partnership, "but I liked it. I started making them for me, and I never thought about my audience. But then a million people watched the last one, and that was pretty cool."

"Try five point six million," Evan said.

"Jesus, I had no idea it was that high."

Evan realized that Miles wasn't being humble; he really had no idea what his stats were like. And that did shed some light on how the man ticked. He lived for his work and his kitchen.

"So you didn't get into this for the fame, obviously," Evan said. "Why did you start?"

Evan couldn't believe it, but Miles flushed. It was almost very nearly a blush. Evan felt his own skin flame hotter in response. "I was bored at work, if you could believe it. And my sister missed seeing me bake. So I posted it for her, really." Miles went a tiny bit darker red and Evan had a sudden visceral image of their bare skin pressed together, damp and warm. "It sounds silly, doesn't it? I made the first video just for my sister, and five point six million people saw the last one."

"It's actually pretty incredible." Evan paused. "And it's just the beginning. The sky's the limit."

Miles leaned back in his chair, and actually laughed. "You really mean that."

Evan rolled his eyes. "Like Reed said, I'm annoyingly honest." What Evan didn't say was that he had believed in Miles almost as much as he'd always believed in himself. The belief was currently a little tarnished, but Evan knew it wouldn't take much encouragement from Miles to bring it—or his ill-advised crush—back to their former states.

Considering how far they'd gotten in the last five minutes by just *talking*, Evan decided they could do an analysis of the old videos later. He didn't want to do anything to remind Miles that he was the interloper trying to take over the show he'd started as a way of keeping in touch with his sister.

That was sort of cute, actually. It made Evan wish that he knew how to bake. Or that he'd had a sister.

Still, it was better to stick to non-confrontational topics. So Evan opened up his internet browser, and another food site that did videos. He turned the screen so Miles could see it. "I didn't know they let you watch those," Miles said wryly. "Aren't they the enemy?"

"It's research," Evan said. "We're going to go through these videos and you tell me everything you like and everything you don't."

Evan figured that criticizing other people would probably keep Miles from going rogue until Evan could figure out a new way to plan the next season of *Pastry by Miles*.

Evan came home to his apartment—and tried not to think of Miles doing the same, only a door away. The first thing he did was pour himself a very large glass of wine.

It was a Tuesday but he had fucking earned this wine. Miles had spent almost three hours complaining about everything in the other videos. He had lots to say, though most of his criticism was culinary-based. Even though the plan was to keep Miles focused on other people than Evan, every time Miles had pointed out something that was wrong, he'd pointedly glanced over at Evan. Basically, he was never going to let Evan forget that his degree was in business and not croissants.

Usually Evan did some form of work in the evenings, but tonight he didn't even want to open his laptop. Miles had managed to make Evan hate his job, albeit temporarily. He was a horrid pain in the ass, and Evan tried to dig up some motivation because he needed to find a way out of this situation. *Not out,* Evan corrected, *he wasn't going to give Miles what he wanted and quit.*

No, he needed to figure out a way to change up the dynamic. He needed something to put Miles at ease and stop feeling like he needed to fight Evan all the time. Goddamn it, he wanted Miles to like him. Even if it wasn't ever in *that* way.

Tomorrow had to be better than today was. If it was any worse, Evan was seriously considering smacking Miles for being an asshole. And that wouldn't make Miles like him any more than he already didn't.

Evan's stomach grumbled, and he opened his fridge with a glare and a wrench. Empty, of course. A half-empty bottle of orange juice and a sad glass jar of mustard adorned the shelves. He was going to need to order in, again. And then it hit him.

He needed to emphasize to Miles that they agreed food was at the center of his videos. What better way to convince him than to put him back in the kitchen?

Pizza first, Evan thought, *plan later.*

Miles poured himself a big glass of red wine and thought, *I fucking earned this.*

He'd known this transition would be hard. He'd spent his entire professional life in prestigious restaurant kitchens where marketing was something the PR reps dealt with so diners would pay hundreds of dollars to eat at the latest and greatest.

Miles had personally always thought of it as an inside joke, something completely made up. Not something real and concrete that people spent time and effort to research. He sort of figured that he'd design the show, film the episodes, and then the marketing guys would come in and figure out what sort of bullshit they needed to say about it so people would watch.

As it turned out, that was not how it worked at all. It turned out that Miles was going to be saddled with some marketing "expert" who would be criticizing and forcing him into changing everything along the way until the end result only vaguely resembled Miles' initial vision.

That Evan guy was determined, Miles thought as he opened his fridge and perused the contents. Cute, because Miles was human and he couldn't avoid thinking it more than once today, but annoyingly determined.

At lunch, Reed had said they'd had the fridge and pantry stocked for him. And it had definitely been done with a chef in mind, with a plethora of fresh ingredients. The apartment itself felt like an accidental luxury, all open rooms and this enormous kitchen with fantastic natural light.

Miles had planned on coming back to his apartment and getting so drunk that he wouldn't have to think about Evan's sour milk expression every time Miles opened his mouth—or his light-brown, crème brulee eyes that reminded Miles of one of his favorite desserts. But maybe there was something he could do to make tomorrow marginally better. Maybe there was a way he could win Evan over to his side. Maybe there was a way to control Evan other than disparaging him. It wouldn't be a hardship, Miles thought as he sipped the wine, he was good-looking, and Miles was attracted to him. Of course, Miles was attracted to most good-looking men, but with all the couples at *Five Points*, there wasn't a reason not to act on it. It wasn't against the rules. He could see Evan flustered and warm, bow tie dangling, sleeves rolled up, a slight dusting of flour on his cheek. Lips swollen pink from Miles' mouth.

It would be easy. Maybe too easy.

Miles turned back to the fridge. Maybe there was a way to kill two birds with one stone.

Chapter Three

"I've been looking for you." Miles looked up to see his brand-new partner standing in the doorway of his cubicle. He still wasn't sure how he felt about the cubicle thing, but he definitely knew how he felt about Evan. Miles gave himself a little mental pat on the back for the annoyed edge in Evan's voice, and then another that he was ignoring how incredible Evan's ass looked in those tight jeans.

Maybe it was petty or childish, but it felt so satisfying. Miles had spent time around lots of egotistical perfectionists over the years, but none of them had ever had a stick up their ass quite the same way Evan Patterson did.

"I've been sitting right here. For at least an hour." Miles leaned back, and enjoyed the way Evan's face struggled to find control. He also just plain enjoyed Evan's face, but those gorgeous brown eyes or his blond hair, and not even the slim, cute body he was showcasing in those skinny jeans could entice Miles to get in bed with someone so uptight.

Evan walked into the cubicle, and glanced down at Miles' laptop screen. He pointed to the left of the laptop, where a neon-green Post-it note read, "Join me in the kitchen when you get here," in what must be Evan's neat handwriting.

Miles thought Evan could have sold his handwriting to some font website, and hipsters would be falling all over themselves to buy it.

"Oh, I didn't see that." Miles didn't even attempt to sound convincing. Anyway, they both knew he was lying.

Evan crossed his arms and his eyes shot bullets. It made him look cuter—and also more terrifying, if you were into that sort of thing. Which Miles was not. *Definitely* not. He'd told himself last night that he wasn't going to try to seduce Evan to control him. This morning, the prospect looked a lot more appealing.

Or maybe that was just Evan.

"What have you even been doing?" Evan asked.

This was the opening Miles had been dying for. "I'm so glad you asked. I decided to do a little show-and-tell experiment."

Evan didn't look convinced. Or amused. Which only amused Miles further. He wasn't usually such an asshole, but he wasn't going to share control of *Pastry by Miles* with anyone, especially a marketing "expert" like Evan. He'd only had to be in his new partner's presence for approximately ten point two seconds to realize that Evan was the kind that didn't give up easily. Thus,

Miles' attitude shift to being as annoying as possible. Miles had a little sister; there was no way Evan could hold out against the pain and suffering Miles could bring him.

Miles clicked on the video he'd been working on. Evan watched it soundlessly and Miles watched Evan. Other than a very subtle eye twitch, Miles gave Evan a handful of points for reigning in his explosion of annoyance.

"You filmed an episode of your show in your apartment last night," Evan stated.

"I did," Miles said unrepentantly.

"You made a Twinkie."

"Actually," Miles drawled, "it's better known as a Ding Dong. And it's a *homemade* Ding Dong. I don't know if you've ever tried the store-bought version, but this one is infinitely better. Tastes a whole lot less like cardboard."

Evan's eye was twitching harder.

"A Ding Dong," he repeated in disbelief. "How did you even film this? With your phone?"

"Yep," Miles admitted happily. "Rigged it up on one of those fake house plants with some duct tape. Had to drop by Reed's office this morning and let him know how much I appreciated such a stocked apartment. And not just the fridge."

"That was me," Evan said. "I stocked your apartment." He was looking like he'd love to march right over and un-stock it. Miles was delighted. He'd anticipated how this might go, and it was going better than even his wildest expectations. He ignored the little voice that said just how much he'd enjoy it if Evan lost it and threw him down on the desk.

He also ignored what came next in that little fantasy.

Miles shot Evan his most charming smile, but the recipient did not look particularly charmed. "Oh, thank you. It all came in handy, as you can see."

"I can definitely see that." Evan leaned down, and Miles caught a whiff of his cologne. Something tart and lemony. It suited him. "Now you're going to come with me to the kitchen, and we're going to figure out how to work together. On a video of you doing something impressive that isn't a Ding Dong."

"You don't think that would be cute?" Miles asked, and thought maybe he'd taken it a step too far because the look on Evan's face was suddenly not playing around. Having worked in very tough kitchens and then Terroir, Miles was used to people wanting to kill him. He was not used to people who looked like they wanted to kill him slowly, and might enjoy it the whole time.

"Okay," Miles added. "I can do that." He was still chalking this up as a win because anything that put that look on a man's face was worth the effort it took to rig up a phone on a fake ficus tree.

"I know this isn't easy for either of us. But I do think we can make it work." Evan looked like he was repeating something out of a handbook for crisis management. The problem was that he also looked like he meant it. Miles tried to ignore the pulse of guilt at how he'd deliberately tried to rile him up, and mostly failed.

"If you say so," Miles said. He didn't see either of them relinquishing control to the other anytime soon, and he had a feeling that Evan liked compromise just as much as Miles did—basically, not at all.

"I do." Miles was pretty sure Evan was grinding his teeth together. Then he turned and stomped right out of the cubicle.

Miles was still seeing that look of Evan's—the one that promised a slow and painful death if he didn't follow—so he followed.

And if that also meant he got a nice back view of those skinny jeans, he wasn't exactly complaining.

They got to the kitchen, and Evan breezed right by the schedule board that he'd so helpfully and earnestly pointed out yesterday. Miles had just enough time to see that they definitely had not been scheduled for this morning.

Evan stopped by one of the long counters, and gave Miles a frank look that shouldn't have been hot, but apparently was. Miles didn't have a history of liking confrontational men, but either his tastes had changed, or he apparently found Evan a lot more attractive than he wanted to admit.

"Let's see what you can do," Evan said. He gestured around the kitchen. "This is your domain. Bake me something."

Miles ignored the jibe about what he could do. It wasn't worth his time to refute it, and they both knew it. Bastian

Aquino wouldn't tolerate someone in his kitchen who didn't know what he was doing.

"What do you like?"

"Me?" Evan sounded disbelieving, like he couldn't imagine Miles wanting to personally bake him something. And honestly, Miles didn't want to, but he had a feeling there was only so much he could fight back against this arrangement without making Reed pissed at him. Reed, while admittedly giving up Garnet, was still *Reed Ryan*. The thought of pissing him off was not a pleasant one.

"You said, and I quote, 'bake me something.' Tell me what you like."

Evan waved a hand. "Oh, I don't really like sweets. So, anything, I guess. It doesn't matter."

There was roaring in his ears as Miles tried to process this statement. "You . . . don't . . . like . . . sweets."

"Are you deaf *and* intractable?" Evan asked archly.

"No, I'm just trying not to . . . cry or something," Miles muttered. "You realize what I create isn't exactly the same as a bag of M&M's or bag of Oreo cookies."

"Of course I do."

Miles tried to keep his temper leashed. It wasn't easy, probably because it felt like Evan was pushing all his buttons, even the ones he liked having pushed. "Tell me what you might like if you liked sweets."

"Apparently once when I was four I ate a whole bag of Reese's peanut butter cups. I vomited them all up afterwards, but I did eat them." Evan didn't even act like this was a horrifying memory.

"Perfect," Miles said, the finished product already emerging in his mind. His recipes usually started with the end product, and worked backward. Each step was a way to achieve what he'd already conceived in his head.

Right now, he was imagining a fluffy deeply peanut butter-y cookie, dotted with the sharp bitterness of dark chocolate chunks.

Evan whipped out a pad and started writing. "What are you doing?" Miles demanded.

"Taking notes," Evan claimed. "This whole experiment is to figure out how you work. I already know how I work. The end goal is to try to mesh something together of the two."

Miles raised a dubious eyebrow. "You really think we can compromise?"

"Not really," Evan admitted. "But I've never given up, ever. I'm not about to start." He hesitated. "What are you doing now?"

"Standing here?"

Evan made a grumpy sound that shouldn't have been as cute as it was. "In your head, silly. What are you *thinking*?"

Miles had never talked about his process before. Everyone had a slightly different one, and nobody usually cared about the intricacies, as long as the end result was good. "I usually construct an idea of what I'm baking in my head first. Then work backwards to figure out the exact recipe steps."

Scribbling away in his notebook, Evan nodded. "What's the idea you're creating today?"

"Peanut butter cookie with dark chocolate chunks," Miles said.

"Now that wasn't so hard," Evan shot back with a sly, challenging look that Miles told himself he hated. He never lied to himself, but he knew he was now.

"Supplies?" Miles asked, changing the subject. He didn't want to trade flirty quips; he wanted to prove to Evan that there was no way they could figure out how to work together.

"What, you haven't already familiarized yourself with the kitchen layout and pantry?" Evan snarked right back. He definitely sounded bitter over Miles filming his own video.

Okay, he probably deserved that. Though baking that Ding Dong had been pretty damn satisfying—almost as satisfying as Evan's reaction to it—it was still on the tip of his tongue to apologize. Only the thought of leaving Terroir, moving to LA, and somehow losing control of *Pastry by Miles* in the process, kept him silent. Ignoring why his base instinct was yelling at him to treat Evan nicer, he trailed after the other man, who pointed out the tucked-away pantry and the big commercial fridges against the far wall.

Evan returned to his pad, scribbling with his eyes down as Miles methodically went through and picked out his ingredients. Setting everything on the counter and beginning to sort through so he could get his *mise en place* set up, he glanced over at his partner.

He knew Evan wasn't going to tell him and so there was no point in asking, but Miles found he couldn't help the question. "What are you writing?"

Evan didn't even glance up. "Terrible, dreadful things."

Miles rolled his eyes.

"I thought you'd already deigned this experiment a failure before it even began," Evan continued. "So why do you even care?"

"Maybe I want to know all the terrible, dreadful things."

Evan looked up and even across the room, his dark eyes felt piercing, right through all the skin and muscle and into his chest.

"First off, you spent probably four hours making homemade Ding Dongs. I'm not sure you deserve to know."

"Six," Miles said, and it was technically true, but it also did what he'd intended, which was to get Evan's attention away from that stupid notebook again.

"What?" Evan demanded. "You spent *six* hours on those stupid Ding Dongs?" He sounded even more affronted than he had when he'd first found out about them.

Miles shrugged. "I'm a perfectionist. I have to make a recipe more than once to get it right."

"How many times usually?"

"Last night? Four. Today? We'll just have to see."

"Well, you have the kitchen for three more hours today," Evan said unrepentantly. "So it's however many batches of cookies you can bake in that time."

"Only three?" Miles knew he was pouting. He was also painfully aware that they had bridged a snarky, sharped-edged back-and-forth that vaguely resembled flirting.

"It would have been four if you didn't waste an hour this morning not coming to the kitchen when I told you to."

Miles returned his focus to the mixing bowl in front of him. If he only had three hours, he needed to focus, and stop bantering with Evan. If that was even what they were doing. Maybe it wasn't bantering if it was one-sided. And Miles was sure it was one-sided. Evan didn't look like anything ever distracted him from work.

Especially someone Evan intended to control. He talked big about compromise, but Miles had a feeling that Evan had zero experience compromising. Probably as far as Evan was concerned, all compromise meant was that you'd conceded.

Miles wasn't great at it either, but even if he had been, he couldn't do it here. Not with *Pastry by Miles*. Not when he was taking such a risk in leaving the restaurant industry. If he failed here, he might not be able to get another plum job like the one he'd had at Terroir. And Miles knew he'd never get his job at Terroir back.

He wasn't even sure he wanted it back, if it came to that, but the phantom sting of potential failure made him turn away from the temptation Evan presented, and back to his mixing bowl.

Evan was a distraction, and almost certainly the enemy. Even worse, Miles was beginning to realize he might like him more than he hated him.

Miles was fascinating to watch as he worked. Evan was trying to spend more of his time scribbling down notes and ideas versus staring at the other man like a creeper, but it was hard because he totally had a thing for competent people. Watching Miles was like competence porn; he was so instinctual and confident, it was very hard to look away once you'd started.

He'd been trying to keep his questions to a minimum in order to give genius a chance to work uninterrupted. Evan might have been worried about Miles unconsciously changing his process because he was being observed, but there was an innate certainty in every movement he made. Besides, Evan thought darkly,

Miles had had zero compunction about demonstrating exactly what he thought of Evan's involvement in this project.

Rigging up a phone in a fake ficus. Evan didn't know what he could have said or done to make someone so desperate to prove themselves. What Miles didn't realize was that while Evan was committed to making a successful show that appealed to a wide range of audience members, he was also committed to producing a show that Miles could be proud of.

The problem, Evan thought, his eyes returning again to a pair of graceful hands as they cracked eggs, was they were both too determined to be in charge.

It was Evan's natural position, and while he wasn't sure it was Miles', Miles was clearly determined not to relinquish creative control.

Evan still believed they could find a compromise they could both be happy with; the problem lay with convincing Miles of that fact. And, considering what Miles had done when he thought he'd been backed into a corner, it was not going to be easy.

Evan didn't need easy—he'd been living the hard way for as long as he could remember—but easy still would have been nice. It also would have been nice if Miles had returned even an iota of the interest that Evan was trying to forget he felt. But clearly, Evan was alone there.

He usually didn't let himself feel regret, but if he had, he might have wallowed in it a very tiny bit. He might have also wondered what could have been if they'd met in a bar, or a coffee shop or even on Grindr, and *Pastry by Miles* hadn't been this big, looming, impossible thing between them.

Evan looked down and realized he'd doodled a heart in the margin of his notebook. He scribbled it out with such hard pen strokes, the paper tore. When he looked up, Miles was watching him, amusement tilting up the corner of his lips.

"You writing more terrible, dreadful things?" Miles asked.

Ha. If he only knew just how terrible they were. Evan shook his head. "Just an idea that wouldn't work out."

"Those are usually the best sort of ideas," Miles observed.

This was definitely not Evan's experience. Of course, he'd made a habit of always doing the stuff that people said was impossible. Go to school while working three jobs? Transition his part-time internship at *Five Points* into a full-time, paid position? Take care of himself and others when most guys his age were barely able to handle the former?

Unlike the saying, yeah, he'd definitely broken a sweat, but he'd still done it. But those were all things that he didn't share about himself. Especially not at work. Miles would find out that he was a former intern sooner or later—hopefully later, if Evan got lucky—but the rest was going to stay firmly locked away.

"Trust me, this one isn't," Evan said. Because getting Miles to be able to stand him professionally seemed like a tall enough order; to convince him to like him personally wasn't even under consideration.

Miles seemed to digest this as he poured vanilla from a bottle into the mixer. He wasn't measuring, and Evan couldn't help it. "You're not measuring anything," he asked. "How do we replicate the recipe if we don't know the proportions?"

"This is just a test batch. I'll adjust from here," Miles said. "Besides, I might not be measuring everything out, but I know how much I'm adding."

Of course he did. Evan knew odd things turned him on, but finding it hot that Miles was a human measuring cup was weird, even for him.

"Force of habit," Miles added, with a bashful, lopsided smile that would have made Evan's insides clench if he'd let them.

"Must come in pretty handy," Evan said.

"Yeah, at home, for sure. But at the restaurant, we measured everything. Had to follow every recipe to the letter."

"You didn't like that?" Evan was surprised; Miles struck him as a chef who didn't do wild experimentation.

"I hated it," Miles admitted. "I get that diners look for consistency, especially at a restaurant like Terroir, but it got really old. Sometimes I felt like I couldn't take a step out of place without having a ton of bricks come down on me."

"That's why you took this job," Evan said, realizing very quickly what had driven Miles to accept their offer. "You were bored."

"No," Miles corrected. "I was bored so I started *Pastry by Miles*. I was insane, that's why I took this job."

Evan couldn't dignify that with a response, but when he glanced up, he saw that Miles was actually smiling still. "Seriously?" Evan demanded.

"I made you a video of me baking a Ding Dong," Miles said, "do you really think insanity scares me off?"

"Obviously not."

"It's just like I said. Sometimes, the worst ideas are the best ones." Miles folded in the dark chocolate chunks he'd just been chopping off the big block. "Dark chocolate, as dark as I'm using, is probably going to be complete shit in this recipe, but I'm trying it anyway."

Evan's jaw dropped a little. "You think those aren't going to be good? Then why are you making them?" It seemed like a total waste of time and resources to bake something Miles didn't think was going to be good. But he'd done it anyway.

Clearly, this was part of the reason why they hadn't gotten along right away. They both had very different ideas of how to go about a project.

"Because I thought they might actually be brilliant, and I had to know. I made those strawberry raspberry tarts that everyone loved so much eight times before I was happy with them." He gave a careless shrug.

Evan realized that Miles really did not care how long something took before he declared it finished. In a terrible premonition, he could see blown budgets, billowing grocery bills, and an intractable chef whose perfectionism somehow eclipsed Evan's own.

It was not a pretty picture of the future. Even if Evan had been inclined to let Miles take over and control *Pastry by Miles*, he couldn't let it happen because Miles wasn't just fooling around in his own kitchen. There was a lot more on the line now, including, Evan thought with a mental shudder, *his* job.

"How long are they going to bake for?" Evan asked, eyeing the filling cookie sheet with trepidation. If these weren't outstanding, they were going to have to go through this process as many times as Miles wanted until he was satisfied.

"Ten minutes, give or take," Miles said.

Evan scribbled that number down, next to the list of ingredients Miles had used. Miles might be lackadaisical about measurements, but the point of this show was to make what he did accessible to the regular viewer. That meant recipes—proven, tested, *reliable* recipes—that accompanied each video.

"Did you just write that down?"

Evan glanced up at Miles' incredulous voice. "Of course I wrote it down. You might not be measuring, but we need to provide a recipe for the cookies to everyone who watches the video."

Miles wiped his hands deliberately on the towel he'd draped across his shoulder. Evan, in a moment of unbelievably weak hormones, thought it made him look like a romantically temperamental chef. *Delete the romantic part of that*, Evan thought to himself morosely, and braced himself for another round of, "I'm a big fancy chef and I know better than you do because I took a class on how to chop an onion."

"I didn't realize we were doing that," Miles said.

Evan couldn't help but explode. "Of course we're doing that," Evan ground out. "How do you think this site makes the money to pay you? Hits. And you get hits by directing people to the recipe and the site, where we sell ads that pay for all of this."

Miles rolled his eyes. "I'm not an idiot."

The problem was Evan had a temper. A temper that he'd spend a lifetime hiding and controlling and stuffing back into its little box, but a temper nonetheless. And Miles was the most tempting target for it that Evan had run across in a long time.

"Then don't behave like one," he snapped, all too aware that Miles' laid-back, infuriating, patronizing personality was breaking him, a little bit at a time.

Evan did not like being broken. He'd learned to assert control over himself because he didn't always have control over his environment, and Miles, with his annoyingly good looks and bullshit attitude, was taking him right back to a time Evan never wanted to revisit.

Miles didn't say a word, merely turned back towards the counter and began piling dishes into the sink. Evan returned to his notebook and scribbled out the line he'd written about compromise. There was going to be no compromise. He would prove to Miles, one day at a time, that he was the one who was in charge of this show, and it was Miles' job to develop the recipes in a reasonable timeframe, and then stand in front of the camera and charm the women of the world into attempting his recipes.

It would happen because Evan had never failed in his life and he wasn't about to start now. If that meant he had to become an asshole to meet Miles' asshole, and forever ditch the hope that something could have grown between them, so be it.

Miles ran some hot water over the dishes in the sink as the first batch of cookies baked, and then began to re-assemble the ingredients for a new batch. He hadn't tasted the first ones yet, because they weren't out of the oven, but he didn't need to. He'd never made a recipe that couldn't be further perfected.

And Evan could just pry his head out of that exasperatingly cute ass and get with the program.

Ever since marching the two of them into the kitchen, he'd been making noise about compromise, but Miles knew one thing for sure—Evan had never compromised in his life, and he wasn't about to start now. The sour-milk look on his face after Miles had confessed to redoing the strawberry raspberry tarts told him everything he needed to know. There was no way Evan was going to let him be true either to his vision or his training.

And sharing recipes! Miles didn't feel comfortable with that at all. The point of *Pastry by Miles* had never been to make the food accessible to anyone. It had been to express his point of view.

Having to dumb down his processes so the common person could follow along was not something that Miles was interested in doing.

The alarm on the oven beeped, and Miles sauntered off to take a look. The cookies were baking nicely, looking fluffy and full in the middles, and just browning around the outside. He opened the door, pressed on one lightly, and decided it could use another minute. He wanted a firm, cake-y cookie on the inside, but with crisp outer edges.

Miles didn't have to look over his shoulder to know that Evan was writing this all down. He could hear his pen scratching across the pages as if he was doing it right next to his ear. He put in another thirty seconds, just to fuck with him.

He fully expected Evan to loudly and emphatically inquire what good thirty seconds of oven time would accomplish (almost nothing) but his section of the kitchen remained quiet. Miles knew it wouldn't last.

Pulling the cookies out of the oven, he slid them across the counter, and went to grab a spatula and a cooling rack in the equipment pantry. Returning, he saw Evan had moved closer, bending over the pan, finger outstretched, as if he was going to duplicate Miles' movement from earlier.

"Don't touch those," Miles growled. "They're not cool yet."

"You touched them," Evan said, straightening, and looking him right in the eye. Always challenging. Miles wondered if he was even capable of anything else. He had a sudden, blinding idea that sex with him would be fantastic. All that drive and passion and certainness focused on him.

"Yeah, but I knew what I was doing. You don't." Miles acted casual, like he wasn't reeling from the idea of sex and Evan. Frankly, he probably would have thought of it before now, if they hadn't fought from almost the first moment. Miles knew he was attracted to Evan; it had only been a matter of time before he considered it.

"You've made that abundantly clear," Evan sniffed.

"Then don't touch if you don't know," Miles said, trying to keep his temper and rapidly failing.

Evan threw his hands up. "They're just cookies," he said.

"Yeah, and you've made it pretty damn obvious that I have a limited number of attempts to get them right. So," he said, his voice growing hard around the edges, "don't touch."

"For the record," Evan said, returning to his pad and pen, "you're an ass."

Miles knew he really wasn't. Except maybe he was being one now, just a tiny bit. And only because if he didn't assert firm boundaries now, he was going to lose the thing that mattered most to a professional chef: his reputation.

He shoved the spatula under a cookie and transported it to the cooling rack. He repeated this with the rest of the cookies, and then went back to the mixer. "You're making a new batch before you even taste these?" Evan asked incredulously.

Miles refused to even look up from what he was doing. Evan was just trying to get under his skin—trying and unfortunately succeeding.

"Actually," Evan continued, and there was the clear munching sound of a cookie being eaten, "these are actually pretty good."

Miles turned around, to see Evan's mouth full of chewed cookie. "I told you not to touch."

"You did," Evan said. "I'm terrible at rules. Sorry." He didn't sound apologetic at all.

Miles reached over, and grabbed a cookie himself, taking an experimental bite.

"I thought you didn't like sweets," he said.

"I don't," Evan said. "These don't exactly make me change my mind, but they're not bad."

They were more than "not bad," in Miles' expert opinion. They had good crumb, good texture, a solid amount of peanut butter taste, and the dark chocolate was an interesting juxtaposition with the richness of the batter. He made a note to add more salt next time, and to change to semi-sweet chocolate. It had been a decent first try, but he could make better cookies than this.

Chapter Four

"How do you think it's going?" Reed asked, leaning back in his desk chair, looking relaxed because he had no idea how it was actually going.

Evan had a feeling that if he had an inkling, his question wouldn't have been nearly so casual.

"Uh, it's . . . well . . . it could be going better." Evan believed one hundred percent in being truthful and straightforward in business, but he genuinely liked Reed and wanted Reed to not only appreciate his professional skills but to like him too. And the truth about how Miles felt about him and his ideas didn't reflect well on Evan at all.

"What happened?" Reed still didn't look worried. Evan didn't want to tell him he should be, but he really *should* be.

"We're still trying to come to an agreement about the direction of the show," Evan said with diplomacy.

Reed finally frowned, and sat up straighter in his chair. "The direction? I thought we talked about this."

"*We* did." Evan paused. "Miles is very committed to having complete creative control over the content of the show."

"And he does, right?" Reed asked.

Evan nodded. "I keep telling him that there's a very happy middle ground between the production and marketing and the vision he has, but he's not really interested in compromise. Of any kind."

"Do you want me to talk to him?" Reed asked, sounding very much like he did not want to moderate the discussion.

That might be the right way to proceed, but Evan didn't want to fix his problems with Miles by just dragging him in front of their boss and pointing at the part in his contract that said he retained creative control, but had relinquished production control to a *Five Points* representative.

Because that wouldn't really solve anything, and if Evan knew anything about this business, it would only lead to terrible shows that nobody ever wanted to watch.

He didn't just want to successfully produce *Pastry by Miles*—he wanted it to be a fucking smash.

"No. I want to try to fix this without forcing you to intervene."

"Okay, how about this," Reed said, and Evan was reminded that not only did he manage sixteen employees and sub-contractors at *Five Points,* but that he'd very successfully run a high-end restaurant with a full staff in Chicago. "What is Miles' point of view?"

Evan slumped back in his chair. "I'm a super special pastry chef who makes rainbows and orgasms but I won't tell you how to make them. You need to bow down to my superior ability; I'm not going to actually teach you. You just watch my videos to bask in my cute hair and dimples and imagine you could make pastries like I do."

Evan ignored that this attitude of Miles' was what had attracted him in the first place. Or that he'd wanted to be the one Miles gave rainbows and orgasms to.

Reed chuckled. "I hate to tell you that nearly every chef is like that, to some extent."

"Oh, and I forgot," Evan added. "You must also let me follow my beautiful chef muse, even if that means baking fifteen batches of cookies. When the first batch was plenty fine."

"I thought I smelled cookies," Reed said, then sighed. "I warned you this is how chefs are."

"You did. But I've worked with them before—you, and Quentin and even others. And nobody has ever been this stubborn and difficult."

"You've never worked with me in a kitchen before," Reed corrected warmly. "Trust me when I say that I'm probably way more difficult than Miles."

Evan was plenty loyal to his boss, but he was also a realist. "How would I convince you to compromise?"

"Tell me your vision for *Pastry by Miles*."

That was the easiest thing Reed had asked since he had sat down. Reed had seen him walking by the open door of his office and had waved him in to discuss the progress of their newest show. Evan had learned after working for Reed for over two years that he hated formal meetings and much preferred organic conversations.

Evan had been actively trying to avoid this organic conversation, but the only way to get to the break room was to walk by Reed's office.

"I want a great pastry chef who is willing and *wanting* to teach the housewives and teenagers and bored retirees how to bake with skill and conviction. I want clear, easy-to-follow recipes, paring down difficult concepts to easy steps. Miles should want to help people, not condescend to them."

Reed didn't say anything for a long moment. "Finding a compromise there is going to be tough, Evan."

Evan knew it. It was why he had spent the last two hours alternatively wanting to beat Miles' head and his own against a wall.

"But I think there's hope in even the most dire situation," Reed continued, which Evan thought was probably total bullshit. He was probably just hoping that they didn't kill each other in the next few months. Evan had read that leadership manual before. "But if you do need me to intervene, just say the word."

"I will," Evan said, getting up from his chair and feeling more frustrated than he had before sitting down. It was well and good to be able to accomplish the impossible on a regular basis because he put his head down and got shit done, but it would've been nice for Reed to acknowledge just how impossible of a task this was.

Unfortunately, the task began with convincing Miles to consider compromising his artistic vision. And Evan had no freaking idea how to do that.

Reed wished him luck again, and Evan stepped into the hallway and right into Mr. Artistic Vision himself, thunderclouds in his eyes.

"What the fuck do you think you were doing in there?" Miles demanded, in a hushed, angry whisper that was not nearly as effective as he probably thought it was. He sounded raw, almost betrayed. Which, as far as Evan was concerned, was a serious overreaction.

"None of your business," Evan said.

Miles gaped at him. "You really mean that, don't you? You really mean to make me some sort of pastry Julia Child Joan of Arc, don't you?"

Evan rolled his eyes. "The problem with eavesdropping is that you have no context for anything I said."

"Oh, no, I heard it all," Miles challenged. "I heard what you said about me. All about my insufferable ego. And then how you want to bring it down to earth. *Bury it.* That's never going to happen."

It had been a long day. Scratch that—it had been a long *two* days, and the blame for that could be laid directly at the feet of the man in front of him. Without Miles' ego, they could've already been working towards filming their first episode. Instead, Evan was trying to figure out a way to placate it all the damn time. All while not trying to fantasize about what he looked like bent over the kitchen counter.

"Listen," Evan said, grabbing Miles by the forearm and dragging him further down the hall towards the break room, which was certain to be empty at this hour in the early evening. When he reached the room, he dropped Miles' arm like it had stung him. Touching was bad. Touching would expose what he really wanted.

"Listen," he repeated. "I am sick of your bullshit. I'm trying to get something done here, and instead of you even trying to listen, you just keep pontificating about how fucking awesome you are. Get over your damn self."

"Me?" Miles retorted. He pushed a finger right against Evan's chest and pushed him back towards the soda machine. Caught off guard, Evan's back hit the machine and he couldn't escape before Miles crowded right in front of him.

This close, his eyes were definitely thunderclouds. It shouldn't have been sexy; it sort of was.

"Definitely you. You're ninety-nine point nine percent of the problem here," Evan argued.

"You walk around like the hottest thing in chinos, all spreadsheets and calculators and stupid bow ties," Miles muttered. "You don't know a *damn thing*. You don't even like dessert!"

"Not even yours," Evan retorted, which was only sort of true. He shouldn't, but he wanted to taste Miles' dessert more than ever.

Not just his desserts if he was being completely honest.

Miles' brows drew together like two dark slashes against his olive skin. "You're an asshole."

Evan found himself almost pinned and almost breathless. And only mostly because of the argument he was currently having. "It takes one to know one."

Evan could see that he was breathing hard, fists clenched together at his sides. Evan had never considered the possibility that Miles might punch him, because Miles worked in a kitchen, for god's sake, physical violence couldn't be up his alley, and yet, he seemed tempted to do it.

Evan got it. He'd been punched more than once growing up because he was an asshole. Or maybe because he was smarter than his parent of the week, or this month's brother.

"I'm not doing this with you," Miles finally spat out. "I'm not going to let you ruin me."

"Ditto," Evan said. And between the two of them, he was definitely convinced that he was the more determined of the two.

After all, look at what he'd forcibly put behind him. Nobody was more motivated than he was to do this job and to do it to everyone's satisfaction.

He had already come to terms with the knowledge he'd never be able to satisfy Miles. There was no point crying over that spilt milk.

Miles had at least three inches on him, and he leaned in, expression both intense and inscrutable. "Are you even going to tell me what you were doing in Reed's office? I heard you complaining about me."

Complaining? Evan hadn't even gotten started complaining. "At Reed's request, I was giving him a fair assessment of our situation."

"I'm not an egotistical prick!" Miles said hotly. Evan knew just how hot it was, because he could practically feel Miles' very firm thigh pushing against his own. He didn't know how they'd suddenly gotten so close, but he wasn't sure he could complain about it.

Not for the first time, Evan was surprised that his own weakness for someone who did *not* deserve it kept cropping up. He should have been pissed as hell that Miles was attempting to use his height to try to intimidate him. The only problem was it was more of a turn-on than anything else.

Evan wasn't usually this conflicted, and he hated it.

"Then stop acting like it," Evan said. "You've been acting like hot shit ever since you arrived. I don't care if I never went to culinary school, I'm not a moron. I know it sounds crazy, but we might even learn to like working together."

Miles' breath stopped short. They were so close, Evan could hear it, and feel the lack of it against his cheek. There was an awful, horrific pause of total silence, like Miles was contemplating how completely insane it was for them to ever like working together.

Or maybe he was figuring out that Evan had just let one of his closely held secrets slip. He'd wanted so fucking badly for them to be friends. To like working together. To maybe, in some faraway fantasy vision, find something even deeper.

Now Miles probably knew, and Miles was probably disgusted.

Of course, he didn't look disgusted. He was staring at Evan, at his mouth actually, and there wasn't a hint of disgust to be seen.

Evan tensed as Miles' hands slammed on the wall behind him, bracketing his head. And before Evan could demand to be released, Miles' mouth was on his.

It was probably the angriest kiss Evan had ever had. It was raw and anguished and bizarre. Miles' lips crushed against his, moving hotly, desperately, like he had to convince himself or maybe even both of them, that there was no way in hell they could ever get along.

But we're kissing, Evan thought helplessly.

It was nothing like Evan had imagined it would happen. Part of him wanted to slap Miles for doing it now, when they wanted to kill each other. Part of him wanted to melt into Miles, and show him just how much he'd wanted him from the very first moment of *Pastry by Miles*.

It was a problem.

Abruptly, it ended. Really, before it could even begin—or at least before it could begin being anything other than angry and intense. Miles' breath was coming hard now, in fast, furious little pants. His eyes were slanted to the side, like he couldn't even bear looking at Evan. Like maybe he *was* disgusted.

That thought pushed Evan over the limit and he tumbled right off the cliff. He set the heel of his hand against Miles' chest and shoved him, hard, pushing him away. "Get your shit together and start acting like a professional," Evan said.

Miles shook his head, blank confusion still written all over his face. His stupid, cute face. He turned and walked away, leaving Evan shook up and pissed off, his blood hot with no convenient outlet.

That wasn't the worst of the offenses he could lay at Miles' feet, but it sure as hell felt like the worst right now.

The accusation and his lips burned all the way to Napa.

Miles had stormed right out of the *Five Points* offices, and had caught a ride right to the rental car office, where he used some of his signing bonus to rent a car.

He spent the next six hours contemplating every way that he could make Evan pay for his words and trying to forget how Evan's mouth had felt under his. He didn't know how the kiss had even happened, only that it had happened and that his world felt rocked by it.

He hit the town limits right around eleven, and headed straight to Terroir, where, as he'd expected, employees were beginning to drift out the back door.

Wyatt and Xander walked out first, unsurprisingly, because Bastian Aquino could never bear for Kian to be one of the first out of the door.

Miles rolled down the car window and whistled. Xander's head turned his direction, and his jaw dropped.

"What are you doing here?" Xander asked, jogging over to the car. "Aren't you supposed to be Julia Child-ing in LA?"

"That's not a verb," Wyatt said, joining them. "Julia Child is a person, not an action."

"If you're Miles, it is," Xander said, and it wasn't surprising to hear that rough edge of disapproval in his friend's voice, but it hurt anyway.

He'd given up the camaraderie and Terroir for what exactly? Some uptight prick who wanted to make everyone a world-class pastry chef? Miles didn't know what he'd been thinking. To be frank, Miles still didn't know what the fuck he was thinking.

"So why are you even here?" Wyatt asked.

Miles forced himself to shrug casually. "Let's go home, open some wine, and I'll tell you about it."

But as the others piled into Miles' compact rental, he didn't even know how to begin telling them about it. *I thought I'd go to LA and run the town the moment I showed up? I thought I'd get to call all the shots, and now that I can't, I'm freaking out and pulling the ego card? I'm going around kissing my producer when he tells me to get my ego in check?*

What stung the most about Evan's accusations was that they weren't so far from the truth; they hit right in the tender, honest parts of himself. He was being a bratty unprofessional. He was panicking, and that explained some of it, but he was way out of his element and he didn't trust Evan enough to let him guide them in the right direction.

How could you trust someone who made you kiss them even when you didn't like them?

And how could Miles possibly trust him when all Evan wanted to do was teach every man, woman, and child how to make world-class desserts, *and* he didn't even like them?

There was an exclusivity that surrounded chefs like Miles and Wyatt and Xander, and sometimes even Kian. It was a cult that was cultivated by chefs like Bastian Aquino. And what it proclaimed, loud and clear, was that not everybody could join. You had to pass the tests. You had to prove yourself. You couldn't just turn on YouTube and walk in. There was a blood, sweat, and tears barrier that had to be crossed first. It was what made Bastian able to charge hundreds of dollars for a single meal. If everyone could make it, then everyone might, and they would all be out of a job.

Miles hadn't made the rules, but he was expected to live by them. And some upstart guy with spreadsheets and a marketing degree and tight khakis that made Miles' dick ache wasn't going to make him break them.

He'd been gone from the house they'd all shared for less than a week, but already Miles felt nostalgic as they all collapsed on the various sitting surfaces in the living room. They all had their special spot, and Miles still got the particularly comfy corner of the couch.

"Don't worry," Xander said with a roll of his eyes. "I haven't appropriated it yet. I couldn't get comfy in it because the dents in it still match your skinny ass."

Miles never thought he'd miss Xander's snide little comments, but he'd take Xander's mostly open hostility over Evan's insidious back-stabbing manipulation. Even thinking of him now and the innocent openness of his expression right after Miles had caught him red-handed burned.

"I figure this is as good a time as any to open this," Wyatt said, walking into the living room holding a dusty bottle.

"Nate gave that to you, didn't he?" Kian asked, because he hadn't had *that* sort of boyfriend yet, and was still blissfully naïve. Miles and Xander were both too smart to bring up that Nate, Wyatt's asshole sommelier ex-boyfriend, had given him the bottle in his hands.

"Fuck that asshole, anyway," Xander said.

Wyatt's expression grew wistful. "I know you all hated him, but he wasn't so bad."

"Quick," Miles said, "let's drink the wine before Wyatt changes his mind and waxes nostalgic about his relationship with Nate."

"More like waxes nostalgic about what great wine Nate would always buy," Xander added.

Wyatt raised an eyebrow. "Do you want me to open this or not?"

"We've been staring at it for more than six months," Xander said. "And nine before that, when you were still together and you felt obligated to drink it with that dick. Open the fucking wine."

Wyatt made a face but started opening the wine anyway.

"Kian broke our fourth red wine glass," Xander explained when Wyatt brought out three wine glasses and a champagne flute.

"It wasn't my fault!" Kian exclaimed, though out of a kitchen, he was notoriously clumsy.

"And the sky isn't blue," Xander retorted.

Miles took the glass Wyatt handed him, and did a showy little swirl. He wasn't a sommelier like Nate, but he'd taken a few classes about wine, and he could tell from the bouquet that it was pretty good. Maybe not as good as Nate had sworn it was, he thought as he sipped, but pretty damn good.

The problem was that Nate had always oversold everything—and that included himself. It had been a very good day when Wyatt had finally shown him the door. And, *bonus*, he'd gotten to keep the birthday gift Nate had given him a few months before.

"Dish," Wyatt said, leaning forward, elbows on his knees, blue eyes bright in the dim room. "I wouldn't have opened this wine if I didn't think it would loosen your tongue."

Miles tipped his glass in a faux toast. "You're a real giver."

"Seriously," Xander complained. "What the fuck are you doing back here?"

Miles didn't even know where to begin. He didn't want to talk about Evan, but everything started with him. "You know how we all really liked Nate at first, and it took us a long time—some of us a *very* long time—to realize he was a tool?" A round of nods. They'd all been happy when Wyatt had started dating Nate. He was decent and had access to better wine than any of them could afford. Plus, nobody else had dated anyone seriously during the time they'd all lived together. Xander was too mean to date anyone, Miles liked to keep things more casual, and from the very beginning, Kian had this unfortunate crush on their boss he continually denied but was obvious from about a hundred miles away.

"Well," Miles continued, "that isn't what happened with my producer. I pretty much hated him right away." This hadn't really been true then, and it definitely wasn't true now. But it made for a simpler story. Definitely easier than explaining that his feelings were intense and confused. Too difficult to try to explore, even with his best friends.

Kian made an aborted shocked noise. Kian was also too young and too naïve to ever hate anyone at first sight.

"I don't buy it," Xander inserted cynically. "You don't hate anyone right away. That's me, not you."

This was unfortunately true. Miles' first impression of Evan hadn't been hatred; it had been vague interest at his cute ass and velvety brown eyes. And he'd seemed nice and eager to please. Even if nothing he said had particularly pleased Miles.

"You haven't met him," was all Miles said. They'd already had to discuss Nate tonight; they didn't need to rehash all of Miles' poor romantic judgement too—*and* they didn't even know the half of it.

"I can't believe you only lasted two days," Wyatt said with a shake of his head. It sounded like a Xander comment, and it stung.

"I'm not *back*," Miles retorted. But he knew how it looked. He knew how good it felt; how comfortable and routine to sit on this couch and drink a glass of wine and bullshit with his three friends.

Like he'd slid right back into the same life he'd already acknowledged he'd grown out of.

There was nothing to do but take a big gulp of wine, and appreciate the acidic burn.

"Does this mean you have to pay back the money?" Xander asked.

Miles knew he wasn't going to pay back a dime. He was tied up, metaphorically and legally. The rest of his glass of wine slid down his throat with none of the ceremony Wyatt's ex-boyfriend would have required.

He got up from the comfy corner of the couch; suddenly it didn't fit the same way it had. He walked in the kitchen, which looked a little barer without Miles' precious copper pots. The thought stung, and he turned away, towards the sad little cabinet that contained their meager liquor collection—most of which they'd kept to be used in Miles' desserts.

He grabbed the half-full bottle of knockoff Kahlua, and returned to the living room. This time, he didn't take the corner on the couch, but settled on the edge of the arm.

"What are you doing?" Kian asked. Only Kian wouldn't recognize a meltdown requiring alcohol, Miles thought bleakly.

"Getting drunk," Miles said, at the same time as Xander added, "Trying to forget he's already made his bed."

Miles glared over at Xander. It was a little rawer than usual, because he'd already taken two swigs of the terrible Kahlua knockoff and if he'd thought Nate's wine had burned going down, it had nothing on this shit.

"You can't come back," Xander said by way of explanation, and his casual shrug burned even more than the wine and the bad Kahlua combined.

Miles took another long drink, straight from the bottle. "Anyone joining me?"

Wyatt laughed. "We all have to work tomorrow. Unlike you, apparently."

Miles could only imagine Evan's affronted expression when he didn't turn up the next morning, and then the exaggerated annoyance when he used his key to check Miles' apartment and discovered he wasn't there.

He could also imagine the smug edge to his annoyance. How Evan would imagine that Miles had conceded victory.

Miles let more booze slide down his throat and snapped his fingers in Kian's direction. "Go get your laptop."

A wrinkle appeared between Kian's blond brows. "I really don't think you should be making a video now, Miles."

Miles frowned. "I'm not making a video, I'm writing a fucking email."

Xander looked concerned now. A sure sign that everyone was convinced Miles was melting down. Even Miles was convinced, but he didn't give a shit anymore.

He waved with the plastic bottle. He should've stopped at the store and bought some half-decent booze to lose it with. "I'm not going to actually send it," he claimed. "I just want to write it. That's why I'm using Kian's laptop. It never fucking stays connected to the Wi-Fi."

The glance Wyatt gave him was galling. "I don't think this is a good idea."

Miles finished the bottle with a gross belch that tasted of pretty good red wine and bad Kahlua and definite regrets. "It's the best fucking idea I've had in awhile."

Kian must have been at least partially convinced—or maybe he was trying to distract Miles from the liquor cabinet—because he went and got his laptop and reluctantly handed it over.

Miles traded the laptop for the empty Kahlua bottle, which Kian took with a dubious look and an even more dubious sniff.

"You're a snob," Miles told him with a shake of his head.

"I just don't get it," Kian said earnestly. "You're—okay, you *were*—a chef at one of the best restaurants in the world. How can you even stomach bad liquor like that?"

Miles was booting up the laptop and was so focused on the white-hot ball of rage lighting his way that he nearly missed Xander's answer.

"Kian," he said much more patiently than usual, "you wouldn't. But sometimes you want it to burn going down."

That was the goddamn truth.

Miles wanted to burn the whole world down, starting with his taste buds and his throat and his stomach. Next stop, Evan's infuriating ego.

Not once, not *once* in his whole fucking career, had anyone—either a superior or a head chef or co-worker—ever had reason to call him unprofessional.

Miles wanted to burn Evan down because he'd dared to say it out loud and mean it. Even worse, he was *right*.

He opened Kian's browser. The Wi-Fi was currently working, but it was only a matter of time before it went on the fritz. The most consistent thing in this entire house was the inconsistency of Kian's Wi-Fi. It was something Miles was counting on, because while he wanted to mentally deep fry Evan, he wasn't ready to deep fry his career.

Nobody, even Evan Patterson, was enough motivation for Miles to throw away everything he'd killed himself to achieve.

"Are you really sure about this?" Kian asked. He sounded worried. His voice echoed the look on Wyatt's face. Even Xander didn't look completely convinced. Probably because none of them had consumed half a bottle of faux Kahlua.

Knock-off Kahlua was apparently the key to saying *fuck it* to the world.

"Definitely," Miles said. The adrenaline from his fight hours ago with Evan was still coursing through him. It was a physical impossibility but something about Evan kept him alight. Miles didn't want to look too carefully at what that might be. He zoned right onto the outrage and bypassed the rest right by.

"Dear Evan," Miles said out loud as he typed. Badly, but he wasn't sending this, so it didn't matter. This letter was only for him, an attempt to exorcise all his rage. Tomorrow he'd go skulking back to LA, tail sort-of between his legs, maybe not ready to apologize but conceptually ready to compromise. He wasn't ready to face the kiss yet, but he was sure Evan would want to pretend like it hadn't happened.

But first . . . revenge.

Kian opened his mouth to try to say something else, but Miles talked right over him. "Dear Evan," he repeated, "I really hate your face. It's a big fat fucking lie. Earnest and trustworthy when you're really a big backstabber."

"Maybe you shouldn't repeat 'big' twice in one sentence," Xander inserted.

Miles shot him a hot glare. "This isn't a fucking essay, you idiot."

Xander just shrugged, and Miles felt the room begin to spin as he tried to focus on his face. But he dug down deep and returned to his email.

"How about horrible backstabber?" Wyatt suggested.

"Thanks, Mr. Thesaurus," Miles retorted. His fingers were flying over the keys, insulting everything from Evan's stupid bow ties to fake marketing genius to his cute ass—okay maybe that last one wasn't quite an insult. But Miles was trying. He didn't mention the kiss, but it was right there, hidden between the lines. The one thing he wasn't saying.

The problem was the more he wrote, the colder the fire grew, until it felt just about ready to smolder right out. This had been a fucking fantastic idea. He'd managed to exorcise the last of his anger, and he'd really be able to return and try to salvage this whole thing.

And then . . .

"Oh, shit," Miles said, dread spinning through him faster than quicksilver. Certainly faster than the rage had spread. And unlike the rage, it made him sick. Or maybe that was the Kahlua.

"What happened?" Kian asked, scrambling to get over to where Miles sat on the floor with the laptop. Something in Miles' voice must have told him something terrible had happened, because he could move quick when he wanted to, and he was moving fast now.

"I pressed enter," Miles said in a small voice.

"Oh shit," Kian said, which was unusual for him because like the Boy Scout he'd been, he almost never swore.

"What?" Xander was scrambling now, trying to join Miles and Kian as they stared unbelieving at the laptop screen.

"I think Miles sent the email," Kian said carefully.

"What?" Wyatt exclaimed. "How could that even happen?"

"I forgot to mention, I think I fixed the Wi-Fi," Kian said, and he sounded wretched. Not nearly as wretched as Miles felt, and in some other universe, it might have helped that Kian felt bad, but in this one, it didn't. It didn't at all.

His brain was one long fuzzy slow-rolling image of Evan, all peppy and morning-person, opening his email tomorrow and being confronted with one insult after another, most of which weren't even true. Miles didn't even want to think about the spelling and grammar errors. No doubt Evan would return it to him, marked up with a red pen. His eyes would be red too, because as frustrating as he was, he wasn't immune or cold.

He *cared*. He'd wanted a Joan of Arc Julia Child, and all he'd gotten was the asshole half of Gordon Ramsay.

It didn't feel fair at all, even if Miles didn't really like him. It really wasn't fair if Miles decided he *did* like him.

"Maybe we can take the email back," Kian suggested, trying for hope and landing somewhere north of despair.

"Take the email back?" Xander sneered. "It's a good thing you're not on a career path that requires any sort of technical skills. The email is gone."

"Gone," Miles repeated hopelessly.

Someone shoved a bottle in his hand. He took a swig. It was worse even than the fake Kahlua, some sort of sickly sweet orange liquor, but Miles didn't even care anymore. He wanted oblivion because maybe that would kill the shame.

94

CHAPTER FIVE

His mouth tasted like a Russian and a Spaniard had fought over a rotten orange and lost. As Miles gradually fell towards consciousness, he knew only one thing: he'd never be able to drink White Russians or Spanish Coffees ever again. For a split second, that was something to seriously mourn. And then it all came roaring back: the fight, the drive back to Napa, the wine and bitch session with his friends, and then the email from hell. Followed by the faux Kahlua and the fake orange liquor and what he was pretty sure was a drag of shame into the bathroom.

Yep, Miles realized, that was definitely the edge of the toilet his face was resting on. It was a good thing too, because as soon as he got ambitious enough to open one sleep-crusted eye, he got instantly, horrifically sick.

Miles wiped his mouth and settled back on the toilet seat, which thanks to Xander's OCD tendencies, was spotless. It was also a whole lot more comfortable than he'd imagined. And conveniently close to the toilet bowl, which might be making another rapid appearance in his life at any moment.

Why had he come here? He'd known his life here was done—even if the friendships weren't. Had he come so his best friends could plump his ego, even though they'd never done it before? Had he come here so they could clean his wounds? Salve his pride? He wasn't sure, though he knew the decision to get drunk and write the email had been the worst of the bunch.

Never mind that he'd never intended to send it. It was enough that he'd written it, spelling errors and odes to Evan's ass and all. And now Evan had most likely already seen it. The thought was enough to send him back to the toilet, retching helplessly because he'd already thrown most of his stomach up already.

He was fucked, and not even in the fun way.

A brisk knock sounded on the door. He ignored it. He wasn't in any mood for Xander's resigned "you've fucked up your life" bullshit.

"What?" Miles croaked when they didn't go away but instead knocked again, with way more determination. Definitely more determination than Miles felt. He was only determined not to die, and it was feeling pretty touch and go at the moment.

"Miles, are you okay?" It was Kian, and he sounded a hell of a lot more sympathetic than Miles deserved. As far as he was concerned, he wasn't worthy of any of it.

"No," he croaked. Might as well be honest.

"Open the door," Kian said.

"You open it," Miles retorted.

"You locked it, you idiot." That was Wyatt, who was even more protective over Kian than Miles was. "There's someone here to see you."

It was probably Reed, here to fire Miles and demand all his signing bonus back. Some of which he'd already spent on a stupid rental car to come up here and bitch at his friends about how hard he had it. Miles wanted to vomit again, but nothing came. Somehow that felt like the final indignity.

"He's wearing a bow tie, Miles."

Oh god. Even worse. Evan had come here in person. Probably after reading the email. He was definitely here to commit a murder on the parts of Miles that weren't already dead, and he wasn't sure his friends would be inclined to stop him.

Then Miles remembered the kiss, and wondered if he could stay in here forever. He didn't know if he could face Evan, considering what he'd done and then what he'd said.

But Miles knew he should drag himself off the floor and give Evan an opportunity for the murdering to begin.

It was a several-minutes-long process, gently and carefully unfolding his aching body from the position over the toilet, and then hefting himself up using the counter. He flipped on the light and only screamed a little bit, either at the brightness or the horrible image the mirror confronted him with.

He stole Xander's toothbrush and splashed some water on his face, and tried to fix his hair. It was a useless exercise, but

Miles guessed it didn't really matter anyway. Nobody would care what his hair looked like when he was dead.

Unlocking the door, Miles braced himself, but it was only Kian standing outside, a worried crease between his brows. "What are you doing?" Kian hissed.

"I wish I knew," he admitted.

"Well, figure your shit out. Your partner you just insulted ten ways from Sunday is here."

"How did he even get here so fast?" Miles wondered, even though the thinking hurt his brain. It could only be mid-morning because Kian hadn't left for Terroir yet.

Kian just shrugged. "He's in the kitchen."

Miles gingerly felt his way to the kitchen, and when he arrived, was ironically confronted by a vision of what he'd just insulted—or praised. He wasn't sure. But there Evan was, back to him, in another pair of those tight khakis.

It wasn't fair. Nothing was fair.

"So this is where the magic all began," Evan said without turning. Miles didn't think he was a particularly heavy breather, but maybe Evan had sold his soul for magic powers so he could kill Miles and get away with it.

"I'm not sure it was very magical," Miles said, and all of a sudden he didn't know if they were talking about *Pastry by Miles* or their kiss. He took a breath and tried to steady himself. He wanted to cry and apologize and tell Evan just how sorry he was, but there was something deep inside holding it all back. Pride? Ego? Shame? "How did you even know I was here?"

"You used your corporate credit card, it wasn't very hard to track you," Evan said, and there was a hint of a sneer in his tone. Like Miles must be incredibly stupid to not be able to keep his credit cards straight—and Miles thought he was probably right. It *was* stupid and would have topped his most embarrassing list, if not for the email.

That was going to win for a very long time. Possibly forever.

Evan turned around. "God," he said, and there was definitely an audible sneer now, "you look even worse than you smell."

"Thanks," Miles said stiffly.

If he had any embarrassment left, he'd be cringing right now.

"I guess Reed sent you up to fire me," Miles said, uncomfortable with even vaguely referring to the email. He'd already been rightly accused of being unprofessional; he didn't even know what this behavior was. A complete aberration. A panic-induced, ego-driven freak-out. But no, that wasn't even right, because if his ego was where it was supposed to be, he would have spent this morning working to contradict Evan's words, not support them.

Evan ignored the reference. "I came here to get you, not to fire you," he said. "We have work to do, and you're not where you're supposed to be."

It was even tougher to face Evan, knowing he was right. Maybe not on every count, but on every count that mattered.

Sure Evan shouldn't have gone blabbing to Reed, and maybe he should have shared his plans in a less autocratic way, but he'd at least been trying to work out some sort of compromise.

What had Miles been trying to do? Get drunk and write an ode to how much he hated Evan's face but loved his ass?

"Okay," Miles said.

Evan looked skeptical. "Just . . . okay? No arguments?"

"Some . . . discussion can be good for creativity. But you're right, I'm not where I'm supposed to be." Miles had definitely learned that during this little unplanned trip. He was done in Napa, at least for now. He still wasn't a hundred percent convinced he was supposed to be at *Five Points* either, but he'd given his word, and that had used to mean something to Miles.

So he'd go back and no matter how daunting it was for Miles to try to live up to Evan's Joan of Arc Julia Child label, he'd give it his best shot. Basic cooperation was the least he could do after how he'd just insulted Evan.

It turned out part of how Evan had gotten here so quickly was that he hadn't driven.

"What's this?" Miles asked, as the black Lincoln pulled into one of the side private airstrips by the Napa airport.

With a quick phone call, Evan had efficiently arranged for Miles' rental to be picked up and for their travel arrangements. Miles hadn't been listening because he'd still been trying not to vomit. He'd sort of assumed Evan had come up overnight using the car service so he could grab a few hours of sleep.

Apparently not. Miles knew that he had to stop assuming things when it came to Evan, because each wrong assumption was growing more embarrassing, and he didn't have any extra to spare.

"A favor," Evan said succinctly as the car stopped in front of a small white jet.

The driver grabbed their bags from the trunk and followed Evan and Miles to the small set of stairs leading to the aircraft.

"What, no check-in? No ticketing gate?" Miles knew he sounded stupid, but Evan's calm silence, which had lasted from their departure from the rental house to the present was nerve-wracking. He couldn't tell when Evan was going to finally explode and tell him off for the things he'd said.

Evan stayed quiet, and climbed the stairs. The captain was waiting for them at the top, dressed in a navy-blue uniform. It was only then that Miles glimpsed an insignia featuring a fish with particularly nasty teeth on his breast pocket. And he realized whose jet this must be.

Embarrassment felt like a mild word in comparison to what he felt now. He'd heard rumors that someone in the upper management of *Five Points* was married to Colin O'Connor, the famous Miami Piranhas quarterback, but since he didn't really follow sports, he'd assumed those were just rumors.

He'd been so wrong. He and Evan were currently ensconced in comfortable blue-and-white-striped seats with tiny light-blue piranhas woven right into the fabric.

"None of the above," Evan finally said with satisfaction as he took in Miles' stupefied expression. "First class all the way."

Even calling this first class was being modest, and even though they'd only met a few days before, Miles didn't think Evan tended towards humility.

He could only think that this was yet another way for Evan to put him, subtly or firmly, back in his place. A little flare of anger that he knew he had no right to feel burned through him.

He'd been puking less than an hour ago, and his mouth still vaguely tasted like rotten oranges. It was enough of a reminder to swallow back down the retort he'd just been about to dish back. Back at the rental house, he'd made himself a vow that he'd be professional, no matter what, even if Evan pushed his buttons.

How could Miles have forgotten how good Evan was at pushing them?

It didn't matter, he told himself resolutely, he was going to be a professional. After the email, he owed Evan at least that much.

"I guess I should be grateful you came to get me then," Miles said, leaning back into the soft leather captain's chair, trying to act like it was something he did every day.

Evan just rolled his eyes and got to his feet, walking over to a little cleverly disguised refrigerator under one of the gleaming wood accents. Clearly he'd been on this plane before, and that stung even more.

He turned back towards Miles and he had two bottles of water in his hands. He tossed one in Miles' direction. "Thought you might still be feeling it," Evan said. "We're about to take off soon. This might help."

His voice was blunt, but his message was at least semi-sympathetic. It confused Miles, whose head was still pounding. "I wouldn't expect you to care much," he said. He kept expecting Evan to mention the email. Or the kiss. Or both, together, as two actions that didn't make any sense put together.

"I don't," Evan said, with an even blunter delivery. "But Mr. Wheeler will skin me alive if you puke all over his plane."

Miles took a sip of water, grateful even though the anger he kept trying to tamp down kept cropping up. "Trust me, it's all gone. You can keep your skin intact." He ignored the voice inside his head that decided this was a great time to mention what gorgeous skin it was. And that it might be soft if Miles was ever allowed to touch it.

"What a relief," Evan retorted disdainfully.

The desire fizzled. Dealing with Evan was confusing and exhausting and he was already worn out.

He heard Evan rustling around and then the all too familiar staccato punch of fingertips on a keyboard. He was working again, even though they were on a private plane. Miles was grateful though, because that meant he might have more time to gather himself for the apology he still needed to make.

Too many damn things were floating in the air around them and until they addressed them, he didn't know how they would ever get anything done.

I really hate your face. It's a big fat fucking lie.

He'd just close his eyes for a minute, to collect himself, and then he'd figure out his apology. It wouldn't be as complicated as a *Napoleon* or his famous *Paris-Brest* even. Pastry was difficult, people were easy—usually, anyway.

❧❧❧❧❧ ❧❧❧❧❧

"Rise and shine, sweetheart." The voice, edged with derision, could only belong to one person.

Miles' eyes snapped open and Evan's face swam into view.

I really hate your face.

What a joke his little drunken charade was turning out to be.

"Are we back?" Miles asked groggily as he pulled himself upright. The chairs were so cushy it felt like they were sinking their padded claws into you.

"We're back." Evan was already facing the door, bag in hand, looking so proper and together that Miles wanted to swear. No doubt his hair, already a wreck, was a rat's nest on his head, and he didn't want to think what his clothes smelled like.

"Great." Miles tried to sound enthused, but definitely didn't pull it off.

"Don't worry," Evan said, not even bothering to glance back, "we'll drop you off at your place first, so you can wash that horrific smell off. And then you'll be coming in. We have work to do."

"I would've come back today, I swear," Miles said, because the apology was still an unformed, cloudy mirage in his head and he couldn't seem to wring solid, concrete words from it.

"Of course you would have," Evan said in clipped tones.

Miles knew he was lying.

True to his word, Miles was dropped off at his apartment. He showered, letting the hot water beat him into defeat. As he got ready, his face frosted in the foggy mirror, he told himself that he could be a professional. He'd been a complete professional every single day of his career until he'd come to *Five Points*. Letting fear get the best of him was stupid.

By the time he'd walked to the office, his head was a little clearer and he'd discovered a deep-seated determination not to let Evan push any more of his buttons.

He'd just settled in with his laptop to check the email he'd missed when Evan popped his head around the corner of his cubicle.

"Marketing meeting in the conference room, you're already five minutes late," was all he said in clipped, straightforward tones.

Personally, Miles thought every meeting they'd had so far could be categorized as a "marketing meeting," but Evan just tilted his head, tempting Miles to challenge him. And Miles wasn't stupid. If Reed knew about the email, he'd already be fired.

Reed might preach more touchy-feely now, but he was still the same man who had run Garnet with a velvet-covered iron fist and the expectation that everyone brought their A game every single day. Which meant that Evan hadn't told him about the email.

Miles didn't like blackmail, whether it was inferred or directly stated, but he couldn't be pissed because he'd handed it to Evan on a silver platter.

"Fine," Miles ground out, and picked up his laptop to follow Evan.

When Evan opened the door to the conference room, he was a little shocked to find it was full. Lots of employees, including

Reed, were sitting around the table. He and Evan were able to grab two of the last free seats right before it started.

What followed was the most interminably boring bunch of bullshit that Miles had ever sat through. There were multiple presenters, and everybody had slide decks with more charts and keywords and strategies than Miles had ever wanted to see.

His head was still pounding behind his eyes and he'd barely gotten any sleep, but every time he even briefly considered closing his eyes, he saw Reed sitting across the table, taking attentive notes and asking questions that seemed to be relevant.

Plus, there was Evan beside him, no doubt ready to pick up on any wavering from Miles.

It was like being bored to death.

When the torture was finally over, Reed stopped by and clapped Miles on the shoulder. "I couldn't believe it when Evan said you'd expressed interest in coming to one of these. I only come because I don't have a choice. But I guess you really meant it when you said you wanted to reach the people."

Miles could only nod mutely. Miserably. In acute pain and wishing he could inflict even a tiny bit of it on the man next to him.

He couldn't. Never mind his own vow to stay professional, he knew if he took even the tiniest step out of line, Evan would bat him right back with the email.

Grinding his teeth together, Miles forced himself to smile. "Working in the kitchens doesn't give me many opportunities to see stuff like this," he said, which was all true. And he'd been one hundred percent okay with that situation.

"I'm impressed," Reed said, and he sounded it too, which was even worse. Normally Miles craved approbation from his bosses, but not like this. Not for something he basically loathed.

Miles didn't have to look over at Evan to see the smug smile on his face as Reed departed.

"Lunch?" Miles asked, aware of how desperate he sounded. He didn't really care about food yet, but coffee was going to be a necessity.

"We have another meeting," Evan said.

"I didn't really have to come to this one," Miles said slowly as they walked towards one of the smaller meeting rooms. "Did I?"

Evan just shrugged. "I thought it would be educational."

"If you understand what they're saying, probably it would have been," Miles grumbled. It was clear that Evan wasn't going to trip up and admit that the meeting had been clear punishment for the email—or maybe for the kiss—or that he was essentially blackmailing Miles into compliance.

Evan was too smart for that, which Miles sort of admired and definitely hated.

"So, what's this meeting about?" Miles said, slumping into a chair.

"We only have a few short weeks to plan your first slate of episodes before we have to film," Evan said, and that hard, determined edge to his voice was back. "We need a plan of attack. *Now.*"

"Okay, tell me what you think Joan of Arc Julia Child would do," Miles said, because he might as well hear the worst of it, all completely spelled out.

Evan flipped open a folder. "I'm glad you finally asked." Even this statement was pointed at the end, like he was insinuating Miles should have asked that right away. And frankly, Miles probably should have. Except it wasn't entirely Miles' fault because he'd never really done this before. As his producer, wasn't it Evan's job to guide him?

Miles watched Evan as he gathered papers and tried to bury the seething resentment that somehow Evan had wanted him to fail. But that didn't make any sense either, because hadn't Evan picked him? Not Reed?

Miles didn't know what to think anymore. So he decided that if he'd asked the question, he might as well listen.

"Joan of Arc Julia Child, as you put it, is essentially a pastry course built into the first season. Each episode is a dessert that showcases a particular type of technique, and we work forward from there. The idea is to build on knowledge, but I'd like it to be accessible to anyone, at the same time."

Miles ran a hand through his hair. "That's what I've been trying to tell you, it *can't* be accessible to just anyone."

"Why not?" Evan retorted. "Anyone who can read can follow a recipe."

"It's not all about following a recipe," Miles countered. "Or else we'd just be publishing recipes online, and not filming videos. There's technique that you can't teach through words."

"Then *teach*," Evan challenged, dark eyes spiking with temper across the table. "Or . . . is that something you aren't capable of?"

"What I'm trying to fucking tell you is that I don't care about people learning how to bake," Miles said, all too aware that even though he was trying to listen, trying to understand, he was beginning to lose the control over his temper. It was funny, even Xander had never provoked it the way Evan did. Until this job, Miles would have insisted he didn't even have a real temper.

"Then what do you want to do?" Evan questioned, still even and calm.

"I want to bake what I want to bake," Miles said testily.

"Why can't we do both? It's not that great of a restriction, showcasing one technique each episode. And it's not like you didn't have restrictions at Terroir."

"Yeah, well there's a reason I'm not working there anymore," Miles mumbled.

"So, if I asked you what you wanted, you'd tell me you want to make videos that don't do anything except look pretty and impressive. Bolster your ego, so to speak."

Miles had never thought of it that way before, but put the way Evan did, he certainly sounded like a petty egomaniac. It wasn't an attractive look, and they both knew it.

They both knew Evan was going to win this round.

And really, Miles justified to himself, Evan was sort of right. There was a small restriction on each episode, but there wasn't any reason he couldn't go a little wild and crazy. And maybe the wilder and the crazier he went, he might pay back Evan for painting him into this corner.

"No," Miles said. "That's not really me." He could tell from Evan's face that he was definitely not convinced of that. "We'll try it your way."

It didn't sting as much he'd expected, saying those words, but Evan's smug face still needed something—a punch maybe? But that wasn't right either, Miles thought as Evan started taking notes. No, something else, something to surprise him.

It shouldn't have surprised him when the thought of kissing Evan popped into his head. Evan already had an ass he admired—which unfortunately they were both aware of now—but nothing would probably drive Mr. Bow Ties up the creek more than something messy and complicated, which was what all sexual relationships were, as far as Miles was concerned.

Definitely worth considering, Miles thought.

Miles landed on the couch with a heavy oof. It had been an extremely long day and he was exhausted but he still dragged out his phone from his back pocket. He felt a pulse of shame when he noticed that he hadn't texted Gina since telling her with many emojis and exclamations that he was moving to LA. Of course, she hadn't texted or called him either, but she was in college. He'd never been but he had a feeling you were so tired when you finally hit your bed, regular correspondence was basically impossible.

His fingers hesitated over the keys. Finally, he typed out a quick, **you free to talk?** and sent it.

He was so tired, it was a genuine worry that he might fall asleep before she replied, but instead, the phone rang almost immediately, jerking him awake.

"Big brother," Gina crowed on the other end of the phone. Miles switched it over to speaker and laid the phone on his chest. "Long time no talk."

"How is your philosophy class? Did it improve at all?"

She laughed, and he couldn't believe how much better he felt, just hearing her voice and her high-pitched giggle. Something tight in his chest loosened.

"No, not really." She paused. "What's up?"

Miles felt a little bad about not talking to her for three weeks and then dumping his horrible situation on her, asking for her advice, but he couldn't go to Xander or Wyatt. Kian would look at him uncomprehendingly. There was only one person he always felt he could go to, and she was listening right now.

"I think I fucked up, Gee."

"Do you think it was a mistake to move to LA?" she asked quietly.

"No. Yes. I don't know. That's not exactly it. LA was the right choice, I don't think I shouldn't have come. But everything after I showed up. That's the problem."

She sighed, sounding like she'd been around the block a hundred times and knew the score. "Who is he?"

"How do you know it's a he?" Miles squawked. "It could be the job. It could be my boss."

"No. Definitely not. Because *one*, you're ridiculously good at your job—crazy intimidating good, if I'm being honest—so there's no way it's the job. *Two*, you already told me your boss was Reed Ryan, and he didn't ever strike me as an asshole you couldn't get along with. I mean, you get along with *Xander*."

Miles regretted introducing his sister to Xander for so many reasons.

"Did Xander tell you about his crush on Reed? Is that how you know about him?"

Miles could feel her disapproval radiating through the phone line. Even her silences could say a hundred words. He'd always envied that about her. He knew he tended to be both too open and not open enough; charming but opaque.

"Don't you remember when he was on *Kitchen Wars*?" Gina asked, referring to a reality TV show that Miles vaguely remembered and definitely hadn't watched. The name probably only sounded familiar because Xander had likely DVRed it and then had refused to delete it. Especially if Reed had starred in it.

"No?"

"Right," Gina said with amusement, "I always forget that it's Xander who has a crush on Reed, not you."

"Thankfully not. Considering he's now my boss," Miles retorted. He really hoped he had distracted her from the topic at hand—the mysterious *he* she had already correctly identified—by the topic change. He'd initially wanted to ask her advice, but now that he was talking to her, he realized he didn't know what he would even ask her. Besides, talking to her had already made him feel better, like none of this was truly permanently fucked, and he could still salvage it.

He loved his little sister a whole damn lot.

"So, who is he?" she persisted, and Miles groaned out loud.

"You're not very good at subtle," Gina pointed out with a laugh. "I can always see you changing the subject from a mile away. So who is he?"

"He's my producer," Miles reluctantly admitted.

"And?"

"And I was stupid." Miles didn't really want to detail every way he'd messed up with Evan, but knowing Gina, she'd drag it out of him.

"Big bro," Gina said patiently, "you're stupid about a hundred times a day. Did you hit on him? You hit on him, didn't you. Like five seconds after meeting him."

He couldn't exactly blame Gina for coming to that conclusion, because if he hadn't been so on edge when arriving at *Five Points*, he probably would have taken one look at Evan and done exactly that. But he'd been scared and worried and apprehensive, and so afraid those would show, he'd done the exact opposite.

"Not exactly," Miles hedged. "I sort of insulted him. And then kept insulting him."

He could tell Gina was speechless because there was a long, loaded silence.

"Who are you and what have you done with my brother?" Gina finally asked.

"He was afraid he was out of his depth and acted like an idiot," Miles said.

"Then he should *apologize*," Gina reprimanded, sounding so much like their mom, Miles had to do a double take.

"Yeah, he didn't do that," Miles said.

"So, he should start there," Gina said. "And then he should definitely stop referring to himself in the third person, because that makes him sound even weirder than he already is."

"Noted," Miles said with a laugh. He definitely felt lighter. He wasn't sure how he could even begin to apologize to Evan for what he'd said, but he knew Gina's advice was sound. It was Gina. It couldn't be anything else.

"Good," Gina said.

"How is that guy in your philosophy class?" Miles asked.

Gina groaned. Miles couldn't help but think that the sound they had both made when confronted with their nemeses—Miles with Evan, and Gina with Philosophy Class Guy—were eerily similar.

That could be because they were related, or it could be for an entirely different reason.

"Believe me, I feel you," Miles said.

"How can you want to kiss someone and kill them all in the same breath?" Gina demanded to know.

"I really don't know. When I figure it out, I'll get back to you." He paused. "And no kissing! I like to think of you as one of those nuns in the *Sound of Music*."

He could hear the force of Gina's eye roll over the phone. "You're an idiot," she said. But there was so much love in her voice, he squeezed his eyes shut against the sudden wave of emotion.

"I miss you, Gee," he said. "We need to figure out a way to hang out. Soon."

"Soon," she promised. "But I've got a midterm to study for, so I'd better go."

"Good luck on your test," he said.

"Thank you." She hesitated. "And, Miles?"

"Yeah?"

"Just fucking apologize."

Miles knew it would be so much smarter to just listen to his sister, but he already knew he wouldn't. The only way he intended to apologize, after the way Evan had manipulated and blackmailed him today, would be if he could leverage it as a way to control the producer.

After all, he'd never admitted to being a smart man, only a driven, determined one.

CHAPTER SIX

As far as Evan was concerned, Miles' agreement to do things his way was just a little too easy.

Sure, he'd strong-armed him, half-drunk and one hundred percent nasty-smelling, like an orchard gone bad, into Colin O'Connor's jet, then dragged him to the marketing meeting that Reed regularly said was the worst day of his week, all while walking a delicate line between outright and only inferred blackmail.

And sure, he'd had to wake up at six this morning after a mostly sleepless night, tossing and turning and agonizing over what Miles had meant by kissing him. And then he'd had to read the email Miles had clearly gotten wasted and then written, probably because he'd kissed him and didn't know what to do about it. But in between the not-very-imaginative and poorly written insults had been some insights into both Miles-the-Chef and Miles-the-Man.

After all, was something really insulting when it started with the playground taunt of "I really hate your face"?

Evan didn't really think so.

Even if Evan had actually been offended by the email, he still would have used the material the same way. The sick look on Miles' face this morning hadn't just been the bad liquor talking; he'd clearly been overwrought with guilt and confused as hell.

Guilt, Evan thought with satisfaction as he swept into the *Five Points* kitchens the next morning, was the best fucking motivator in the whole world. Better than love or revenge or whatever petty shit those comic book villains were always preaching about.

They could keep their world domination via childhood insecurity. Evan was going to take guilt and shame right to the bank.

Lucy, the kitchen manager, called out good morning from her spot on the other side of the gigantic space, where she was probably writing up next week's kitchen schedule. Even if she hadn't been, Evan still would have smiled big and waved. As it was, he smiled extra big because it was a fucking fantastic morning.

His espresso had been the perfect blend of hot milk and bitter, rich coffee and he'd slept like a baby the night before. But most importantly, he'd finally fixed his problem.

"Hey."

Evan looked up to see his fixed problem staring at him inscrutably.

"You look better," Evan said judiciously. Now that Miles was no longer a thorn in his side, Evan was fine with being civil. Besides, Miles could hardly look worse than he'd looked yesterday. So his statement also had the bonus ring of truth.

"Actual sleep and no booze works wonders," Miles pointed out.

There had been a tiny worried part of Evan that had been concerned that after a good night's sleep, Miles might recant his agreement of the day before. Or even worse, decide he wanted to talk about the two major events of the last forty-eight hours. But when Miles stayed silent, Evan forged on with his plan.

"I'm going to suggest," Evan said, "that we use the peanut butter dark chocolate cookie recipe as our first episode of the series. It's a strong introduction to your point of view as a chef—your sort of high-end, low-end combo that you used with the strawberry raspberry tarts that went viral—and it's a great introduction to basic concepts of baking, like creaming together butter and sugar and sifting dry ingredients."

Miles looked grudgingly impressed. "That's not a bad idea."

Evan couldn't quite help the chiding look he shot Miles' direction. He had a problem being a little smug after he knew he'd won, and this morning was no exception. "If you'd give me half a chance, you'd learn that I have more than a few of those."

"I told you yesterday I'd listen," Miles said, a grumpy expression crossing his face. But unlike the inscrutable, lofty frowns of earlier this week, this one was almost adorable. Like a pissed-off cat.

"We talked yesterday about you coming up with a list of higher concepts you thought would come across good on video."

Miles pulled a crumpled piece of paper out of his jeans and slid it across the counter. It was a sunny morning and the tall windows in the kitchen were all open, lightening his eyes and making them tougher for Evan to read. But if he had a guess, Miles looked the way Evan felt: smug.

Scanning the list, Evan had to admit that Miles had done a really good job. Which didn't surprise him all that much, because he'd personally selected Miles for a reason. They'd gotten off to a bit of a bumpy start, but there was no reason everything couldn't go smoothly from now on.

"This is good," Evan said.

"Don't sound so surprised."

Evan glanced up, surprised at the hard, defensive edge to Miles' voice.

"I know I haven't shown it here, but I'm a professional," Miles said and there it was again—the little thread of shame for the way he'd behaved earlier.

Evan couldn't have planned it better if he'd orchestrated the whole damn thing. He wanted to break into a song and dance of victory.

"Of course you are." Okay, if he sounded a little patronizing, then it was payback for, "I really hate your face."

"Which of these would be good for the next episode in the series?" Evan continued.

"They're actually in order—or the order I'd suggest they be in," Miles said, shoving his hands in his pockets.

"Thoughtful," Evan said approvingly. "Next up is chocolate croissants?"

Miles nodded. "And even better, last night I thought of an even better way we can learn to cooperate."

Later, Evan would come to think of this moment as the one where he stumbled and fell over his own ego.

"You're teaching me all about marketing," Miles said, oh-so-innocently—so innocently that Evan should have realized what was coming, but he was too busy celebrating such an easy win. He should have known that anything too easy to believe was just that—*too damn easy*. "And so I thought I could teach you how to bake. Starting with these recipes. You want me to teach an average person. I figure," Miles said, flashing another one of those charming smiles that made the housewives across America fall in love with him, "you're about as average as it gets."

Evan didn't know whether to be pissed off or very reluctantly admiring over the way he'd just been out-maneuvered. It was almost a masterstroke of genius, and from the lack of smugness emanating from Mr. Ego, it was hard to tell if he even realized he'd struck gold.

As far as Evan was concerned, that was the worst part of all. If you were going to meet Evan on a field of victory and snatch it out from under him, then you'd better be damn aware you'd done it.

"Average?" Evan asked, definitely conscious of how his voice crept up at the end of the word.

"If you want me to teach anyone, then I sure as hell better be able to teach *you*," Miles said. And suddenly, there was just a flash of the egotistical chef Evan had come to know.

Evan had never failed at anything in his life. He definitely wasn't about to start now.

"Sure," he said breezily. "I'm sure you can teach me."

Evan had fully expected another kitchen session observing Miles and taking notes. He hadn't anticipated touching any-thing—unless it riled Miles up again—and so he'd worn one of his favorite bow ties, a beautiful summer-blue plaid.

The last thing he expected was Miles to take a few steps closer, and reach up, resting one of those slim, capable hands on his shoulder, then edge towards his throat. Evan might have worried Miles was finally going to strangle him, except those fingers were hesitant but sure of their destination, which was his bow tie.

"This needs to go," Miles said, and Evan wasn't sure he imagined it, but his voice seemed lower, almost gravelly. Earthy. Evan might have imagined it was sexual, but he couldn't quite reconcile the Miles who wrote, "I really hate your face," and had kissed him like he was attacking him, to someone who might be sexually interested in him. It didn't compute.

And yet here Miles was, fingers capably and nimbly undoing his bow tie and gracefully tugging it out of his collar. He still couldn't seem to form words—maybe that was the sheer shock of Miles choosing to touch him, maybe it was that his actions fulfilled so much of what Evan had daydreamed about before they'd ever met—and he stood in silence as Miles thumbed open one collar button and the next, with efficient movements.

If Evan hadn't had sexual fantasies about Miles' hands before now, he definitely was going to now.

Miles Costa was undressing him.

It seemed too unreal to be actually happening, but Evan could feel the floor under his feet, and the brush of Miles' breath on the skin he'd exposed.

"There," Miles said softly, and Evan swore his voice wobbled for a second. "Much better."

"I thought it was the khakis you didn't like." Evan knew only the most shocking event would have forced him to refer to the email and the things Miles had said to him. He figured his slip was pretty justified, considering what had just happened.

"They're distracting," Miles said, but instead of continuing that line of thought, he turned away and headed towards the supply pantry, leaving Evan confused and sort of bereft. He wondered that if Miles kissed him again, if it would still be so angry.

He didn't think it would be.

When Miles returned, he was carrying an apron, which he handed to Evan. "You don't wear one of these," Evan said skeptically. It turned out he was far more interested in Miles undressing him than encouraging him to put more clothes on. And that was definitely a problem.

Miles gestured to his worn t-shirt and jeans. "Besides," he added, "I'm the professional, remember? I'm teaching you."

Evan shouldn't have found anything endearing about Miles bringing up one of their main conflicts, but there was a self-conscious, almost wry, edge to his voice that made it obvious how embarrassed he was about the whole thing.

And he *should* be embarrassed about that email, Evan thought as he plucked the apron from Miles' hand with barely another glance. "If it's a requirement, I'll be happy to wear it."

He only looked down after he'd tied it around his waist. "Wait," he stuttered, "this isn't . . . this didn't come from the kitchen."

"Kiss the Cook" was emblazoned across the front in bright red letters. Miles only grinned, the curve of his bottom lip all the evidence Evan needed that he was far too pleased with himself.

It occurred to Evan then that while Miles had come in today, prepared to deal and to compromise, he'd made some plans of his own. Teaching Evan to cook wasn't a spontaneous idea he'd just come up with. He'd planned for this to happen, even to the extent of buying and bringing this ugly apron in for Evan to wear.

"Looks good," was all Miles said before he turned away, but that was enough. Evan had already seen the amusement in his gray eyes, and he had to force down the answering blush.

"Thank you," Evan said stiffly.

He would've had to be dead not to be affected by some of the things Miles said and did. The reluctant attraction he felt had come through loud and strong, in between all the silly insults and the angry kiss. But Evan already knew it would be dangerous to let Miles kiss him again. Maybe too dangerous, especially not when Miles had just proved that he was perfectly capable of arranging his own manipulative plans. Evan would never know if anything that developed between them was real or if it was just Miles trying to gain the upper hand in their power struggle.

That was why it couldn't happen at all.

Evan picked up the paper Miles had scribbled the show ideas on and pointed at the first line. He needed to remind both of them that this was a professional—not personal—relationship. "This is what we're doing today?" He hesitated, already thinking of how he'd stumble over the French. "*Pain au chocolat?*"

"*Oui, pain au chocolat,*" Miles answered absently, absorbed as he arranged the ingredients he'd just fetched from the pantry on a rolling cart.

Unlike Evan, French rolled off Miles' tongue naturally. Evan was reminded that one of the bullet points on his resume was several years studying and working in Paris at one of the great *patisseries* there.

Evan had never been to Europe. His childhood had definitely never afforded him a chance to travel, and he'd spent his entire adult life clawing his way up by his fingernails. There had never been time or money to indulge any of his fantasies.

Hearing Miles speak such careless and perfect French was another reminder of how different they were, and how Miles could never find out just how different.

"Do you speak fluently?" Evan asked before he could swallow the question back. Like he needed any more vivid dreams of those long, pliant fingers running across his skin, hypnotic murmurs of French in his ear.

"Not as much as I should," Miles admitted. There was a hint of a smile on his lips, like he knew what Evan was thinking—and he couldn't, Evan knew that, but there was still a fearful thrill that he might still figure it out. "Everyone kept speaking English."

"Well that was a waste," Evan said.

"I'm assuming you don't," Miles said.

Obviously Evan didn't. The way he'd butchered the pronunciation of the recipe name would have given that away instantly. He spoke a little Spanish, because you'd have to be painfully isolated not to pick up some, and also because he'd taken the language courses required by his university.

"It's a goal of mine to learn another language," Evan said.

Miles rolled his eyes. "Of course it is."

Evan was instantly reminded of all those years of being made fun of because he'd had the nerve to excel in school, because he'd had the nerve to want *better* for himself. Why wasn't that cool? Why did Miles, who'd certainly done some excelling of his own, find that lame?

But Evan had long learned there was no point in asking those questions. He'd do whatever he believed he needed to do, damn everyone else. He pushed the hurt away because there was no point in wondering why Miles would judge him for it too.

"What are *pain au chocolat*?" he asked, carefully attempting to copy Miles' effortless accent.

"Chocolate croissants," Miles said. "And they're important because learning how to make pastry dough is vital to French baking. Also because they're delicious *and* impressive."

Evan was definitely impressed but he kept his lips pressed tightly together because he wasn't about to tell Miles that.

"We begin," Miles continued, "by putting the basic dough together." He gestured to a gigantic glass bowl that he'd placed on the counter.

Evan walked over to the bowl. He was only going to follow instructions and mix some stuff together in a bowl. How hard could this really be?

"I don't suppose you have this recipe written down yet," Evan said.

Miles smiled and leaned against the counter, a little closer than Evan felt comfortable with, his gray eyes the warmest they'd been since he'd arrived at *Five Points*. He was a long, lean temptation and Evan needed him a little further away. A little more unattainable.

"I'll walk you through it," Miles promised. "Flour first." He pointed to a big metal bin.

Evan tugged it over to the bowl and opened the latch. "How much?"

"Four cups." Miles pointed to a variety of measuring cups and spoons that he'd laid out at the workstation.

Picking up the cup measure, Evan tried not to be self-conscious as Miles watched him intently measure out four cups of the flour and dump it into the bowl.

"No," was all Miles said, picking up the bowl and dumping all the flour back in the container. "There's a way to measure flour correctly when baking." He leaned over and suddenly was right in Evan's personal bubble, forearm brushing against his chest and plucked the measuring cup from his hand. Despite fighting his attraction, Evan knew he was breathing heavier, while Miles, who was just as close, didn't seem to be affected at all. Evan didn't know whether to remind himself of what Miles had said in the email or to try to forget it completely and believe the charade Miles was playing at.

"We fluff up the flour first," Miles said, voice casual but precise as he took the metal cup in his hand and with a few flicks of his wrist, churned up the flour. "We want it light but uniform. Flour can clump together, making the measurement imprecise."

Then he handed the cup back to Evan. Flour sifted gently over his fingers as he dipped his hand into the container and tried to replicate Miles' movements. "Now," Miles said, snagging Evan's wrist, his fingers making a loose bracelet around it, "you dip the cup in and level it off with your other hand."

Flour was coating both their hands now, specks sifting down across the counter as Miles guided Evan's movements. Finally there were four new cups of flour in the bowl. The amount seemed very similar to Evan, but Miles was the expert, and if he said this was how flour should be measured, then he'd do it.

"Half cup of cold water," Miles said, releasing his wrist gently, more flour sifting to the counter, to the floor, even onto Miles' jeans. He seemed unconcerned. Evan hadn't thought he'd ever be grateful for the apron, but he sort of was.

Evan sorted through the selection of measuring cups, and he'd just found the right one when Miles' voice stopped him again. "Nope," he said. "Those are just for dry ingredients." He gestured to the nestled glass measuring cups on the side. "*These* are for wet ingredients, like water."

Not about to let Miles stop him again, Evan slowly measured water from the faucet into the cup, ducking down so his eyes could double-check the liquid had rested exactly at the little red line.

Miles gave an approving little nod as he poured the water into the flour. "Same amount of milk," he said, and Evan dutifully measured that too.

"Wait," he said, as he was pouring the milk in, "didn't you make all sorts of excuses when I asked you the other day about measuring? You didn't measure anything in those cookies."

"You've got to learn the rules to break them," Miles said a little smugly.

Evan was tempted to tell him he was an asshole, but that wasn't exactly in the spirit of cooperation and compromise they were working on right now. Plus, if he'd actually said it, it probably would have come out disgruntled but endeared, like he found Miles' insistence on teaching Evan how to measure kind of adorable.

And it wasn't. Not even a little bit. His heart just hadn't gotten the memo from his brain yet.

He dutifully measured out the sugar, and then the salt, per Miles' specific instructions, and then poured out the packet of yeast into the bowl.

"Last ingredient," Miles said, pushing over a small glass bowl filled with butter. "This is really important—more important than measuring things right. Some recipes call for room temperature butter. Others call for cold butter. You need to make sure you follow the instructions. That can make or break a recipe."

"Like I have a recipe I'm actually following," Evan grumbled.

Four days ago, Miles probably would have shot something grumpy and ill-tempered right back, but this time his smile was as soft as the butter. "You're following *my* recipe," he said, and his voice edged just enough on proprietary that despite all his good intentions, Evan went hot all over. It felt like he'd just been blasted by the heat from an open oven, but there wasn't one. Only Miles.

How had Evan ever thought he was cold and unfriendly? The man could melt chocolate at a hundred paces. Evan wanted to believe it had something to do with their unspoken attraction, but he knew better. It didn't have anything to do with him. Not really. It was all about who was going to be in control, and Miles just wanted it that bad.

Badly enough to bother charming Evan, when, if Miles had been paying attention at all, Evan had been charmed—despite his best intentions—from day one. From the first moment he'd watched a *Pastry by Miles* episode, if he was being painfully honest.

"Well, what does *your* recipe say?" It was stupid to flirt back, but Miles' charm made it too easy.

"Soft," Miles murmured, easing closer, and *god*, yes, that was his finger, brushing casually yet purposefully against Evan's arm. He was probably touching more flour than skin, but even that teasing touch was enough to shoot lightning up his nerves.

It nearly killed him, but Evan took a step away, disguising his need to put some breathing room in between him and the gorgeous man next to him by grabbing a thin flexible spatula from the pile of equipment Miles had set out earlier.

"Just plop it in?" Evan asked and even he was impressed by how cool he sounded when the reality was so much different.

Miles still smiled though, like he knew the truth, and Evan hiding it only added an extra edge of anticipation. "Yep, right in the bowl. And then we get to the fun part."

Evan was almost afraid to ask what the fun part was. But he did because he needed to have some kind of plan of how to resist Miles going forward. "What's that?"

"You mix it up." Miles eyed the spatula in Evan's hand. "And not with that."

"With my hands?" Evan squeaked. "Isn't that unsanitary?"

"Not if you wash them first," Miles said.

Evan did, spending a lot of time unnecessarily scrubbing, like a dose of water and soap could extinguish the fire that Miles kept trying to start.

"You're trying to clean them, not take the skin off," Miles pointed out, leaning over near the sink, eyes bright with amusement. Evan kept telling himself that Miles couldn't read his mind or understand why he was doing anything, but it was getting tougher to believe it.

"Just want to make sure they're clean of laptop cooties before I shove them in the bowl," Evan retorted, reaching for the paper towels next to the sink.

"But laptop cooties are my favorite," Miles said, his lips forming a crooked, lopsided smile and his eyes crinkling.

This was the most blatant lie Miles had told him yet, and it had the opposite effect than he'd probably anticipated. Instead of enchanted, Evan felt cold and clammy, like he'd just sobered up.

No matter how much he liked Miles—and desperately wanted Miles to like him back—the truth was Miles was only trying to charm him so he could have the upper hand. Miles thought the stuff Evan did with his laptop was pointless and a waste of time.

"How should I mix this?" This time it was easy for Evan to drag his attention back to the task. He should have been happier, but he wasn't.

Miles' expression was perplexed. "Mix . . . it?"

"Never mind," Evan huffed. "I'll figure it out." He stuck his hands in and started swirling the ingredients together. Way too quickly his fingers were caked with the sticky flour mixture.

"Wait," Miles said and Evan hesitated, still fingers-deep in the gluey mass. "I think . . . I think maybe we need to approach this differently."

Evan hoped the glare he shot the other man said pointedly that he had *tried* to ask ahead of time, and Miles hadn't understood.

"I know, I know," Miles murmured as he approached Evan, a little like he was trying to calm an upset dog, "it'll be fine. We'll figure it out."

"I don't think so," Evan retorted. "I think we're pretty fucked." His voice wobbled on the last word as Miles reached in and plucked out one of Evan's hands. Whenever Miles was in the kitchen, his own hands were always quick and efficient—certain. Now, he took his time, carefully and thoroughly cleaning off the caked-on mass of sticky flour off each finger.

It couldn't be impersonal, because there was so much touching—way too much touching for Evan's peace of mind—but it felt even more intimate with Miles bent over his fingers, so meticulously making sure every bit of the "dough" was off, his lashes dark against his cheeks as he concentrated on the task.

"I'm sure . . . I'm sure I could manage," Evan stuttered helplessly. He was caught. Literally. Metaphorically.

"Almost done," Miles said, his soft voice still roughly hypnotic, pinning Evan in place even further. He could have moved. He could have protested—he *should* have protested. But the truth was he didn't want to stop touching Miles, even if it didn't mean what he wanted it to.

"Why don't we start over?" Evan asked. "We've got lots of ingredients."

"Because I was slow and you were too fast? There's no reason to. We can salvage this." Miles glanced up, his gray eyes almost green in the light, and it was like he could see right through Evan and all his token protests. Like he meant something else by his words. Like maybe he was admitting he'd been too slow out of the gate and was just now catching up.

"There," he finally said, releasing the second hand. The sticky mass was mostly gone, but Evan knew he needed to wash them off still. And then they needed to do whatever Miles came up with to salvage the half-mixed ingredients.

But he didn't move, and neither did Miles, even though their hips had somehow aligned. If they took a step closer, more than just their fingers would touch. Evan had a sudden flash of memory: Miles crowding him close against the wall when they'd argued only a few days ago. Then, he'd been hot with anger and the indignity of having Miles push him around. Now, the anger had faded and all that remained was an indelible memory of Miles' body against his. And the memory was filled with a whole different kind of heat.

It was annoying that even when Miles was an ass, Evan somehow found him irresistible. Evan figured that must be a commentary on his poor taste in men. Nice men didn't register; it was only when someone went out of their way to be a dick that he paid attention.

"I didn't mean it," Miles murmured, and that was the worst of all, because that was his doughy fingers brushing his cheek, and if he leaned in another few inches, they might be kissing.

The very last thing on earth that Evan wanted to discuss was the email, and he definitely didn't want it to be used against him, especially not when it was only fair and equitable that Evan get to use it against Miles.

After all, it hadn't been Evan who'd up and run away and then gotten drunk and written a nearly incoherent email filled with vague insults and even vaguer compliments.

The good news was it was the push Evan needed to pull away and put some space between them. He turned towards the sink and told himself that he imagined Miles' disappointed face. "Tell me," Evan said briskly, scrubbing with more cold water, "how do we fix it?"

"I don't know, I'm trying," Miles said, and there was too much raw honesty in his voice.

Evan looked up and his own was sharp in response. "I meant the dough."

"Oh. The dough. Right."

Evan ignored how sulky Miles sounded. Was that all he thought he needed to do to fix things between them? Some charming lines and some vague flirting? And a few moments where he considered kissing Evan again?

Yeah, *no*.

Miles had made Evan's life hell since he'd showed up at *Five Points*, and then he'd gone out of his way to insult him.

Finishing up with his hands, Evan wet a paper towel and scrubbed at his face, sure that Miles' fingers had left some traces of flour even though they'd only brushed his skin for a split second. It had been long enough.

When Evan returned to the workspace, Miles was staring into the bowl like it held all the mysteries of the universe. "I think if we mix with a spatula to get the mixture into a rough dough then we can knead it by hand."

Evan picked up the spatula and gently, carefully mixed the dough until it came together into a ball. He wasn't taking any more chances for Miles to ingratiate himself. Mistakes were an opportunity for Miles, and Evan wasn't giving him any additional openings.

"That's good," Miles said. The murmured intimacy in his voice had lessened somewhat, and Evan *was* glad. It was exhausting to fight the attraction all the time. Sometimes he just wanted to get some stuff done without all the distraction.

Shoving his hands back into the dough, Evan copied Miles' demonstrated kneading techniques until Miles pronounced it ready, and got another bowl out, to set the dough into. It went into the freezer to chill.

"What now?" Evan asked.

"Have you ever eaten a croissant?" Miles asked.

"Of course I have." Evan tapped a foot impatiently. It felt like they'd wasted hours, even though it had only barely been one, if the clock on the far side of the kitchen wasn't lying to him.

"Then you know about the flaky layers it has. We need to create that, and to do that, we use a sheet of cold butter, folded in between layers of dough. When the croissants bake, the butter evaporates and creates pockets of air in the dough."

"Which makes it flaky." This baking thing, Evan thought, was a lot more complicated than he'd realized. He re-thought what Miles had said. "A *sheet* of butter?"

Miles shrugged at Evan's astonishment and pulled over a single sheet of waxed paper, on which was spread a thick even layer of butter. "I came in early and made this, and chilled it," he said. "It needs to be very cold, or else it'll all just melt into the dough. It's like pie dough."

When Evan continued to look at him blankly, Miles continued. "You know, like the pies you bake on Thanksgiving? You need cold fat mixed into the dough to prevent it from being tough."

Evan knew what Miles was getting at, and while he had no intention of sharing just how far his Thanksgivings had been from family pie-making, he couldn't exactly pretend like he knew what Miles was talking about.

"We always had store-bought," Evan said, which was only partially a lie. He remembered years when he'd been fortunate and lucky to get a piece of store-bought pie. Homemade pie was a figment of his imagination, a dream that he'd never gotten to share.

"It's the same concept," Miles said. "The water in the butter or the lard evaporates in the heat of the oven, leaving the dough pocketed and airy. Here," he handed a rolling pin to Evan, "let's roll out the butter a little while the dough finishes chilling."

Evan felt like he did a really good job getting the butter perfectly flat and even, as Miles grabbed the dough. Finally, his A-plus personality and perfectionist instincts were coming in handy in the kitchen.

The dough was far trickier to roll out. Miles kept tossing flour on the marble and insisting Evan flour his hands and the pin so many times that he was sure that flour had made it past the apron to his clothes beneath. Good thing he didn't have any other meetings scheduled for today.

When Miles felt like he had the dough flattened enough, they worked together to carefully transport the butter from the wax paper to the dough rectangle. This time, Miles didn't offer to lick the residual butter off his fingers, and Evan shouldn't have been disappointed, but he was a little.

He certainly thought about offering to return the favor as Miles lifted one of his hands to his mouth for a surreptitious lick. But that would be insane and Evan prided himself on his sanity.

"Now, fold the sides of the dough over the butter, like a Christmas present." Evan held his breath and waited for Miles to try the same thing he had with the Thanksgiving pies, but he didn't. Which meant nobody else in the office had blabbed and Miles didn't know yet. A small blessing.

"We're done?" Evan asked hopefully after the folding was complete.

Miles shot him an incredulous look. "Not even close. The dough needs to be re-chilled, and then we'll re-fold to make more layers. And then rinse and repeat."

Jaw dropping, Evan stared incredulously at the man next to him. "How many rinse and repeats?"

"Four? We'll see how it looks at four," Miles said, piling up bowls together and walking over to the sink. "Pastry isn't a race to see how fast you can get something on a plate."

"Or in my stomach," Evan grumbled. "Am I allowed to work at non-baking tasks in between layers?"

Miles waved a hand as he started running hot water in the dishes. "Whatever you want."

Checking email usually didn't fill Evan with quite so much excitement or anticipation, but he was so ready to get back to the familiar, he nearly forgot to take off his flour-dusted apron before venturing back to his cubicle to retrieve his laptop and his notes.

He could only imagine what the reactions would have been if he hadn't detoured to quickly shed the ugly apron and brush off his clothes. He left the bow tie lying on the counter next to his notepad, and considered it a worthy sacrifice for a little bit of Miles' trust.

The problem was that Miles wasn't just after trust. That much was becoming very obvious, and even though it was difficult to imagine a world in which Evan could resist him forever, he still had to make a decision about giving in.

What would it mean? What would it look like? How could he make sure he maintained the upper hand while giving in?

Since he'd turned eighteen, Evan had been professionally ambitious and personally careful. It was a combination that served him well until now, and he saw no reason to throw caution to the wind. If he was going to let Miles—and himself, if he was being very honest—have their way, he needed to at least do it on his own terms, in his own way.

Laptop in hand, Evan swung by the restroom and when he was washing up, gave his face only the most perfunctory look over. Even with the briefest glance, his flushed cheeks and bright eyes gave away the story.

Miles evoked all sorts of emotions in him—frustration and annoyance and impatience, but also something warmer and more indefinable. Something he'd always avoided because he wasn't sure he could control it, and until this moment, that had felt like the scariest risk he could have taken.

This time it felt scarier *not* to take it, like he didn't know what he was missing out on if he let it pass him by.

CHAPTER SEVEN

WHEN EVAN LEFT THE kitchen to grab his laptop, Miles did the dishes and stared at his reflection in the window in front of the sink.

There was no shame in needing to give yourself a pep talk every now and again, but Miles felt weird that he didn't need any sort of pep talk at all. Didn't people usually need to psych themselves up when required to cozy up to someone for mercenary reasons? James Bond never flinched, but James Bond was a manwhore with zero conscience.

Miles didn't like to think he was that sort of person, but when faced with the prospect of using Evan's attraction to give himself the upper hand all he felt was pure, unadulterated excitement. He knew his own feelings about Evan were conflicted, but maybe the lack of shame he was feeling meant he wasn't really conflicted at all.

He was pretty sure that meant his heart or his mind or maybe just his dick was engaged on some level. *And that made it better, didn't it?* his conscience insisted.

It wasn't going to be all for show, on some level it was real for Miles and that should have been all the green light he needed to close the deal. But instead of prodding him into action, the thought made him hold back when Evan returned to the kitchen with his laptop and that stupid folder bulging with notes, half of which seemed to be pages torn from the precious notebook that barely ever left his side.

It was the same sky blue as the bow tie he'd removed earlier, and they both sat, innocent but inherently dangerous, on the kitchen counter.

"Do you want to go over some of the stuff I have?" Evan asked, and unlike his normal, ball-busting certainty, he seemed hesitant. Like maybe he'd reconsidered just how good of an idea so much flirting was.

Miles' dick certainly thought the flirting had been fantastic, and nothing in the world had been hotter than uptight, always-confident Evan uncertainly digging his hands into a bowl of dough and looking to Miles for instructions on how to deal with it.

He hadn't realized that was going to be a turn-on, but Miles wasn't stupid. It added a flair of authenticity to the charm he was trying to pour on, so he used it.

The real question was if it only had the ring of truth or it *was* the truth. Miles had claimed, not even a week ago, that he could never be attracted to a man with such a stick up his ass. He was not happy to discover he might have been wrong.

The only explanation was that Evan, like any decent mold, grew on you after awhile.

"What do we need to go over?" Miles tried to play it casual, but he sounded equal parts apprehensive and excited.

"Oh, tons of stuff. A whole bunch of tiny details, all pointless by themselves, but it all needs to be decided."

"Like?"

Miles had spent most of his teenage and adult life playing it casual with guys he liked. He didn't do serious relationships, or usually relationships at all. He'd never felt the need because casual came naturally to him.

Casual was not coming easy to him now, as he sidled up to where Evan was perched on a stool, sorting through his folders. He leaned against the counter, and railed at himself for looking like some sort of practiced gigolo.

Maybe he *was* James Bond, he'd just never realized it.

Evan wrinkled his nose. "You don't have to be so tense. I'm not *telling* you the decisions, we're making them together."

"Right, yeah, of course."

Costa, he told himself firmly, *you sound like a fucking moron. You can barely string together a sentence. When did he get to you like this?*

Apparently between one breath and the next, in the time it had taken for Evan to stick his fingers in the dough and then throw Miles a single beseeching look.

Miles wasn't James Bond, he was a romance novel heroine straight out of the bodice-ripping 1980s.

"For example," Evan said, pulling out a single sheet with a bunch of scribbles, "how do you feel about the title?"

Evan had very straight posture, his spine stiff even when he was sitting on one of those uncomfortable stools. Miles had never really noticed before, or if he had, he'd marked it off as a character flaw, but now he couldn't stop noticing. And all that ramrod posture made him want to do was tear off Evan's shirt and see what his back looked like, pale and firm, as he bent over the kitchen counter.

Maybe it was Miles who was the bodice ripper.

"The title?" Miles was having difficulty giving coherent answers, and Evan was looking at him a little like he was crazy. More than usual, anyway.

"Of your show. *Pastry by Miles?*"

"I'm not changing the name."

"I know that," Evan coaxed, "but what about a subtitle for this first season?"

"What, like *Pastry by Miles: Joan of Arc Julia Child Teaches You How to Bake?*"

"Not exactly," Evan sniffed.

"Then what?"

"Like, *Pastry by Miles: Baking 101*."

"I sort of like that," Miles admitted begrudgingly. There was a part of him that still recoiled in horror, of course. He wasn't Joan of Arc Julia Child; there was a part of him who was always going to be an inherently selfish slave to his own creativity. But the idea of helping others find their potential was growing on him. He'd drink another bottle of faux Kahlua if Evan found out, though.

"I thought you might." Miles told himself that Evan's smug tone of voice was not in any way attractive. He wasn't very convincing.

"What else?"

"Well, I took the liberty of having the graphics department make some mockups of the new title, just to see what you thought."

Evan pulled some other brightly colored pages out of his folder and slid them across the workspace.

Miles knew graphics were not his strong suit. The logo he'd pulled together last year for *Pastry by Miles* was barely acceptable. Which was why it was so easy to get excited about having a professional take a crack at it—or at least that was what he used to justify it to himself.

"These are great," he said, leaning over and carefully examining the options one at a time.

"We can change them, or mix them, or really, anything we can think of. If you don't like any of them, we can even start over,"

Evan rambled, and Miles looked up at him, and realized, like a light turning on in a pitch-black room, that he was nervous. Uncertain. Worried that Miles wouldn't be happy with his initiative.

That was to be expected, because Miles hadn't been happy with any of his initiatives until now. It was completely Miles' fault that Evan worried about his reaction—because, and this was a bitter pill to swallow—none of Miles' reactions had exactly been reassuring.

Obviously, Miles had seen Evan before, but at this moment, it was like he was seeing him for the very first time, separate from his own fear-tinted glasses. It felt like he'd just been dunked in very cold water.

"I think some of these could really work," Miles said.

Evan smiled, any momentary lapses in self-confidence gone. "Agreed. This one is my favorite," he said, pulling one particular graphic, the font curling around a series of rainbow-tinted circles that evoked the famous French *macarons*. A series of episodes that Miles had done on *macarons* inspired by famous adult beverages had been very popular; probably his most popular episodes before the strawberry raspberry tarts. He still got people messaging him that they'd never thought of making a strawberry margarita *macaron*, or one inspired by a White Russian, but that he'd changed the way they saw pastry.

Those comments had probably been part of the problem, Miles realized. Somehow he'd gotten insufferably smug. There was self-assurance and then there was conceited arrogance. Somehow he'd fallen on the wrong side of that line.

He wanted to apologize—to his credit, not for the first time this week—but that apology, like all his others, still stuck in his throat.

"Did you know that three quarters of *Five Points* clamored for Reed to make those *macarons*?" Evan asked, almost to himself, like of course Miles knew.

"Did he?" Miles asked.

The expression on Evan's face grew conspiratorial, and it shouldn't have been so cute, but it was, undeniably. He leaned closer, bending over the drawings between them. "Reed claimed he was too busy, but his boyfriend, Jordan, admitted to me that he spent three weeks trying to perfect them, and finally gave up."

Reed Ryan had attempted to duplicate his recipes and failed? Miles didn't know whether to be flattered or embarrassed. Suddenly it seemed very stupid to not provide people who wanted to duplicate his creations the recipe.

And sure, he'd worked at Terroir, but Miles had always prided himself as being laid-back and down-to-earth, at least as far as chefs went. He certainly had never been as bad as Bastian Aquino, whose ego he'd gotten to witness with a front row seat.

"*Macarons* are tricky," Miles said, which wasn't a lie. They were notoriously difficult to master, and even he sometimes baked batches that just didn't turn out for reasons he could never pinpoint. "I'll make some this weekend and bring them in." He hesitated, because even though Evan had claimed not to like sweets, maybe he could extend a peace offering in lieu of an actual apology. "Did you want to try a particular flavor?"

Evan shot him a triumphant look, like he'd just been waiting for Miles to ask. "The lemon drop. Of course."

It felt as easy as breathing to reach forward and trace the bright yellow circle on the logo. "One of my favorites."

Evan just sniffed. "Well, you have *some* taste, apparently."

"Does that mean I should pick that particular logo?" Miles challenged. But he couldn't help but miss that the sniping they were doing today was far more playful and anticipatory than the sniping of the last two weeks.

It left Miles breathless and fairly certain that he had almost nothing in common with James Bond after all.

"If you want to. It's ultimately your show. But," Evan said, with more than a little defiance in his own voice, "it's the best choice, by far."

"And probably the idea that you came up with," Miles finished smoothly.

Evan looked surprised and annoyed—definitely not as pleased as Miles had hoped when he'd thrown that line out. "So much shock I can do my job properly," he retorted.

"I figured they put the best with the best."

Evan just rolled his eyes. "And there's the Miles Costa I've grown to know."

"Be nice, or you won't get any *macarons*. Or any *pain au chocolat*."

This time Evan seemed to completely forget that he didn't like sweets, because he sighed with exasperation at Miles' threat. "What?" he asked defensively. "They're taking an eternity to make, surely I should get something out of all this time and effort."

The beeper on Miles' phone went off, pinging loudly. "And that's our cue for more time and effort. Time to re-fold the dough."

This time Evan didn't make a movement to go grab the dough from the blast chiller, but Miles let him go, as he scribbled more into his notebook, seemingly absorbed in making notes on the new logo.

It was an easy five minutes of work for Miles, who got twitchy if he couldn't get his hands into some sort of dough every day.

When he got back to where Evan was perched, he had opened his laptop and was typing furiously into an email window. Miles peered over his shoulder. "Anything good?" he asked.

"Sending some final notes to the graphic designer," Evan said. "I told her to bump the brightness of the colors up a bit, I want something bright and almost candy-colored. And to make the font a bit less fanciful. I feel like the rainbow *macarons* are enough on that front. She'll probably send a few options for us to look at."

Miles rubbed his neck and tried not to look sheepish. "I'm not very good at this part, I should probably default to your expertise."

It was worth admitting that he wasn't very good at something to see Evan's face light up. "Of course," he chirped happily. "If you're sure you trust me not to pick something hideous."

"You picked me, didn't you?"

Evan's smile evolved into a self-satisfied smirk. "That's right, I did. Besides, in case you were worried, I have fantastic taste."

"What else do you have for me?" Miles asked.

"Do you watch *Dream Team*?" Evan shot the question over as he typed furiously away at his laptop. Miles knew enough to see he wasn't working on another email. It was hard to bite back the sudden demand that Evan tell him what he was writing—it wasn't easy to trust Evan when he'd said all that to Reed—but Miles knew he needed to.

"*Dream Team*? The cooking show with that baker from LA and Landon Patton? The one where they spent three quarters of the time flirting and not actually cooking?"

"That's the one." Evan didn't look up. "They're gearing up for rehearsals in the next week, because the next season of their show starts filming."

"And?"

Evan looked up, and he didn't look thrilled. "And that means our kitchen time goes way down, because they're stars and we're the low men on the totem pole."

"What?" Miles demanded. How was he supposed to create recipes and test them and make sure he was able to actually teach people if he didn't have access to the kitchen?

"Believe me, I know. How are you supposed to create recipes if you can't get in the kitchen?"

Miles stared. "That was fucking eerie. How did you know I was thinking that?"

Evan shrugged. "You're predictable. Chef, kitchen time—more important than anything else. It's not hard to connect the dots."

"So what are we going to do about it?" Miles asked, trying to keep his voice level. Evan might be responsible for some things he didn't like, but he wasn't responsible for this. This was, apparently, out of his control. "I'm assuming, since you're you, you have some sort of plan to deal with this."

"Yes," Evan said. "Of course I do. Even though I just found out about this."

"Just now?"

Evan shot him a challenging look over his laptop screen. "Literally thirty seconds ago."

"Oh, so that *was* an email you were typing so angrily," Miles said.

"No. Well. Yes. Sort of. I was sending a message to Reed. Getting permission for us to work from home. Or rather, permission for us to work from *your* home. You've got a good kitchen. Not fantastic, but it should be good enough for our purposes." Evan skewered Miles with another incredibly direct look. "After all, you made that Twinkie at home, didn't you?"

"It was a Ding Dong," Miles corrected.

"Whatever." Evan threw up his hands in frustration. "This is my solution. I wish I had something else, but it's what we've got."

"Would begging help?" Miles asked. "I can be pretty persuasive."

Evan's incredulous glance didn't instantly puncture his ego. Nope. Not at all.

"Okay," he admitted, "*usually* I can be pretty persuasive. Better?"

Evan gave a sharp nod. He was still typing like each key he hit was a punch in the face of the people who had demoted their kitchen time to zip, nada, *nil*.

"No," Evan finally said, with a sigh, fingers finally drifting off the keyboard, "it wouldn't help. *Dream Team* trumps all."

It wasn't like he hadn't heard of *Dream Team*—Miles didn't live under a rock. But he hadn't really paid attention to how popular it was. Or cared, until he was suddenly faced with losing the kitchen time he needed.

"We can work around this, right?" Miles asked, and he didn't even try to hide the desperate edge to his voice. The part of him that was still terrified and needed any reassurance he could get. He'd never imagined asking for it from Evan, of all people, but maybe that had been his problem when they'd first met.

"Of course we can. Working from your place, and we'll still get some time in here but it'll be shorter and it'll be either early or late."

The one thing Miles felt confident about was that Evan was definitely as committed as he was to making this show a success. Of course how they got to that success was still up for debate, but he could never doubt Evan's commitment.

The timer on his phone dinged again, and Miles went to the fridge to pull out the dough. It felt right to be working on something right now, as they tried to muddle through this new hurdle. Whenever he'd struggled with anything cropping up in his life, he'd always gone to the kitchen.

In the kitchen, if you put flour with leavening, you got dough, and if you baked the dough, you got bread and pastries and rolls. There was a logically reassuring certainty about baking—like Miles was asserting control when he didn't have any.

"How many more rinse and repeats do we have left?" Evan asked, not even looking up from his laptop.

"One more, and then they bake," Miles said.

"I find it difficult to believe that anything is worth all this," he said primly.

"Wait and see," Miles insisted.

"You keep saying that." Evan rolled his eyes. Miles couldn't even see his whole face, but he'd begun to discover just what Evan's voice sounded like when his face did that cute little scrunchy thing that always accompanied an eye roll.

Miles shouldn't, but he couldn't help imagining feeding Evan little bites of hot, flaky, buttery pastry dotted with the rich, dark chocolate and him moaning with pleasure as the flavors hit his tongue. He couldn't help it because he was just a man and Evan was wearing him down with each cute scrunchy face and every snarky retort.

Miles was befuddled because those weren't supposed to be things that attracted him. They weren't supposed to be things that attracted anyone. But somehow those things—and a growing list of others—had caught him and now he wasn't just flirting because he was trying to out-James Bond James Bond. He was flirting because he couldn't do anything else.

And that was a problem, mostly because Miles had been incredibly dumb and had kissed him like he was trying to eat him alive and then had sent an email that would have turned off the most understanding and forgiving of people.

Evan was definitely not that understanding or forgiving.

"Miles, Miles, *Miles.*" Evan's voice hit him suddenly and Miles realized that while he'd been daydreaming, trying to figure out how to get Evan to eat from his fingers and *like it* and also forget all about that very unforgettable email, he'd been trying to get his attention.

"Sorry," he said.

Evan threw his hands up in frustration. "Did you hear anything I just said?"

"No?" Miles put on his most charming sheepish expression and hoped that would melt the exasperation on Evan's face. It didn't. Not even a dent.

"I said, tomorrow we should get what you need at your apartment to make it baking-friendly."

"Right, yes, we can do that." Miles realized after he'd said it that *we* had to be a misnomer. Because Evan had no clue what he needed at his apartment to make it "baking-friendly," whatever that meant.

"You'll put the list together?"

Miles saw an opening and even though this attraction confused the hell out of him, it didn't confuse him enough to not take advantage of it. "You said, *we*," he said, with a faux leer that Xander had once said made him look like a creeper. But that was Xander, and Miles took everything he said with a massive grain of salt.

The look in Evan's eyes when he glanced up was dismissive. "Like I would know what you need to bake stuff," he said. "You make the list, and we'll go get the stuff tomorrow. You—list; me—corporate credit card."

"Let me guess, you're also in charge of the budget."

"Yes, and no. Reed just sent me a message and said we could work from your place, *and* he'd foot anything that didn't seem excessive." Evan looked rather self-satisfied at that, and Miles couldn't blame him. He also couldn't deny that even though a week ago, that smug look would have made him crazy, today, all it did was make him want to wipe it off. With his mouth.

It wasn't so much a problem as it was . . . complicated.

The timer on his phone went off again, and this time he dragged Evan off his barstool, ignoring the pulse of electricity under his skin when his fingers closed around Evan's forearm.

He was slender, but he had muscle tone under all that smooth skin, and that was an image that Miles didn't need to have when he was trying to explain to Evan how to roll out the dough for the final steps.

"A big rectangle, like this-ish," Miles said, gesturing with his hands. Evan just stood there, looking at him levelly, his arms crossed across his chest, which might be a way he stood all the time, but right now, only emphasized to Miles that he'd somehow missed that Evan was all lean muscle he desperately wanted to see.

He'd thought this was complicated, but the more he sunk into this new understanding of Evan, the more difficult Miles realized the situation really was. Because he wanted him, much more than he'd ever imagined.

"Maybe you should give me an actual dimension," Evan retorted frostily.

"We'll work on that," Miles coaxed. "It'll be great, just . . . more flour. Lots of flour. We don't want the dough to stick to the counter."

"Not after we've spent four hours in this torture chamber," Evan snarked.

Miles knew it had been frustrating at points, but he thought they'd had a pretty solid morning. He was a little offended that Evan had just referred to the kitchen as a torture chamber. Because that made Miles the head torturer. Yeah, complicated was probably an understatement.

"Just . . . flour the damn counter," Miles said.

Evan did as instructed, but only after tying the apron back on, which surprised Miles. That had been a silently acknowledged instrument of torture (apparently) and here Evan was, voluntarily putting it back on. Of course, he was probably more worried about the state of his clothes than the stupid apron.

The rolling went pretty well; Evan had good technique; he was slow and careful and even with the pressure. Miles stood a little ways behind him, and made all the right encouraging noises and tried not to check out his ass in those pants.

He remembered a point when he'd made fun of those khakis. Now he just wanted to worship them. Or at least what they contained.

"How's that?" Evan asked, standing back and eyeing the rectangle of dough critically. Like this was a life-and-death situation. And baking could be tricky, you often had to be extremely precise, but this was the easy part of the whole thing. It was tough to fuck this up, but Evan never let up on himself for a single second. He had the most A-plus personality that Miles had ever encountered.

"It's fine," Miles said, and pointed to the knife. "Now trim the edges, and cut into four equal strips."

Instead of grabbing the knife, Evan turned around and there was fire and brimstone flashing in his eyes. Miles stood there shocked, because even at the worst, even when they'd been trading insults in the break room and even after Miles had sent him the worst email in the history of emails, Evan hadn't looked at him like that.

"Do you mean to tell me," Evan said, voice low and frustrated, "that we're only getting *four* croissants out of this?"

Miles knew he should have doubled the recipe. But it had seemed easier at the beginning to keep things small and relatively simpler.

"Uh, yes?" He remembered after answering that Evan was easily within reach of both a knife and a rolling pin. Both of which he could use to extract his revenge on Miles.

"*Are you insane?*" Evan hissed. "*Four fucking hours on four croissants?*"

"I thought it was more about the experience and the journey. Besides, you said you don't even like sweets." Miles was torn between groveling and also throwing up an arm to protect against the inevitable attack with the rolling pin, which Evan was still gripping.

"I don't." Evan was still shooting fire from his eyes. It shouldn't have been sexy; it was. Miles couldn't explain that or anything else that had happened today, but logic was overrated. Maybe he should just go with it.

"Right, well, let's continue cutting the dough then. Four even strips." Miles wanted to power through this, and maybe then they could finally get them in the oven, and he could see his fantasy come to life. Evan, putting his food in his mouth.

"This is ridiculous," Evan ground out. But he still turned back to the work surface and began to cut the dough.

"Noted," Miles retorted. But he knew the difference was stark. This time, he sounded amused and not angry. Not like before. He wondered if Evan was paying close enough attention to care. Or if it even mattered.

Evan didn't say anything else, just absorbed the instructions on how to roll up the chocolate bar in the middle of each dough strip, and then brush with a beaten egg.

"And now, *finally*, the oven," Miles said.

"Why do people even do this?" Evan wondered, and Miles thought it was probably a rhetorical question, but he was going to answer it anyway. At least so Evan might absorb some of why baking was so vital to Miles.

"Because once you've tasted the real thing, not the chemical-flavored, soggy, sunken artificial croissant, you won't want anything else."

"I thought you were going to feed me some sort of bullshit about pride in your work."

"That was next." Miles smiled weakly.

"Right, how long in the oven?" Evan asked, picking up the tray and walking it over to the oven. Miles was only a little ashamed, but the sight of him holding a tray of baked goods was undeniably a turn-on.

"Fifteen minutes," Miles said.

Evan absorbed that, and then immediately ripped off the apron. "I'll be right back."

Thirteen minutes later—Miles totally didn't time Evan on his watch or anything, because that would be creepy—he returned, holding two cups of coffee. From the good coffee place that was a block further than the Starbucks in the first floor of the building.

"I figured if we were having first class *pain au chocolat*, we might as well indulge in better coffee." Evan handed Miles his cup with a shrug, like he was trying to downplay his gesture. Maybe he was just trying to downplay that it meant anything deeper.

But Miles already believed it went deeper.

"Thank you," he said, right as the timer went off.

The *pain au chocolat* came out of the oven a beautiful burnished golden brown, crisp edges, with the scent of butter and chocolate wafting through the air.

Evan stared at the tray and seemed to be fighting himself. "Don't you want to have one?" Miles asked innocently. He'd been sure Evan would be on the pan before they even cooled, desperate and eager to prove to Miles that he was wrong. That it wasn't worth the time and effort to bake a *pain au chocolat* from scratch.

"Maybe we should wait for them to cool a minute," Evan said.

"They're perfect just like this," Miles argued. Reached over and deposited one in Evan's palm.

"Hot," Evan complained, but he still lifted the pastry to his mouth and took a single bite. In Miles' fantasy he'd been feeding him in tantalizing little bites, waiting until Evan begged him for more. But this was good too.

Evan's eyes drifted over the first bite, and the expression on his face as he chewed and swallowed was *very* good. There was undeniable bliss, and Miles knew if he'd been able to hold it back, he would have. It made the success even sweeter.

"Good?" Miles asked innocently.

Setting the pastry on the counter with careful, deliberate movements, Evan turned towards Miles. There was something conflicted in his face, like he was doing all of this against his better judgement.

Miles understood that feeling far too well.

"How do you do that?" Evan asked plaintively.

"Do what?"

Evan threw his hands up. "Be so damn good at this. Win me over to your side when I know just how much I want you to be wrong and I know just how stubborn I am."

Miles took a step closer even though Evan's expression was telling him he'd better stay right where he was. "You wanted the best," he said, and his voice was shaky. "Why are you so disappointed you got it?"

"I'm not, I'm not," Evan tried to protest, but he'd already said enough and the green light was flashing in Miles' head. Evan might pretend to be aloof and uninterested, and might fight this every inch of the way, but he felt the exact same pull Miles did. And this time, Miles wasn't going to fuck it up by being angry.

It wasn't going to go away; in fact, it was only getting stronger. Miles usually acted on instinct, and he did now. There were only three steps between him and Evan, and he crossed them in a blink but he still hesitated when he'd reached his destination.

Evan's eyes were huge in his face, wide and shocked as Miles slid a hand around the back of his collar. But he didn't pull away and he didn't say no. Miles had been sure he'd need to argue his case harder, spend longer trying to erase the memory of their first kiss and then the email.

But instead Evan held his ground and held Miles' gaze and waited for him to close the distance between them.

Miles kissed him. It took an achingly long moment for Evan to respond, to reciprocate. A heart-stopping moment when

Miles thought that maybe he'd judged everything wrong and that hadn't been the green light he'd secretly been dying for.

Then Evan's mouth moved against his, sluggish and hesitant at first, and then his tongue was slipping between his lips and he tasted just as he'd expected—like chocolate and coffee and butter—and like nothing he'd ever anticipated—sharp and charged, like the red wine that grew high up in the hills of Mount Veeder at the edge of the valley.

It was fierce and hot and the power of it blew out every fuse in his head, giving Miles no time to get his kissing shit together. His hands had just drifted up Evan's arms, and he was wondering if it was too soon to go for his cock, when Evan suddenly pulled away. His face was flushed, his eyes on the floor.

But he was breathing hard, the rhythm an echo of the ricochet of Miles' heartbeat.

The only thing Miles could think was that he needed another chance, another shot, because that couldn't be the last time it ever happened between them. A week ago he hadn't even liked this man, and now he couldn't get enough of him.

Had Evan changed or was it Miles who was irrevocably altered? He didn't know, and he wasn't sure it mattered.

"This isn't happening," Evan said resolutely before Miles could catch up and make sure that he knew everything he'd done was definitely okay. More than okay. Actually, perfectly fucking splendid.

"It just happened," Miles said frankly. "Come back over here, and it'll happen again." This was more the reaction he'd been expecting after the first kiss, and for it to happen now, after the mind-exploding second kiss, was unexpected and frustrating.

Evan shook his head emphatically. "This is the worst idea in the history of ideas. You don't even like me. I don't know why you decided to flirt with me, but apparently I can only take so much before I fold."

"I do like you," Miles said, even though it sounded stupid.

Evan shot him a look that said loud and clear that he definitely thought it sounded stupid. "Okay," he said, clearly not convinced. "But it's still not happening again. This is a major distraction that we don't need. And I don't really like you either. Or your face." His expression grew downright challenging.

The problem was that Miles didn't believe him at all. The other problem was that Evan still believed he'd meant that email.

"Fine," Miles said, unconcerned. Evan might be talking big right now, but Miles knew what it felt like when someone wanted him, and Evan wanted him. Miles just had to wait until Evan was done fighting with himself. It wouldn't matter how long it took, because Miles knew he was going to get what they both wanted.

Chapter Eight

Not even five minutes after the kiss, the kitchen was overrun by Lucy and Steph and Chloe, Lucy's crew of prep assistants. Evan tried not to think what they would've thought if they'd come in just a tiny bit earlier and caught him kissing Miles.

Or Miles kissing him.

Evan still wasn't sure exactly how it had happened, only that it had happened at all, and if he was being very honest with himself, the world had shook and the floor had rocked and when he'd opened his eyes again, nothing was the same. It was the first kiss he'd always dreamt he'd get from Miles, and he'd let himself be persuaded into it because he'd imagined it would be like the first time.

It hadn't been anything like the first time. It had been dreamy and wonderful and perfect.

It couldn't happen again, but Evan could already tell from the determined glint in Miles' eyes that he wanted it to. That he believed it was only a matter of time before Evan gave in and let it happen again.

Miles thought he knew Evan, but all he'd seen was the professional surface he'd spent years cultivating. He didn't know anything about the steel inside that had been forged through even more shitty years making the best of bad situations.

And he'd seen enough in those situations that he wasn't going to let himself be swayed into a situation where he liked Miles and Miles just thought it was convenient and easy and a simple way to convince Evan to go along with whatever he suggested.

Evan was never going to be the guy who fell for that and then let it drag on. It was necessary for Miles to understand that now.

He scrolled through his email, pretending like he was actually working, while he listened to Lucy and her minions divide up the remaining *pain au chocolat* and exclaim all over the place about how talented he was, how innovative, how flawless his execution was.

Evan could see the remaining half of his abandoned *pain au chocolat* on the other counter, and he had a visceral memory of how much he'd really hated Miles when he'd taken that first bite. He'd hated that everything Miles had said was true, and he'd tried to hate that smug look as Miles watched him discover all his truths.

The final, and worst, truth being that he didn't hate Miles at all.

It was just ironic that Lucy and the assistants were so excited about Miles' talents, when Miles had only been tangentially involved. They wouldn't be squeeing all over the damn place if they'd discover Evan had made the *pain au chocolat* they were currently ingesting.

"Someday," Lucy was saying, "I want to take you to this little bakery down the street. The *choux* are a revelation. And I want to pick your brain as you figure out how they do it."

Evan tried not to grind his teeth together as Miles talked with Lucy. He shouldn't have been jealous. He and Miles weren't exactly friends, and Miles was a decent enough human being that Evan couldn't deny him workplace friends. Even if they weren't him.

"Are we done?" he asked as he stood, gathering his papers, notebook and laptop. "I have a meeting." He didn't have a meeting, and if Lucy went and looked at his schedule later, she'd know he'd manufactured a reason to escape.

Miles glanced over, and Evan steeled himself against the silent apology in his gaze. "Yeah, of course, if you've got to split, I guess I'll see you tomorrow."

It wasn't his proudest moment, but later as he collapsed on his couch, feet and brain and heart hurting, he realized what he'd done. He'd given Miles all the advantages, all the power, all because he'd run away.

What he should do was get up, and go right over to where Miles was probably in his apartment, cooking something delicious, and take some of that power back. His heart and something deeper, a fault line that ran right through the core of him, quaked at the thought. He could *do* something. It was a huge risk, the sort of unimaginable risk that Evan couldn't have conceptualized even a few months ago. But the promotion, even as uncertain as it was, had begun to give him the sort of solid foundation he'd always craved.

And once life had become less of a rat race towards one goal or another, always something necessary and vitally important, Evan had become unbearably aware of all the couples that surrounded him. And the contentment their happy relationships gave them.

He'd seen Reed grow confident and happier the longer he was with Jordan. He'd watched Nick worry and stew and pray as his husband, Colin, had figured out where he wanted to play football next. He'd seen one of Lucy's assistants blossom as she fell in love with her girlfriend.

Love was something Evan had only vaguely heard about, because any kind of love was constantly in short supply in the homes he'd grown up in. There were always more important priorities.

But he'd fulfilled those priorities and they weren't yelling at him anymore. He was clothed and fed and had a solid roof over his head. He had money in the bank. He wasn't living a terrified hand-to-mouth existence anymore. He could afford to be exploratory, even if the possibility scared the shit out of him.

But even the fear wasn't enough to stop him. Even the promise he'd made to himself only an hour earlier that he wouldn't let Miles kiss him again.

That was the thing. He wasn't going to let Miles do anything. He was going to be the one doing the kissing this time. The thought was fucking terrifying, but Evan had never let fear stop him.

"This is probably a mistake," he told himself as he got to his feet and went to look for shoes. "This is almost definitely a mistake."

Yet he still found the shoes, shoved his feet in them and still tromped one door down the hall.

Miles answered on the third knock, looking very surprised to see Evan on the other side of his doorway.

"Sorry about earlier," Evan said in a rush because suddenly he didn't know what to say. He didn't know how to go from the awkward realization he was standing on Miles' doorstep to kissing him like he wanted to. His lack of any experience besides just sort of falling into bed with people had never seemed daunting. It was now.

He didn't have a clue how to seduce someone. It seemed to come naturally to Miles, because when he wasn't pissing Evan off, he was trying to charm him—usually successfully. Evan didn't do that; Evan *couldn't* do that.

Miles lifted an eyebrow. "Are you apologizing *again* for kissing me back? I didn't think you had a bad time on the second try." He was holding a whisk in one hand, and he had flour on his shirt.

"I'm sorry," Evan said because all he could do apparently was apologize. And even he knew that apologies usually weren't preludes to anything sexy. "I interrupted you . . . cooking something."

Miles pushed the door further open, and just shrugged. "Is it an interruption if you do it regularly enough? Besides, I'm making dinner, you might as well come in if you haven't eaten."

Evan had been in too much of a hurry to escape the office and his inconvenient, annoying jealousy to grab food on his way home, and his fridge was empty except for three bottles of fancy mustard and half a bottle of sauvignon blanc. His stomach rumbled as he stepped into the apartment and he smelled something buttery baking.

"You eat too much butter," Evan said as he toed his shoes off near the front mat.

"At least butter's natural. It isn't processed shit," Miles called from the kitchen.

This apartment was basically the same as his own, except for the kitchen, which Evan could acknowledge was drastically different.

Not the layout. Not the countertops, not the appliances. Just the flour dusting the countertops, and something delicious sautéing on the stove, and the general appearance of a room being used.

Evan mostly used his to unbox takeout containers and to reheat the leftovers the next day.

"You want some wine?" Miles asked, gesturing to the bottle on the counter. "I've actually been to this winery, so I can vouch that it's pretty good."

Evan had just graduated from buying the very cheap wine at the grocery store, the wine that was a whisper above the box wine and the huge jugs of white zinfandel. He'd never actually been to a winery; in fact his only trip to Napa had been the six hour round-trip he'd made to collect Miles.

It wasn't like he didn't want to expand his horizons—Reed was always coaching him to do just that—but horizon-expanding took money and, until recently, he'd never been in any position to indulge.

He poured himself a glass of the cabernet sauvignon and sniffed it, carefully swirling the glass like Reed had taught him the first time he'd taken him to a nice restaurant for dinner.

"It is pretty good," Evan admitted. Even to his relatively uncultured palate. And it might give him the liquid courage to close the few feet of distance Miles was giving him.

"I know the sommelier who's in charge there," Miles said, and his voice grew grittier as he stirred the pan on the stove and then pulled it off the heat.

Evan almost asked if it was an ex-boyfriend but Miles seemed like he was going to tell him even if he didn't really want to know about all the people Miles had kissed before him. Especially not when Evan was planning on doing more kissing.

"You know Wyatt?" Miles asked, shaking the sautéed veggies in the pan and carefully stirring them into the bowl on the counter. "My old roommate?"

Evan barely remembered anything about his trip to Napa, except the lighter fluid stench coming off Miles and the guilt in his eyes. But he nodded anyway, even though all he had was an impression of a big guy, built like a linebacker with sun-bleached hair.

"Yeah, it's Wyatt's ex. Good sommelier. Terrible boyfriend." He hesitated as he pulled a partially baked pie crust from the oven, which explained the deliciously buttery smell in the apartment. "Got us some great wine though. Not that this one is spectacular, but he was connected, you know?"

Evan had learned really fast that some people—okay, *most* people—didn't want to know about how he wasn't connected at all. Or about his shitty childhood. Or about how he'd clawed his way up the ladder to success. He'd been on a handful of very terrible dates where he'd been at least partially honest when asked, and afterwards, he'd figured out that when people asked, they weren't asking because they actually wanted to know the truth.

Miles poured the contents of the bowl into the crust and sprinkled some sort of cheese over the top.

"What are you making?" Evan asked, because changing the subject seemed like the best plan he could come up with at such short notice.

"Veggie quiche with some really good fontina I picked up at the farmer's market," Miles said, like everyone came home from a trying day and whipped together a gourmet meal.

Sometimes it felt like too much for Evan to dial the number to the local Chinese restaurant.

Miles must have caught Evan's eye roll because he smirked. "Are you going to tease me now about the good fontina from the farmer's market?" He was leaning over the counter, eyes sparkling under the lights, looking too delicious for words, even with the flour dusting his t-shirt. *Especially* with the flour dusting his t-shirt.

"It just was such a cliché. You're like a walking chef cliché ninety-four point six percent of the time."

He didn't look concerned about Evan's accusation, though, and Evan couldn't help but be a little surprised. Two weeks ago, that comment would have gotten Evan a sour lemon expression and some biting remark back.

"Why are you being so nice?" Evan wanted to know. He wanted to know even more, like what Miles wanted from him, but he thought he'd start small. Simple.

"To you? Especially when you seem to enjoy making fun of me?" Miles shrugged, clearly unconcerned by the sudden shift in their relationship. "I'm not sure. Why does it matter?"

"It matters because it matters."

"Some things don't require you to overthink them. Just like some pastries shouldn't rise too much. Or that a dessert can be too sweet, but can never have too much chocolate."

"Life advice from Miles Costa. You should change career paths." Evan knew he got bitchy when he got defensive. "*Finding Your Best Self by Miles.*"

Evan ignored the twinge of hurt in Miles' eyes.

"Hey, I never promised I was some sort of expert. I sort of fall into most things," he said, voice still easy, "and when I got out of my own way, this seemed pretty obvious."

"I can't do that. I don't do that." Evan hesitated, confessions teetering on the edge of his tongue, but he held them back. "If something isn't going to work out, if something looks like it's going to fail, I make sure it doesn't." He didn't want this to fail, but he also didn't know how to make it a success.

Show me how, he wanted to beg Miles, but his pride would have stung far too much to ever admit that out loud.

"You know," Miles said casually, "that explains a lot about you. About how you are with your job."

Evan turned away, twisting the stem of his wine glass. "I thought I was the luckiest person in the world when I got a paid internship at *Five Points* my senior year of college. It was the best opportunity I was ever going to get, and I jumped at it."

"And you worked your ass off," Miles finished. When Evan glanced up, he was smiling ruefully.

"What?" Miles asked with amusement. "Don't tell me you've changed that much."

Evan flushed and nodded. "I haven't. I did everything they asked me to do. And it wasn't glamorous stuff, we didn't do any videos back then. Not like now. The culinary department didn't even exist. Most of the staff writers had assistants. I was an assistant to the assistants. And that makes it sound even better than it was."

"How did you end up working for Reed?" Miles asked. "He's never struck me as the sort who would get a new job and demand an assistant."

"Oh god, no," Evan breathed out. "That didn't even become official right away. I had started helping out here and there on the *Dream Team* set, this was right before I graduated from college, and I really wanted to transition from a paid internship to a full-time paid position. And I thought if I made myself an expert, the guy you went to for everything related to that show, I might *make* myself a job."

"So you helped Reed when he came on."

Evan leaned over the counter, wondering how, in a week, he and Miles had gone from hating each other to reluctantly working together, to conspiratorially trading work stories and sharing a bottle of wine as Miles cooked.

For the very first time he let himself think, *I want more. I want this all the time.*

"You and Reed have more in common than you realize," Evan confessed.

"We're both brilliant chefs?" Miles' incredulous look left Evan feeling warm inside. Too warm. He took a gulp of wine before belatedly realizing that was not going to help at all.

"Other than that," Evan said. "When he started, he was fucking lost. Jordan helped, of course, especially with his *Dream Team* producing duties. But the rest of it? I found myself doing a lot of stuff he asked me to help him with."

Miles leaned over the stove, pulling the oven door open a crack to check his quiche. Evan tried to ignore the way his t-shirt rode up his back, exposing a tempting slice of bare skin.

He failed. He wanted to reach over and touch that skin. He wanted to know what it tasted like under his tongue.

"So how long did you officially work as Reed's assistant?"

Evan hesitated. "Are we really having the conversation we should have had the first day you showed up? Right *now*?"

"You just knocked on my door. We're having a nice glass of wine. I kissed you today and we both liked it." Miles shrugged unrepentantly. "It makes sense to start over, as much as we can."

Evan couldn't believe his nerve, but Miles did seem to do that: float through life, unconcerned and not heavily bogged down by regrets or complicated situations. He was a surface person; Evan was desperate for roots. They were probably not the most obvious match, and Evan knew that, but sometimes fate was crazy like that. You wanted the wrong person, even if you knew he was the wrong person.

And then, suddenly, like a light flashing on, it didn't even matter.

Evan reached over and grabbed the hem of Miles' t-shirt and jerked him closer. "Then let's start over," he said, and kissed him.

It probably wasn't the best line ever. It wasn't even the most successful line, but that didn't matter because Miles' mouth was on his. Pleasure roared through Evan like a freight train. He hadn't even realized how much he'd wanted until he could just take, so he did.

He fisted his hand in the hair that he'd been watching and wanting for eight months, and it was just as soft and necessary as Evan had imagined it would be. It also proved handy to use as a directional force because Miles went just where Evan wanted him, sliding right back against the counter, his mouth a hot brand against Evan's.

It turned out that seduction was easy when you just took what you wanted. Evan took Miles' mouth, his hair, and then his body as his other hand slid right down his back, fingers testing and touching every lean inch of muscle the way his eyes had for the last week.

It was also easy when you didn't think, when you let the fire of desire consume everything—every fear, every worry, every quietly murmured doubt.

Evan flipped up the hem of Miles' t-shirt, and slid his hand right up the skin of his back.

It felt even more incredible than he'd imagined, and then Miles moaned, something wild and free and unhinged, like he was torn apart by Evan kissing him, by Evan pursuing him.

It wasn't like Evan didn't think he was worth wanting; it was more complicated than that. And Evan didn't want to do complicated right now. He'd done complicated his whole damn life, and right now a really cute boy was kissing him and beginning to sort of grind against his thigh, his hard cock definitely mirroring Evan's own.

It was so easy to just say, *fuck it.*

When Evan broke the kiss with a gasp, Miles' lips were red and wet, the same color as the raspberry strawberry tarts he'd made that had started everything. And it was so easy to tangle his fingers deeper into Miles' curls. Evan had barely even begun to push when Miles tore the floor right out from under Evan and sunk to his knees.

Yeah, Evan definitely wanted that, but he'd also never conceptualized that it was a thing that could actually happen.

He watched as Miles unbuckled his belt with legitimately trembling fingers. Something Evan had always been sure only happened in overwrought porn. But his own fingers didn't feel so steady either, so it could definitely happen, especially when the moment felt like this and you were so close to the edge you could tumble right off with only a gentle nudge.

There was no time to worry. No time to second-guess. Miles already had his cock out, pleasure spiking as he stroked it expertly with those long, slender fingers that Evan had already been fantasizing about for months.

Then Miles lowered his mouth, and Evan stopped thinking at all. There was only a fuzzy haze of bliss blanketing everything, and for the first time in what felt like forever, Evan just let himself feel it. Up until the moment his cock slipped out of Miles' mouth and he realized that Miles was babbling helplessly as his fingers reached back and gripped Evan tight by the ass, each of his ten fingers branding him.

"God, your ass in these pants," he was mumbling, "I love it so damn much."

And like the worst nightmare in the world, a single, blinding flash.

I really hate your face.

Evan tried to push it aside. He worked really hard, so hard in fact, that he felt himself grow the opposite. And then the flare of embarrassment as he couldn't help but flash back to every single damning word of that email. All those disparaging, drunk, stupid words.

He wrenched his body away, his softening dick falling from Miles' worshipful fingers.

Evan couldn't look down, couldn't see Miles' face as he realized everything was wrong.

His fingers were still trembling stupidly as he stuffed himself back in his briefs and zipped his fly. His belt buckle was hopeless and he just left it dangling uselessly.

"What's going on?" Miles asked softly. Carefully. Like he was afraid he'd spook a wild animal.

And it was Evan who was the wild animal; the wild card who'd just lost his mind and let Miles blow him and then lost the whole train because he couldn't forget—not really, not when it counted—that Miles didn't really like him.

Evan remembered too many homes he'd lived in, where the kids' faces would change the moment he walked in the room. And then how they'd suck up later that night, begging for Evan to do their homework for them.

He remembered every single time he'd gone to bed with that sick feeling in his stomach. Needed for something but never really liked. Never respected. Always used.

It turned out that it didn't feel different even if he was the one doing the using.

"I can't do this," Evan said, and to his own shock, his voice was steady. Rock steady. Like his belt wasn't dangling undone, and Miles wasn't still on his knees in his kitchen.

"It just . . ." Miles said, and then hesitated. And yeah, Evan didn't know what to say either. How else did you address the elephant in the room that the guy you were blowing suddenly and inexplicably lost his hard-on?

"It happened," Evan said with a hard edge, and forced himself to turn back and meet Miles' eyes straight on. To take in his position and remember that it was Evan who had put him there. "It's not going to happen again."

"You're the one who showed up on my doorstep!" Miles exclaimed, pulling himself upright.

"Yes, well, I wanted to check in with you before tomorrow. And now that I have, I'll be going," Evan said. He picked up his wine glass, letting the rest of the alcohol slide down his throat. It didn't help. He set the glass on the counter with a decisive click.

"Wait," Miles said. "Don't go. You haven't even had dinner yet."

"That's your dinner, not mine," Evan said. It hurt, realizing that it was probably never going to be his dinner. But the short-term pain was easier than the long term; he'd learned that the hard way.

"Why are you being like this?" Miles asked, and yeah, he was definitely annoyed.

"I'm being this way because we cleared the air, we had a nice glass of wine together, and now you want more out of me. But it's not going to happen. This wasn't some sort of impromptu date."

"You can't ignore this," Miles protested. "You wanted it too. I know you did." He didn't even have to say, *I had your dick in my mouth and it was hard and you wanted it. You wanted to come.*

"But I am ignoring it," Evan said, pulling the door open, "I'm exercising my right not to deal with this."

Evan shouldn't have been surprised that Miles followed him right out the door, socks and all. Really, he should have just kept going and not stopped, therefore tipping Miles off to the fact they lived next door to each other. A fact Evan had been very determined to keep to himself.

"What are you doing?" Miles stood, shock on his features as Evan pulled out his keys and proceeded to unlock his door.

"Going home," Evan shot over with a challenging look.

"You live next door," he stated incredulously.

"*Five Points* owns this building. Reed got me a good deal when I was looking for a new place."

"Just like my 'good deal,'" Miles said wonderingly. "I wondered why it seemed so convenient."

Evan rolled his eyes. "You should read your lease a lot more carefully. This place is rented to you as long as you're an employee of *Five Points*."

Miles didn't look phased for a moment, and Evan figured that was because he'd never been desperate and on the edge of homeless. If it ever happened to him, he'd learn to read his leases.

Tapping his foot impatiently, Evan asked, "Are we done here?"

It was so sudden, Evan would tell himself that was why he didn't see it coming. Except that Miles uttered some stupid line first about, "one more thing," and that should have been all the warning Evan needed that he was going to take another three steps, cup Evan's chin in one beautiful hand, and kiss him again.

Later, Evan would also tell himself that the reason he didn't stop it right away was because he was so surprised, but how could that really be true after what had just happened?

So if Evan fell into the kiss, let his head be tipped back against his door, let his mouth be nearly ransacked by Miles' mouth, let himself wonder if that was his slightly salty taste, then that was his own damn fault.

Then Miles broke the kiss way too soon, leaving Evan wanting more and again and *everything*, but it was all useless, and Miles' lips, wet and red, superseded anything else.

"You weren't supposed to do that again," Evan said unsteadily, because the blood had left his brain again and taken a fast route to his cock. He shifted his hips away from Miles, because even though he'd probably already felt his hard-on, Evan didn't need him to gloat about it. Yes, it was back. No, this still wasn't happening.

Miles placed a finger right on his damp lips to shut him up. "I know what you're about to say," he said, "and I'm just going to stop you there, before you say it."

Evan glared, but Miles didn't move. "Besides," Miles said, with a cute little shrug that Evan wanted to hate, but didn't, "we both know everything you were about to say was some bullshit you're trying to believe and that I don't believe at all."

Evan backed up a step, and then another, even though this was *his* doorway. Miles' hand fell to his side, and he was free to insist that Miles was the one who was full of bullshit, but for the first time in a long time, he didn't know how to refute something so blindingly obvious.

"Don't ever do that again." Evan crossed his arms over his chest—because, *defiant body language* and also it kept Miles at arm's length while Evan tried to figure out what to do with him.

"Kiss you?" Miles raised an eyebrow. "Blow you? I'm happy to do both again."

"Shut me up," Evan corrected. "Besides, I'm hardly the one who needs to stop talking. Or *typing*."

Evan's bomb hit Miles just the way he'd expected it too. Hard. And it left a trail of guilt and shame in its wake. It should have made Evan feel better, but it turned out that he didn't like seeing Miles look like a kicked puppy. The aggressively charming, certain-of-his-own-charisma Miles was a lot more fun. Evan licked his lips, and tried not to think about why that might be.

"I should really . . . apologize for that," Miles mumbled.

"For what?" Evan asked, loudly and clearly. "I'm sorry, I didn't quite get that."

"I was an asshole. I wrote some asshole things. None of which I really meant, by the way. And I'm sorry."

Evan shot him a level stare. "Five point seven points for execution, three point eight points for technique. And don't even get me started on sincerity."

"What?" Miles exclaimed, a little of his fight coming back. "I totally meant that. I *am* sorry."

"And yet it took you days to apologize." Evan paused. "Now that we've established that I'm good enough to blow, but not good enough to apologize to, I'm going in my apartment now. Move."

Miles conceded the doorway with a shambling, ashamed motion that made Evan feel even guiltier. And it wasn't his responsibility to feel guilty! He wasn't the one who'd written that email and then not apologized for it. Anything he wanted to ding Miles for, he should be free and clear to ding away.

It didn't matter that he'd spent the last week convincing himself that the email meant nothing and that he hadn't cared that Miles had sent it, because it was clearly all bullshit.

It mattered. Miles mattered.

Desire was fine and good when everyone had a good time and got their rocks off. But sometimes desire was slippery, and you couldn't get a handle on it.

It shouldn't have been a big deal. Miles had given Evan half a blowjob. He'd been enjoying himself so much he'd ached with it. Had been tempted, with Evan's dick in his mouth, to slide his hand down the front of his pants and hump his own palm.

It was tempting to do it now. Miles still didn't know what had stopped him after he'd gone back to his own apartment, and he'd spent the rest of the night sulking. He didn't know what was stopping him now.

Maybe because what he wanted was something he couldn't have, and the idea of settling for his own hand felt paltry in comparison.

If he couldn't have Evan, maybe at least he could think about him. Miles imagined that tight rounded ass naked, spread out for him on his bed. Evan, glancing back, desire written all over his face, pleading for Miles to touch him.

No. Miles shredded that fantasy, unhappy with it as he palmed himself through his boxer briefs. He was already hard—had barely gone soft since he'd been on his knees in the kitchen—and there was a damp spot in the cotton.

It would be so easy to get off. He just needed the right image. The perfect image. Miles rolled through them, one after another. Evan bending over, Evan on all fours, Evan on his knees, Evan with a cruel smile on his face as his fist wrapped around Miles' dick.

Pleasure arched through him as Miles shoved his underwear aside and gripped himself. That was what he wanted. He didn't want Evan on his knees for him. He wanted Evan owning up to every bit of his own power and control. He wanted Evan completely in control and completely under Miles' spell.

It was rougher than Miles usually liked, but that added to the swirl of fantasy in his own head. Evan, smiling with a hint of teeth as he worked him over good, thumb swiping over the head and making Miles moan.

Miles was making himself moan, but suddenly that didn't matter. It was Evan doing it. Evan was in charge. Evan was wringing this pleasure out of his body. Only Evan.

He couldn't even enjoy the hot burst of pleasure from his orgasm because he was already panicking about what it meant.

He wanted Evan, but Evan was pissed off. Evan might even hate him a little. And he might have a legitimate reason. Miles groaned and grabbed a handful of tissues from the bedside table. He should feel more relaxed now, his problem taken care of, but instead he felt edgier than ever.

What could he say to Evan so he would forgive him? Was it even possible or was Miles chasing after a pipe dream? Was he going to be resigned to forever fantasizing about Evan in his bed and never actually having him?

Evan didn't hesitate when he got back inside his apartment. He immediately headed for the shower and sanity. Stripping his clothes off, he turned the water on as hot as he could stand.

He ducked his head under the spray and hissed as the water beat down over his forehead.

Evan had known it was a mistake a long time ago to start thinking about Miles while jacking off. He'd always been afraid it would make things weird between them if and when Miles came to work at *Five Points*. It turned out that, ironically, Evan thinking about him while orgasming was hardly the weirdest part of their relationship.

He gave himself a tentative pump, and yeah, he was still hard, and still definitely into at least *thinking* about Miles while getting off.

Maybe he wasn't ready yet for Miles to actually be involved, but it was still so easy to just let his mind drift and settle on an image of them together.

Him bent over the kitchen counter, Miles sliding into him slowly, just thick enough to make him ache and feel it the next day. His hand caressing his back, letting him know how much he cared, even as his cock made sure Evan knew just how much he wanted him. Evan's hand sped up on his own dick, rough and careless, as he chased the pleasure he imagined Miles could give him.

It was over too soon, but Evan knew he'd been too worked up to last. He could still feel the ghost of Miles' mouth around him, and how wet and warm it had been. And that last thought was all it took to blow his load against the tile wall. He let out a groan, and wondered, just for a second, if Miles could hear. If Miles would know what he was doing.

If Miles was maybe doing the same thing.

Chapter Nine

Evan was pissed. Miles had (very) belatedly realized this last night, and had spent the morning realizing just how pissed he was.

The thing about Evan was that he wasn't like anyone else Miles knew. Nobody else could have been that angry and just hid it all, so completely, even the person he was angry at didn't know. Nobody else could have kissed him, and been as hard as he was, lost to the pleasure Miles was giving him, and feel the anger he did.

Miles felt incredibly stupid that he hadn't seen it before, but then he reminded himself that Evan must have worked hard to conceal it. It wasn't like Miles was incredibly oblivious. The truth was that Evan hadn't wanted him to know, and then suddenly he was practically shouting about how it had been too many days with too few apologies.

A tiny voice whispered in the back of Miles' head that Evan must be high maintenance, which was why he was so hot and so available, and yet so damn difficult, but Miles didn't think that was really it. There was something else going on, and Miles was determined to figure out what it was.

Even if Evan ended up right, and nothing else ended up happening between them, he still wanted to know. Which was a state of mind that Miles wasn't used to. He was used to not really caring too much about anything that wasn't in the kitchen. Now the joke was on him, because his life had been in a state of chaos ever since he'd met Evan, and he still couldn't walk away.

It would have been way easier, Miles reflected miserably, skulking behind Evan as he pushed the cart through the restaurant supply store.

"I can practically hear you back there pouting," Evan announced as he examined the list Miles had complied, and compared it to the display of whisks before them.

It was a sad state of affairs that they could be in his personal heaven, and Miles could barely even motivate himself to look at the tempting array of culinary tools in front of him.

"Are you going to let me pick out whisks?" Evan demanded when Miles didn't answer. "Or are you going to do your job?"

Last night, when he'd pulled the quiche out of the oven, he'd stared at it, realizing that he didn't want to eat it alone, even though when he'd decided to make it, he'd never even dreamt that Evan would show up at his door.

That was the problem with Evan. He burst in, and when he left, nothing was the same. There was an Evan-sized hole in the life that Miles had always considered very satisfactory.

It wasn't fair, but it was the bed he had made, and now he had to deal with it. Miles reached over to the whisks and grabbed a handful without even really looking at them, tossing them into the cart.

Evan shook his head and did that cute little half eye roll that usually meant he wanted to do some big production of an eye roll, but decided it wasn't worth the energy.

"When we're making . . . Twinkies or dongs, or dings, or whatever the hell you bake," Evan said snidely, "and you need the *right* whisk for the job, I'm going to remind you of this moment, and how it's all your fault."

"Believe me, I'm sure I won't need that reminder," Miles retorted fervently. "Probably because you'll never let me forget it."

"Only you," Evan said, pushing the cart forward with purpose, "would be annoyed I was pissed you didn't apologize after insulting me."

Miles wanted to find the even keel of the last few days—when they'd compromised and even found a way to work together—but it was completely lost. Maybe it was the kissing. Maybe it had been the almost blowjob. Maybe it was the anger simmering right under the peaceful surface. But it wasn't going to go back to how it had been only yesterday. That much was obvious.

It wasn't right, but he silently blamed Evan. Maybe if he hadn't kept his fucking mouth shut that he was angry then Miles would have apologized right away and prevented all this.

"Do we need anything else?" Miles asked, and gave himself a gold star, because at least he was making an attempt to converse politely.

Evan leveled him an incredulous look. "It's *your* list."

"Yeah, but it's in *your* hands," Miles retorted.

To Miles' surprise, Evan did actually look down and review the list. "I think we've got it all. Oh no, wait, we need silicone molds still."

"Joy," Miles muttered under his breath, even though silicone molds were usually something he really enjoyed.

If Evan ignored that comment, and instead pushed the cart over to the right aisle, then Miles told himself they were definitely better off.

Fifteen minutes later, they were checked out and just about done packing the bags into Evan's small compact.

"I have a lunch meeting," Evan announced when they both got in the car, "but after, we can head over to your place and work all afternoon. That good with you?"

Miles bit back a snide comment that he didn't really have a choice. He'd thought when he left the restaurant industry, his schedule would stop being dictated by someone else. It turned out that wasn't the case.

But instead of bitching, he nodded. There was some recipe research he could do while he waited for Evan. He'd planned on doing it last night, but after Evan left, he'd been in too much of a bad mood to do much of anything, including eat a slice of the quiche he'd been so excited over.

"Good." Evan sounded pleased with himself that he was back in control. Miles didn't like it, but he also didn't know what to do about it.

They stopped by Miles' apartment and unpacked the bags of supplies. Maybe Evan didn't want to fight anymore either, because by the time they made it to the *Five Points* office, the biting tension of earlier had been replaced by a frosty silence.

Miles wasn't sure it was an improvement, but he also didn't know how to fix it. So he kept his head down and when Evan grabbed his laptop from the cubicle next door, Miles acted like he wasn't even there.

When Lucy found him an hour later, he was pretending to do recipe research, but instead knew he was just staring broodingly at the laptop screen.

"You look down," she said, and the kindness in her voice was so welcome, he couldn't help but turn towards it.

"Rough few days," Miles admitted.

"We're heading over to the good coffee place, you want to come with?"

Lucy hadn't ever invited him to accompany her and her kitchen minions before, but it was a no-brainer for Miles to say yes. First, he loved the good coffee place. It was better in every way compared to the Starbucks downstairs. Second, Lucy had worked at *Five Points* since the inception of the culinary department. Almost as long as Evan. Maybe she knew something about why he was so damn prickly.

Maybe he should have asked Evan himself, but Miles figured he had already tried that last night, and while it had worked for a little while, Evan had eventually clammed up and then he'd run away.

"Oh yeah, I could definitely use a pick-me-up," Miles said and shut his laptop.

While they were waiting for the elevator to take them down to the ground floor, Lucy looked over with a compassionate smile on her face. "Evan running you ragged?" she asked, tucking a lock of short honey-blond hair behind one ear.

Evan had told him once that Reed had hired Lucy a few years ago, when he'd struggled to handle both the kitchen management duties and the producing aspects of his job. Miles had been surprised to learn that even with her efficiency and obvious skill set, she didn't have any formal culinary training.

"It's tough reconciling two visions for one show," Miles said as they stepped on the elevator together.

Lucy gave him a sympathetic grimace. "I can only imagine. Evan is pretty driven and usually very sure that his vision is the right one."

"Yeah," Miles said awkwardly. He wanted to ask, but he also didn't want to go on record as *asking*. "I didn't realize the extent of it until last night. I didn't know he'd started at *Five Points* as an intern."

"Oh yeah," Lucy said as they stepped off. Her two assistants, Steph and Chloe, were waiting outside the building. Steph hadn't even taken her work apron off, and it was dotted with bright swatches of some sort of red berry mixture. "He surprised everyone, but I don't think he ever surprised himself. He always knew he'd get the producing job. The rest of us just came on board a little later."

"Are you talking about Evan?" Steph piped up.

Chloe was lagging behind, typing something frantically on her phone. "Her girlfriend," Lucy whispered with a cute little smirk as she nudged her shoulder against Miles'. "They're practically inseparable and very adorable."

"Yeah," Miles said, at the same time that Lucy said, "He's feeling a little overwhelmed by Steamroller Evan."

"Steamroller Evan?" Miles' eyebrows raised and he hoped—*prayed*—that he wasn't breaking any sort of unspoken professional conduct to gossip about his producer outside of the office. But he was desperate for any sort of insider information he could use to convince Evan they were both on the same side. And also, that Miles *didn't* dislike him, no matter what that email might have made Evan believe.

"Shhhhh," Chloe said, proving that while she'd been texting, she'd also been listening to the conversation. "You know he hates it when you call him that."

"I don't care," Steph said stubbornly, "if you get in his way, and you won't get out of it, he'll absolutely steamroll you."

Three sets of eyes turned towards Miles as they entered the coffee shop, and he threw up his hands. "Ladies, let me get some caffeine first."

Unfortunately he didn't get much of a reprieve, as there was actually nobody in line.

When he ordered a muffin with his coffee, Lucy leaned over and whispered in his ear, "Don't get the banana walnut, get the white chocolate cranberry. Trust me."

He was picking at the wrapper, waiting for his cappuccino when Chloe and Steph came up to him. "So," Chloe said, "is he as hard to work with as I'm imagining?"

"It's not that hard," Miles said, which was sort of a lie, but he also wasn't going to throw Evan under the bus with the kitchen staff when they already called him Steamroller Evan. "It's actually nice to work with someone who has a passion for the details, for making sure that you're as successful as you can be." And that *was* true, and Miles had not even realized it was until this moment until he'd had to find something good to say.

"You can't tell me that him wanting to always be right is easy," Steph piped in.

They had him there. "No," Miles admitted. "It isn't always easy."

"You know why he has to be right. He's always trying to prove that him getting hired full time wasn't some fluke," Chloe said.

Miles frowned. "Why would it be? He got an internship and got offered a job because he worked hard."

Lucy approached, carrying a paper pastry bag. "He didn't tell you?"

It felt like everyone knew something that Miles didn't, and he was suddenly, blindingly sure that what everyone knew that he didn't was something vital.

"I don't know what he hasn't told me," Miles said flatly. He shouldn't feel embarrassed that Evan hadn't confided anything about his job history, even though they were supposed to be working closely together, but he was.

"It's okay," Chloe said, laying a sympathetic hand on his arm. "He's just so private. I'm not surprised he didn't tell you."

"What, that he's an axe murderer? That he's secretly hoarding chicken nuggets in his apartment?" Miles retorted.

"I'm just surprised he mentioned the internship and didn't tell you that it's an internship exclusively for foster kids who've been able to attend college," Lucy said softly.

"Foster kids?" Miles couldn't believe that Evan wouldn't have told him that he'd been a foster child, but it made sense that he hadn't. When had Miles ever been receptive to that sort of confession? Before or after he'd told him he hated his face?

"He tries to pretend that he didn't get the internship because of that," Steph said. "I guess because he's ashamed of it or whatever."

"Steph," Lucy admonished softly, "we've talked about this. Whatever reasons why Evan doesn't want to talk about his past are his own." She turned to Miles. "But I did think you should know, since I didn't think he'd tell you himself."

"I appreciate it," Miles said. He'd rather have heard it from Evan himself, but he had a feeling that would have been a long time coming—or not at all. And this felt like the big break that he'd been waiting for; the mysterious information that Evan had been holding back that Miles had desperately needed to understand how and why he ticked.

"I know it doesn't seem like it," Lucy said apologetically, "but I *do* encourage those two," she gestured to where Steph and Chloe were picking up their coffee, "not to gossip about everyone. Especially Evan. He doesn't like it, and frankly, neither do I."

"It hasn't been easy, working with him," Miles said, finally breaking down and admitting the truth. "We've been struggling."

"He's a great person, funny and smart and irreverent, but you do have to break through his shell."

Miles didn't want to tell Lucy that mostly what he'd done since arriving at *Five Points* was do things to reinforce Evan's shell. For example, that email had given it pretty much bulletproof coating, and he was still trying to figure out how to de-militarize it.

"I'm working on it," was all he could say. He didn't want to admit that a lot of the struggle was his own fundamental misunderstanding of the situation on day one, and how he'd acted like an unprofessional ass since then. He was trying to change, to start over, but he was beginning to think there was no way to do that—all he could do was try to move forward and be better.

And then Miles went and got really stupid. "But you don't have to sell him to me," he said, not even recognizing that conspiratorial edge to his low voice, "I really like him. Even if he can be tough to work with sometimes."

Unfortunately, Lucy understood exactly what he'd meant. Miles almost wished she was a little less sharp on the uptake. "I thought you might," she admitted. "When we walked in yesterday, I could feel . . . undercurrents."

No matter what Lucy might say about gossip, he knew it happened. It happened everywhere, at every workplace. It had even happened at Terroir, despite Bastian Aquino's notoriously hardcore anti-gossip policy. And nothing got people talking quite like a juicy workplace romance.

Evan was definitely going to kill him.

So much for starting over and trying to be better every day.

"Ah, well, you know. Adversarial relationships and all," Miles tried to joke, but the look Lucy shot him made it very clear she understood exactly what was going on and no amount of denial or *just kidding!* was going to convince her otherwise.

"We picked up your coffee!" Chloe said to Miles as she and Steph walked back to where he and Lucy were standing. "We're all ready to go."

"Oh good," Miles said, glancing at his watch and realizing he was about to be five minutes late to meet his *adversarial relationship*, "because I'm about to be late."

⊰⊱⊰⊱

"You're late," Evan said, head bent towards his screen, fingers not missing a beat as he typed furiously.

"I know, I'm sorry, I thought I'd grab a coffee." Miles slid into the chair next to Evan, but Evan still didn't look up.

"Oh, thanks for bringing me one too," Evan said levelly, even though he had to know that Miles only had one cup in his hands.

"I . . . uh . . . didn't know you wanted one?" Miles said sheepishly. He'd made it back into the building two minutes late, and then had raced to Evan's cubicle, only to not find him there. He'd made the rounds, until one of the writers stopped him and said Evan was in the conference room, still working after the meeting had ended.

Why hadn't it occurred to Miles to bring him coffee? He liked the good coffee place as much as anyone else. It was probably because instead of actively trying to charm anyone in particular, Miles just fell into bed with willing people and had never wanted someone who didn't want him back—or wanted him but fought it. Miles knew he was going to have to learn to be more aware and less selfish if he was ever going to convince Evan to consider dating him. A great almost-blowjob wasn't going to cut it. Not with Evan.

Sex was probably off the table now, even though Miles knew Evan wanted it. Miles wasn't familiar with the sort of self-denial Evan practiced; if he wanted someone and the feeling was mutual, sex happened. It was an easy way to live, and an easy way to get off. Everything about Evan was complicated, but Miles wanted him anyway. Inexplicably.

"I'm sorry I didn't bring you coffee," Miles said when Evan remained silent, typing away, the staccato of the keys all the response he probably deserved.

"It's okay." Evan paused. "I wouldn't expect you to be looking out for other people. Me, especially."

And yeah, that was galling. Especially galling when Miles had spent the last half an hour discovering that nobody had probably ever really looked out for Evan before. It probably wouldn't take an extraordinary amount of effort to make him feel special and considered. And Miles *still* couldn't figure out how to meet even the lowest of expectations.

"I'm sorry, I'm . . . I know it isn't an excuse, but I was with Lucy, and Chloe and Steph and . . ." Miles hesitated, trying to find the best way to say, *sorry, we were gossiping about you and they told me you were a foster kid and I wish you had told me yourself.*

All Miles knew was that was definitely not the way to break the news.

"And they told you all about me, I'm sure." Evan's voice was still painfully level. It was like he'd hidden every emotion behind some very high, very thick wall, and Miles, who thought maybe he'd been making at least a little bit of progress, struggled not to feel disheartened.

"Yeah, that was something they mentioned. And when they did, I couldn't help but wish you'd told me yourself. Just last night we were talking about how you started here, and you didn't mention it."

Evan's head snapped up, and Miles recoiled at the fire blazing in his dark eyes. "Why? So you could figure out how I worked? How to manipulate me better? I'm sorry, but that's personal information and I don't just share it with anyone."

"I'm not just anyone," Miles insisted. He could feel himself stepping onto unsure, potentially dangerous ground, but he was so tired of Evan retreating. This time he wasn't going to let him; he was going to chase after him.

"Right. I must have missed the memo where you were anything more than the talent I'm supposed to be producing,"

Evan said, and Miles realized his voice wasn't cold, it was hot with anger. And maybe that wasn't the best emotion for him to be expressing, but it was something, and Miles was so sick of beating against that cold wall.

"We kissed, I had my mouth on your dick!" Miles couldn't help but exclaim.

"Yeah, that turned out so well," Evan retorted.

Miles shot to his feet, frustration spreading through him. He knew he needed to keep his temper in check, because letting it run wild hadn't gotten him anywhere. But Evan pushed every single button of his like he owned them. "It's not like I forced you to kiss me. That was your choice. You did that, and you can't take it back."

"I keep telling you I am!" Evan's voice was rising, and now he'd stood and Miles had a sudden déjà vu of their argument in the break room before he'd gone running off to Napa.

"Your words sort of lose their effect when your hand was in my hair and your dick was literally in my mouth," Miles snarled.

"Good thing all I have to do with that is remember that email you wrote to me, and I'm as soft as I've ever been," Evan said bitterly.

"What email?"

Miles whipped his head towards the doorway and the new voice. Reed Ryan was standing in the entrance to the conference room, arms crossed across his chest, and he looked confused and determined and also definitely a little pissed off.

"Now look at what you've done," Evan hissed. "Can't keep your mouth shut for five seconds put together."

Miles couldn't believe Evan was blaming *him*; after all, Evan had been the one to bring up the email this time.

"What email?" Reed demanded when neither Miles nor Evan answered the question.

He turned towards Evan. "I knew things weren't going well, but I didn't know you'd reached the point of sending each other nasty emails or yelling at each other in the conference room."

"It's not . . . I mean, it's sort of . . ." Evan paused, trying to compose himself. "I was handling it."

"By not telling me," Reed said sternly.

"It's my fault, sir," Miles spoke up. He didn't think he'd called anyone but Bastian Aquino *sir* in his whole career, but right now, Reed was almost as scary as his ex-boss.

Reed frowned, his expression morphing between annoyance and overwhelming frustration. "I don't remember saying it wasn't your fault." His gaze fell back on Evan. "What I don't get is why you would keep it a secret, Evan."

Miles could hear Evan grinding his teeth from a few feet away. "I told you, I was handling it. I dealt with it. *Was* dealing with it."

Reed's expression softened, even as Evan forged ahead, and Miles realized as he listened to one excuse after another that he'd never heard Evan caught up in indecisive rambling before. He'd always known what to say before this moment.

"I was pretty sure it didn't mean anything, and we were getting past it—I thought I was getting past it—and I am, I know it didn't mean anything. I know Miles didn't mean it. He was drunk and stupid and well, really, really stupid. You know when someone says something mean and you know they aren't saying it because they believe it, but because they don't know what else to say? That's how it felt. It was all there between the lines. And the grammar mistakes. And the spelling errors."

Evan only stopped because Reed held up a single hand. "Can I read this email before I decide it was nothing?"

"No," Miles and Evan both answered at the same time.

Reed looked surprised. Miles thought he really shouldn't have been.

"It's private," Evan said stubbornly.

"Like Evan said, I was drunk and really stupid. Incurably stupid. And I said some stuff that I'm not proud of, but I also said some stuff . . . it is sort of private," Miles added, under no delusion that his stupid drunk words could still remain between him and Evan.

Reed Ryan was going to find out that he really hated Evan's face, and really loved his ass in the tight khakis he wore. Basically, Miles was going to have to move back to Napa because he was never going to get over the shame of it. Every time he saw Reed—his *boss* and also, the ex-owner of Garnet and a culinary god—Miles was going to have a nightmare flashback to his stupid drunk words.

Miles thought he'd explored all the humiliation he possibly could when Evan had read that email. Unfortunately, there were still embarrassing depths to which he could plunge.

"I want to read it. Now." Reed's tone brooked no disagreement, but Evan still opened his mouth to keep arguing. Miles elbowed him hard in the side.

"Give it up," he hissed under his breath. "No point."

"I deleted it," Evan said anyway.

"All this time you were so *subtly* blackmailing me with it. That god-awful marketing meeting. Compromising! Joan of Arc Julia Child! And you fucking *deleted* it?" The outraged words leapt out of Miles' mouth before he could stop them.

Evan turned towards him, shock written all over his features. "Are you insane?" he hissed.

Reed only shook his head. In disgust or frustration, it was hard to tell.

"You." Reed pointed at Miles. "You still have it. You sent it after all. I want you to forward it to me, and then join me in my office in ten minutes." He turned and walked out, leaving no room for arguments, and Miles at a loss for words.

"Go delete it right now. I don't know how, just do it," Evan hissed.

"I really think we've made this bed and we have to lie in it," Miles said, realizing a little too late that he shouldn't be using phrases that had the word *bed* in them. At least he hadn't said they'd made their kitchen counter and now they had to lie on it.

Evan threw up his hands in frustration. "Do you really want your *boss* to read that email? Really? I thought you had an ounce of self-preservation. Because I definitely do not want *my* boss to read that email."

"Trust me, I don't. But I'm not showing up in his office telling him I just deleted it. That would be worse than him reading it."

Evan shot him a look. "Are you sure about that?"

Miles' resolve crumbled a little. "Not entirely."

"Then go delete it. This is your fault. Therefore, it's your job to fix it."

"What if it can't be fixed?" Miles said, because he couldn't help but think that. Maybe he'd fucked up this situation beyond solving.

Evan rounded on him, as fierce and angry as he'd ever been. "*Everything* can be fixed."

Miles didn't think he could agree, but he also felt sick and every second he and Evan kept fighting over this made him feel worse. It was impossible not to see Evan's words through the frame of the knowledge he'd just learned about how he'd grown up alone and unwanted.

The one thing he knew was that he wasn't going to delete the email. Would it be humiliation heaped upon embarrassment for Reed Ryan to read it? Absolutely. But there was a sort of poetic justice to the automatic cringe that Miles felt every time he thought about it. He shouldn't have written it, and he definitely shouldn't have ever sent it. He should have apologized the morning Evan had showed up in Napa to drag his hungover ass home. Everything that came after this was payback for all those mistakes.

Evan knew the moment he walked into Reed's office that Miles hadn't done as requested and deleted the email. Reed's face said it all. Evan knew he should've watched Miles delete it, instead of escaping to the bathroom to try to compose himself for the lecture to come.

Because even if Miles had deleted it, Evan knew they were both in for a lecture the likes of which he'd never seen. Reed had a fierce temper, and even if he'd never seen it, he'd heard terrifying stories about it. Until this clusterfuck of a situation, Evan had been more than a model employee—he could even say he'd been Reed's best employee. There'd never been a single excuse for Reed to unleash his infamous temper.

Until now.

"Evan, sit down." Reed's voice was deadly calm, but Evan could also see the awkwardness in his expression. Yeah, he'd definitely read all about how Miles hated his face, and how much he appreciated the tight khakis Evan favored.

Evan did what he was instructed, because in the bathroom he'd come to mostly the same conclusion as Miles: it was pointless to keep fighting this. It was going to happen.

"I've read this email," Reed said, still very calm. Too calm, as far as Evan was concerned. "I'm not very happy about it."

"I'm sorry, I can't apologize enough," Miles cut in, but Reed shot him a single, deadly look and he shut up fast. Evan wished he could recreate that look and get those same kinds of results. But it turned out that Miles had more self-preservation than Evan had ever imagined he did.

"Do you know why I hired you?" Reed asked.

"Because I was good?" Miles said.

Evan barely held back a bitter chuckle. Miles had no idea how good he was. Or how fucked.

Reed leaned forward on the desk, his muscular forearms distracting but the look in his dark eyes was intense enough it was tough to even look at his arms. "I hired you because I believed you were a professional. That you'd started *Pastry by Miles* even though you were working at Terroir because you wanted more. That you were willing to work your ass off and sacrifice whatever it took to make sure you got more. That's why I promoted Evan specifically to produce your show. Because he's always, ever since he started here, done exactly that—gone after *more*. And I thought this drive would unite you, but all it's done is divide you. And that's a damn fucking shame."

Evan swallowed hard. He'd thought the same thing, once. He still wanted to believe it was possible, that they weren't doomed to fail, but the further they got down this angry, bitter, vindictive road, the more out of reach success felt.

Part of this was his own fault. But fault seemed so petty right now, when everything they'd built individually was threatening to fall around them.

"Apologies don't seem adequate, but that's all I have. And a promise to do better. To be better. To work with Evan better." Miles certainly sounded earnest, and Evan realized that was part of his charm. You genuinely wanted to believe him, even when you knew he would probably fail to deliver. That was definitely Evan's fault; he kept believing and kept letting himself be seduced into certainty, when nothing was certain.

"That's something." Reed, on the other hand, did not sound particularly convinced. He was a hard guy to win over, though, which was something Evan had always liked about him. And *still* liked about him, even though that particular trait was probably going to be enough to torpedo Evan's continued employment at *Five Points*.

"Evan?" Reed continued. "Do you have anything to say?"

What did you even say when you'd been saying too much from the first moment? Evan didn't know.

"I'm sorry, I should have told you about it earlier," Evan said. "But I think we can still make this work." That was mostly a lie, but Evan had always been a great liar. He didn't like lying to Reed, because he'd always respected him so much, but some things were more vital than honesty.

Evan had just clawed his way up to this point. He'd worked his ass off. He wasn't going to lose everything now over a little dishonesty.

"What I want to see," Reed said, "is a test. Proof of you two actually working together towards something. I want evidence. I want something I can watch and I can see how it's going to work if *Five Points* moves ahead and buys into this show for a season of episodes. Right now, I can't see that happening. But if you prove to me that you can, then you'll get my full support."

"You want a screen test?" Evan asked and he couldn't help but sound dubious. Miles was not ready for a screen test. *Evan* was not ready for a screen test.

"I want proof." Reed sounded solidly convinced. He was probably not going to be convinced by whatever footage they could cobble together.

Evan felt the death knell of all his hopes. He and Reed had agreed when Miles signed that screen tests wouldn't be necessary because he already had on-camera experience and his rapport with the camera was fantastic.

"Okay," Miles said, and he sounded so sure and so casually okay with the challenge that Reed had presented to them, Evan felt a little sick. Didn't he know what they were getting themselves into? Didn't he care about the amount of work he'd just committed himself to? "You'll get your proof. I promise."

Chapter Ten

"Are you insane?" Evan hissed at Miles as they walked down the hall from Reed's office. It didn't even feel like the first time he'd asked this exact same question this exact same way in nearly the same spot.

And didn't that just say it all?

Miles shot him a look like maybe Evan was the crazy one, but there was no way that was the case. "Maybe we shouldn't do this here," he said softly.

He had a good point, but Evan wasn't feeling magnanimous enough to admit it. Instead, he pointed towards the big double doors that led to the elevator bay. Wordlessly, Miles followed Evan to their cubicles, and they packed up their laptops. Evan also grabbed his big folder of filming notes, and they decamped from the office, walking the few scant blocks to the apartment building they shared.

Miles unlocked his door, and the first thing he said, when they were finally alone, was, "Are you hungry? I've got lots of leftover quiche from last night."

Evan decided the question he'd asked earlier applied even in locations that weren't the hallway outside of Reed's office.

"Food? That's what you want to talk about right now?" Evan's voice was inching upwards, both in volume and in pitch. It was a testament to how upset he was that he didn't even try to stop the inevitable.

They'd been on the cusp of a huge blowout in the conference room, and Reed had merely interrupted them. Maybe if they finished the fight, they could buckle down and finally get some work done.

But Miles shot Evan an incredulous look, and after setting his laptop on the kitchen counter, walked right over to the fridge and opened the door.

"Okay," Evan admitted, which was not easy for him to do. "I guess we do need to talk about food. Not whatever happened in here last night. Not your fuckups. Not my hang-ups. We need to figure out how to convince Reed."

Miles flipped the oven on and slid the pie plate, suspiciously full, into the oven.

Maybe Miles hadn't been able to eat either, after Evan had left. Evan had ended up with a liquid dinner, comprised of whatever remaining wine he had left in his apartment, followed by a shot of vodka from his freezer, and a restless, mostly sleepless night, punctuated by sudden and annoying bouts of accidentally turning himself on by dwelling on what had nearly happened.

"It's not going to be that hard," Miles said.

Evan didn't even know what to say. "You did hear him, right? He wasn't lying. He will absolutely need to be convinced. And I know Reed; that isn't going to be easy."

"No, it won't be easy. But he picked me for a reason, and he picked you for a reason. Those reasons haven't changed. We just need to figure out how to make those reasons work together a little better." Miles' gaze slid to the counter. "You know him better than I do. You know how this all works better than I do. So tell me what to do."

"You're really giving me control over this whole thing." Evan couldn't believe after all these weeks of fighting and clawing each other, Miles was just going to hand the power over without a single word of argument.

But Miles shrugged. "I can't go back to Napa a failure. I can't go back to restaurants if this doesn't work out. So it needs to work out."

Evan didn't need another word to convince him. "Okay," he said, flipping open his big folder stuffed full of notes. "Let's start."

"Food first," Miles said. "I've had too much caffeine followed by too much adrenaline. I'm all shaky."

"Fine." The food smelled good, almost better than it had last night, so Evan wasn't going to exactly complain if Miles wanted to feed him.

"Also," Miles said, fidgeting with the frayed edge of a kitchen towel. "I need to apologize. Really apologize," he continued when Evan opened his mouth to say that an apology wasn't necessary. "I was an asshole. I was insensitive. I was thoughtless. And I'm beginning to realize that some of those things aren't new. For that, I'm sorry. I'm going to be respectful from now on. The professional I promise you I can be."

"Apology accepted." Evan figured if they dealt with this, then maybe they could move on. And maybe he should take advantage of Miles' sudden contrition to set up some ground rules.

"But if you're really serious," he continued, "let's write down some ground rules." He opened his notebook to a blank page. "Rule number one, I think is pretty self-explanatory. No kissing."

Miles opened his mouth and then snapped it shut again. Evan was unpleasantly reminded of everything he could do with that mouth, before he pushed those thoughts right out of his mind. Remembering kissing Miles and Miles kissing him was not going to get them a full season pickup.

"Rule number two. No sex."

Miles didn't even react to that.

"Rule number three. No arguments," Miles added.

Evan lifted an eyebrow. "No arguing? You must really have had a change of heart in Reed's office."

"Not just Reed's office," Miles admitted. "I went to grab coffee with Lucy and when she told me about the circumstances surrounding your internship, I realized just how insensitive I've been, when this means everything to you. It means everything to me too. And I can stop arguing if it means we can save everything we've worked for."

Evan felt everything go hot and then cold inside him. Ice cold. Like an ice floe in Antarctica. It hadn't come as a surprise that Lucy had told Miles about his past. She had probably been trying to help, because rumors were flying fast and thick in the office that Miles and Evan weren't getting along. Lucy must have believed that she could assist by cluing Miles in, because normally she didn't encourage gossip.

Evan was still monumentally pissed off that she'd opened her big fat mouth, and he was definitely going to tell her that when he saw her next. They'd known each other and worked together for years now, and he expected better from her. Not for her to sell him and his secrets out to Miles.

"It's nothing," Evan said coldly. "It's less than nothing. Forget what she told you. It's not important."

"It *is* important," Miles argued, heat flashing in his eyes, frustration and admiration and galling sympathy. "I think . . ."

Evan ripped off the notebook page and stomped over to the fridge. He hung it on the fridge with one of the silly magnets

Miles must have brought. This one was a brightly colored neon lobster. "Rule number three," he stated, pointing to the rule he'd written in his neat handwriting.

Miles' dark eyebrows slanted with annoyance and everything he was holding back, but he remained silent, letting the quiet grow until the beep of the oven timer interrupted his pouting and Evan's cold shoulder.

"Eat," was all Miles said, as he slid a wedge of quiche over on a plate, a fork balanced on the edge. "You've got to keep your energy up, and you look tired."

Evan wanted to retort something spiteful, but he buried the spike of heat under the cold wall of ice surrounding him, and merely looked pointedly over at the list on the fridge.

Miles didn't reply, merely walked over to the fridge and scrawled something under the third rule. "Rule number four," he announced, "sarcastic retorts are banned."

"Fine by me," Evan said, even though he felt a pulse of disappointment at losing the banter he'd actually enjoyed trading with Miles.

It didn't matter, anyway. Only one thing mattered now. Not fucking this up again.

"First," he said, between big bites of quiche he didn't really taste, "I want you to go through the cookie recipe again. That's what we'll do for the test. It's the easiest recipe on the list."

There was a mutinous jut to Miles' jaw but he nodded, and Evan watched as he began to assemble his ingredients.

He was right. He had to be right. There was no more room for error.

⁂

Miles watched as Evan ate his quiche and didn't even taste it, then pushed it aside only half-finished. He pressed his lips together and told himself that it didn't matter if this felt all kinds of wrong; it was what Evan wanted.

Or at least what he'd told himself he wanted, though that was a distinction that even Miles could acknowledge didn't matter anymore.

"I made notes last time we baked these cookies," Evan said.

As always, Miles' gut reaction was to correct, to snark just so Evan could snark back. A stupid petty correction that he could use to flirt with the other man. But this time, he kept his mouth shut, even though technically, *they* hadn't baked anything. Miles had baked these cookies by himself, and Evan had just watched—and also, if Miles was being really honest, drove him insane. With sexual frustration. With desire. With need.

"I bet there isn't time for me to teach you how to make them," Miles said, and sue him, he sounded regretful because he really was. The best afternoon he'd spent in forever had been the one when he'd taught Evan how to make *pain au chocolat.*

That was the afternoon when Miles had discovered that maybe teaching other people how to bake might not be too terrible.

Evan leveled him an annoyed look, frosted cold at the edges. "Both of us know that wasn't a serious offer. I'm not here to learn how to cook, and you're not here to teach me."

He was right, but the truth still stung.

Miles turned back to the counter where he'd been assembling his *mise en place* to make sure he had everything he needed.

"We need to finalize the recipe today," Evan announced. "So no crazy experimentation, please."

It was only all those hard years of being shit on by head chefs in kitchens that kept him even-keeled and calm when he nodded. "I'm going to do a quarter dark chocolate, and three quarters semi-sweet," he said. "That should balance out the bitterness nicely. And I'm swapping white sugar for brown."

Evan's sharp nod of acknowledgement shouldn't have hurt, but it did.

It didn't matter, though. Miles wasn't going to be the one responsible for killing off Evan's chances at a successful production of this show. He'd worked hard enough for it, and it wasn't fair for him to lose his shot because Miles was a careless jerk who couldn't keep his fingers under control when he got drunk.

The afternoon passed by achingly slow. Evan didn't question every decision Miles made, he only wanted solid, unchanging ones. And every question was polite, painstakingly professional and about zero degrees.

Miles hated every minute of it. In his fantasies, he might have dreamed about an afternoon just baking and hanging out in his place, and it was glorious. The reality was so much different and so much worse.

Third batch pulled out of the oven, Miles tested a cookie and gave a shrug when Evan asked if this was finally the final recipe.

"You can't tell me you don't know," Evan said, and for the first time, his frustration felt warmer. Hotter. Like Evan was just on edge as Miles, he'd just buried it under so much ice that it took time to melt and show through.

"They taste good." Miles shrugged again, because if Evan didn't get it now, he probably never would. Miles had sworn that Evan was close to understanding what drove him, but maybe after everything, it was safer to assume Evan didn't give a shit. "They taste really good, even, but perfection can't be rushed."

"Perfection," Evan said through clenched lips, "is not what we're aiming for here. We're aiming for good enough."

It felt like something inside Miles died a little with Evan's words. He had to turn back to the cooling rack, fussing uselessly with the warm cookies, so Evan wouldn't see his devastated expression.

"I didn't work so hard to become a chef so I could skate by on good enough," Miles said softly.

"Well, this certainly isn't what *I* worked so hard for either," Evan snapped. "We're all settling here."

It shouldn't have hurt more, but somehow it did. It burned, in a way that none of Evan's other snarky retorts had ever hurt before. Miles turned from the stove and wrenched open the refrigerator and pulled out a bottle of pinot blanc that he'd been saving for a special occasion.

He opened it with quick, efficient movements, and for a brief second, considered not even bothering with a wine glass, just dumping it into his empty water glass, but that felt wrong. Disrespectful of the wine and the effort the winemakers had put into crafting it. So he walked across the kitchen, grabbed a glass, and poured the wine.

"Really?" Evan snapped. "You're drinking? Don't you think alcohol has gotten us into enough trouble?"

"You want a glass?" Miles asked, because even though he *had* sent the email while drunk, it wasn't like Evan hadn't also used the excuse of a glass of good cabernet sauvignon to do something crazy. "Or are you afraid you'll kiss me again?"

Evan's lips compressed together, and he looked angry. The angriest he'd looked since the afternoon had started. "I told you," he said stiffly, "that won't be repeated. It doesn't matter what I drink."

"Then you should try a glass of this. It's special," Miles said, giving the glass a fancy little twirl and watching the golden liquid swirl around the crystal.

Evan made a face, but still went to get a glass from the cupboard, and poured himself a scant quarter of a glass. "What," he retorted when Miles shot him a questioning look. "One of us has to stay sober."

"I can bake drunk, sober, it doesn't matter. You're the one who needs something to loosen up," Miles said, even though he knew what he was risking by saying it out loud.

"I like who I am sober just fine," Evan said, but he didn't even *sound* convincing.

But it didn't matter. Miles had promised he would abide by the three rules—now four rules—hanging on the fridge. Drinking wasn't technically on the list, though it would inevitably lead to breaking one, or all of them probably, but it might also make Evan more bearable to be around during this exercise in torture.

Miles took another bite of cookie, and suddenly it didn't matter so much. It didn't feel like life or death if the batter had another eighth of a teaspoon of salt, or he slightly changed the proportions of dark to semi-sweet chocolate or if he substituted more white sugar for the brown. "Final recipe," he said, and tried to ignore Evan's triumphant expression.

He was supposed to be giving Evan what he wanted, right? All of this done exactly the way he wanted it. But Miles felt hollow. Uninspired. More like quitting today than he'd felt since this whole thing started.

All it took to squash that particular bug was the thought of Evan's face if he gave up and let *Pastry by Miles* fall apart.

Evan's fingers flew across the keyboard, as sure as they'd ever been. And something about Evan's certainty helped Miles believe at least a little bit that they were doing the right thing, taking the right path.

"There, recipe submitted to testing." Evan glanced up. "That's Lucy's minions, in case you didn't know."

"I didn't realize they were going to be testing the screen test recipe." Maybe if Miles had, he would've made another batch, tried another hunch. He didn't want to talk big with his impressive resume, and then fall pathetically short.

"It isn't a requirement," Evan said, "but I thought it would seem pretty dumb to pass the screen test, but not have the recipe tested. Besides, Reed knows when faced with a challenge, I like to go above and beyond. He'll probably expect this, on some subconscious level."

Miles grabbed a plate from the cupboard, slid two cookies onto it, and pushed it Evan's direction. He ignored it, which was a doubly unpleasant reminder: *one*, he didn't like sweets, and *two*, that it didn't matter to him how the cookie actually tasted.

"What's next?" Miles asked, draining the glass of wine. If he had to stand here for another minute and watch Evan type furiously on his laptop, he was going to go out of his mind.

"Remember the wing-wang?" Evan said absently.

"The *what*?" Miles asked.

Evan's eyes shot up to Miles' face. "The Ding Dong, or whatever it was that you called it."

"I remember it. I didn't think we were going that direction."

"We're not. We're going to practice filming, and because we have no equipment, we're going to have to be resourceful. Now where's that ficus you used last time? It'll be steadier than my hands and we're going to want to take this footage apart to make sure you're perfect. It'll be that much harder with the camera jerking all around."

Miles shook his head incredulously and went to grab the ficus from his bedroom. As he dragged it to the kitchen, he realized that Evan had helped furnish this apartment. He'd known exactly where the ficus was and just didn't want to talk about Miles' bedroom. Or *go* into Miles' bedroom.

He didn't think anyone had ever wanted him so much yet spent so much time and energy avoiding the subject of sex. It was a fascinating dichotomy that should have frustrated him enough to kill any interest Miles felt, but instead, it was doing the opposite. This quirk of Evan's made Miles hunt like a detective for any clues, verbal or otherwise, that gave away just how much he wanted. And each discovery was sweeter than if it had been freely admitted.

Miles didn't want to think about what this said about his emotional hang-ups.

Evan had already pulled the duct tape from the supply closet it was stashed in, and he pulled out a GoPro camera from his laptop bag.

"Where'd that come from?" Miles asked as he pulled the ficus into place opposite the big kitchen island.

"The extreme sports department," Evan said.

Miles frowned. "I thought it was just that one guy, and you said he'd been dropped too many times on his head."

"He has." Evan paused, checking the angle of the camera. "He won't even realize I've borrowed this."

The problem was Miles couldn't help but grudgingly admire Evan's determination to get shit done. He was pretty sure they had that in common. That much Reed was dead right on.

If only they could figure out how to align their priorities and stop fighting each other, they could run the world.

"Get behind the island," Evan ordered. "I want to check the angle of the camera."

Miles did as ordered, as Evan made a few minute adjustments.

"Now what?" Miles asked.

"Now, you make those cookies again." Evan paused and Miles wondered if he could make that other set of adjustments he'd wanted to, and if Evan would even notice. "And you make them *exactly* the same. No creative wanderings."

"Just make the cookies?" Miles leaned on the counter. He knew from how many editing hours he'd spent on *Pastry by Miles* videos that he had a not-insignificant charm factor when he stood like this. Evan didn't even blink, he just went right back to his laptop, moving it so he was aligned right behind the camera. Seeing everything it saw.

Maybe, he couldn't help but think, *I'm losing my touch.*

Something he'd considered ever since he'd walked into the *Five Points* offices and hadn't been able to see eye to eye with the cute producer.

"Make the damn cookies, Miles." Evan's voice was cold and hard as steel.

So he made the damn cookies. Again.

Evan knew what the problem was going to be before they even reviewed the footage. Miles was a natural behind a camera, usually relaxed and jovial, even self-deprecating when the situation called for it. His appeal had been one of the more persuasive arguments that had sold Reed on him when Evan had first shown him *Pastry by Miles* videos.

The other persuasive argument had been that they wouldn't need to spend weeks or months getting Miles comfortable in front of the camera. He wouldn't need a single ounce of training because he'd already given himself the best training regimen he could—tons and tons of experience.

But that was before, and this was after—though before and after what, specifically, Evan didn't want to think about—now everything had suddenly changed.

Miles was stiff and awkward on the first video. He spent a lot of time second-guessing both his words and his actions. Even worse, he kept directing hesitant, almost questioning glances at the camera, like he was asking Evan if he was doing the right thing.

This was not the *Pastry by Miles* superstar that Evan had been ready to finish molding.

Evan was at a complete loss. He didn't even want to look at Miles, currently elbow-deep in sudsy water, washing dishes, because then Miles might know how bad things were, and that would make them even worse. He was self-conscious now, but he wasn't aware of it yet. As soon as he became aware of it, it would be even more pointed.

"Was it that bad?" Miles asked, from over at his spot at the sink.

Evan didn't know how he could've given it away, but he was pretty certain that Miles hadn't even looked over at him the whole time he'd been watching the video, and he certainly hadn't admitted anything out loud.

"I don't know what you mean," Evan lied.

"You're totally silent over there. Which means you're usually plotting some sort of world takeover bid. Or how to tell me that all my other episodes were a fluke."

Evan had been definitely worried about the screen test before, because he and Miles saw eye to eye on so little, but when they'd come back to Miles' place, he'd suddenly become an acquiescent stranger. Evan had begun to think that maybe they could pull this off after all, mostly resting on Miles' natural charisma in front of the camera.

And now even that had deserted them.

"They weren't flukes," Evan said, but he wasn't even convincing himself.

The tense line of Miles' back as he scrubbed cookie sheets was proof enough that Evan definitely wasn't convincing him.

"It's been a long week," Evan said. "You're tired. I'm tired. This is a lot of stress. A few more practice run-throughs and the kinks will work themselves out."

Later that night, Evan lay awake in bed, promising to himself that he'd told Miles the truth. He'd been so vigilant when he'd picked the talent he wanted to produce for the first time. He'd followed what felt like hundreds of food bloggers. He'd done research for months. He'd narrowed and winnowed and made at least a dozen pro-and-con lists. He'd kept coming back to *Pastry by Miles* for a reason, and that reason had to be more than how cute Miles was when he smiled, eyes crinkling and so damn bright. It had to be more than when Evan had seen him for the very first time, he'd felt it deep down, right in the gut. More than just that he'd sworn to himself that one day he'd find a way to meet Miles Costa.

It had to be more because Evan had staked everything on his career, and he'd staked his career on Miles. But lying awake, sleepless as the hours ticked by, Evan couldn't help but wonder if he had been wrong this whole time.

The next day, Evan worked both of them like the devil, like a man terrified he was going to waste a single moment of time.

Thirteen times, Miles thought sluggishly as he leaned against the counter, not even caring if it was his good side or he was laid out seductively. He didn't think he could bring himself to stand up.

Despite what Evan had promised to him the day before, and that Miles had sworn to himself that he'd deliver if it killed him, the kinks had not worked themselves out.

Miles got more comfortable, and he'd developed a decent patter as he prepared the cookies, but there was no spontaneity, no life. No *zing*. He knew he felt annoyed and stifled at the man who stared coldly and calculatingly at the camera as he performed. Even when he worked his ass off to forget Evan's existence, Miles couldn't find the spark that had come as natural to him as breathing from the first *Pastry by Miles* video he'd recorded.

Even the stupid Ding Dong video he'd filmed to get back at Evan on their second day was better than the thirteenth run-through of the chocolate peanut butter cookies.

"Maybe we should use the Ding Dong video," Miles said. "I bet you some people would even find it funny."

Evan's expression said it all. He didn't find it funny and couldn't comprehend of anyone who would. And that, Miles thought, was the root of the problem. Evan couldn't unclench for five seconds and fucking *relax*, and his goddamn tenseness had caused Miles to lose his center.

He couldn't get it back, couldn't seem to re-discover it, and even though there was a smooth delivery to the performance (probably because he'd run through it thirteen times), even Miles wasn't delusional enough to believe a rehearsed demeanor would be enough to win Reed over.

"This," Evan said coldly, refusing to rise to Miles' bait, "is the video we're doing."

For better or worse, Evan was determined to stick to his plan, even as he saw it all going down the crapper. Miles didn't know whether to be angry at Evan for his ridiculous stubborn streak or to feel guilty for letting him down.

Maybe he felt both at the same damn time.

"Just so you know, if you tell me to do it again," Miles said, and he knew he sounded as tired as he felt, "I'm going to tell you to fuck off."

Evan looked up. He might be overly stubborn and too determined to stick to the path that wasn't working, but Miles could tell from the hint of despair in his dark eyes that he knew the score.

"No point," he said shortly.

Miles raised an eyebrow.

"Reed just texted me," Evan said by way of explanation, "we'll film the test tomorrow during one of the *Dream Team* filming breaks. Ten a.m."

It was so tempting to lean over, reach into the freezer and grab the bottle of Belvedere that Miles had found the other day. At the time he'd been impressed with the taste of whoever stocked the apartment, but then he'd remembered it was Evan.

It was always fucking Evan.

But they were screwed enough, he was probably going to move his ass back to Napa and beg for his job back. This was no time to be indulging in bad habits and screwing himself over worse. Besides, he'd learned the hard way that sometimes getting drunk only made everything worse.

He didn't even want to imagine what might have happened if he hadn't thrown a hissy fit, drank all that faux Kahlua and typed out an email that he'd never even meant to send.

He definitely wouldn't be standing here, contemplating the end of *Pastry by Miles* and wondering how much groveling he would have to do to get another job.

"You want a drink?" Evan asked and Miles looked up in surprise, wondering how he'd managed to read his mind yet again.

"No? Why do you ask?"

Evan shrugged. "Alcohol seems to be your crutch when things don't go your way."

It wasn't fair but it was true. That didn't mean it stung any less. "Things aren't exactly going your way either."

"Everything will be fine tomorrow," Evan said, but Miles didn't even bother arguing. They both knew the truth of what would probably happen during the test tomorrow. Some things were painfully inevitable, and they'd been on this crash course from the very first moment. "We should both get some rest. We'll cab over in the morning to the studio."

Evan's casual dismissal of Miles and everything they'd shared definitely stung. It might be self-preservation for Evan, but Miles didn't want to live without regrets and he didn't want to pretend that he was okay with this. Even with Evan's cold shoulder of the last two days, he still wanted him. He still wanted the possibility of hope for the future, even if that was at least a little delusional.

It was that thought that gave him the energy to push himself off the counter. He walked over to where Evan was sitting, head buried in his laptop, fingers typing away like it was some kind of barrier that protected him from anything real.

"I'll be out of your hair in a moment," Evan said, not even looking up.

Miles stood there, not exactly patient, but waiting because he was saving his pushiness for something that mattered. "You're not in my hair. I don't want you to go."

Evan still didn't look up. "You just said you didn't want to go through it again."

Miles shoved his hands in his pockets so he wouldn't just reach out and take, mussing up Evan's perfectly styled hair, his still-crisp shirt collar, the omnipresent bow tie. Today's was a leafy green.

"I don't."

Something in Miles' voice must have gotten through to Evan, because finally, he glanced up. There was apprehension in his buttery-brown eyes. Something like fear, even if he tried to hide it. Miles still saw it because Miles was looking for it.

"We talked about this." Evan spit it out, and his eyes flickered for a single brief moment to where the list was still hanging from the fridge.

No kissing.

No sex.

No fighting.

No sarcastic retorts.

Of course Miles had started ignoring number four almost immediately. It had been a natural reflex to try to get a reaction out of the suddenly icy Evan. But he hadn't tried the other three.

He'd worked hard to not argue, to not fight back. It had been even harder to resist pushing Evan on the other rules.

He'd been as good as he could possibly be; he was done with it.

"We did," Miles admitted.

"Then what do you want?" Evan asked, even more defensively than he'd been the last two miserable days.

When Miles had walked over here, crossing the invisible line between kitchen and camera, between chef and producer, he hadn't understood that this was a watershed moment. It was crystal clear now.

Some things were so simple they didn't need explanations. "You."

Evan's jaw dropped. "You really don't," he argued. "Not after everything."

"That's the thing, I want you more after everything. Even after how shitty all these rehearsals have been. Even if I have to go back to Napa and grovel. None of that feels like it matters now."

Evan shot to his feet, hands shutting his laptop, reaching for his bag. Not the reaction Miles had been hoping for. Everyone always said that if you laid it all on the line, if you were honest and straightforward about what you wanted, you got it.

Everyone were fucking liars. Miles couldn't hide his disappointment or the pain he felt as he watched Evan try to escape.

"What if I had never sent you that email?" he demanded. He was so tempted to just show Evan how much he wanted him, but he knew that wouldn't work. Evan had to *know* he wanted it too, even if they both knew he did. He had to acknowledge it to himself, and to Miles. And shoving everything he'd brought into his bag so he could escape was the exact opposite of that.

Evan looked up. Maybe it would've helped that Miles saw the same echo of frustration and pain in his eyes, but it didn't. It made it worse. Like this was their chance, and they were just passing it by.

At least Miles was fucking putting his ass out there. Evan was just running away.

"It doesn't matter. Because you did. And you can't change that." Evan's voice was hard, so hard it sounded like it might crack at any moment.

"I'm sorry I sent it," Miles said, and he knew he sounded desperate. He *was* desperate. "I've never been sorrier about any-thing in my whole life." He meant it. All of it. And it meant nothing.

"Me too," Evan said, and then he was walking out of the kitchen and Miles heard the front door shut behind him.

This time it didn't feel like a bad idea to reach for the bottle of vodka in the freezer and take a gulp, feeling it burn all the way down his throat.

Chapter Eleven

Evan didn't know who he was angrier at; Miles for making him want to believe him, or himself for nearly doing it.

He couldn't sleep. Since he'd left Miles' place, he felt like he'd been half a rationalization away from going back. To telling Miles that he wanted him too, screw how much he might regret it later.

But then he'd probably regret it either way, he thought, as he restlessly switched sides, staring at the bright neon-green numbers of the clock on his bedside table. He'd regret sleeping with Miles, and he'd definitely regret *not* sleeping with him.

The question was which regret was larger and more life-ruining in the grand scheme of things.

It turned out that the answer was shockingly simple; Evan wanted Miles. He'd tried very hard to fight against it, he'd actively attempted to stifle it, to pretend it didn't exist, and part of the exhaustion of the last few days was how much energy it took to deny such an obvious truth.

He was up and out of bed before he'd even thought it through—probably because if he let himself, he wouldn't have gone anywhere anytime soon, and he was done overthinking. It was easy enough to slip on a pair of shoes and scoot down the hallway to Miles' door.

The difficult part was standing in front of Miles' door, waiting for him to open it. It took every ounce of Evan's self-possession to knock, then knock again, and then knock *again*, the whole time praying that Miles hadn't taken Evan's rejection and gone looking someplace else.

After the third prolonged knock, the only thing keeping him rooted in place at Miles' doorstep was a stubborn belief that he couldn't have come all this way, through all this shit, and then at the end, Miles had given up on Evan before Evan could give up on himself.

Finally, the door opened. Miles didn't look happy to see him, in fact, he looked pissed off.

Evan couldn't really blame him for that.

An apology was right there, but at the last second, his dick just took over, and said what he'd been so reluctant to acknowledge: "I want you, I do."

A frown creased Miles' handsome features. "Now? You're going to get me up in the middle of the night, and tell me that *now* you've finally decided you want me?"

Evan hadn't considered that this wouldn't be easy. That Miles would expect some sort of groveling after all the overtures that Evan had rejected.

"Yes." Evan usually didn't *do* groveling. Pride was a hard-won possession, and he wasn't about to give it up, even for Miles.

Miles must have realized this, because after a long, heart-stopping moment, he pulled the door the rest of the way open, and Evan didn't move because he couldn't.

The reason why it had taken Miles so long to come to the door was because he'd already started without Evan. Probably because he'd never imagined that Evan would show up, interested in the bulge he was packing in those tight black briefs.

That was where he had been very wrong; Evan was more than interested. He licked his lips, mouth suddenly dry, and looked his fill. Miles' solid, slim chest, the tenseness in his biceps, the sweat beaded around his hairline, the mussed curls, how his fingers kept clenching and unclenching. The tautness of his abs as he held himself still and refused to cover up.

Evan approved because he shouldn't ever. He was gorgeous, a barely contained storm in that laid-back body.

"I didn't think you'd come back," Miles said, voice calm but with a tense edge.

Evan wasn't going to argue when there were so many better things he could be doing with his mouth.

Urgency propelled him forward, through the doorway, almost falling against Miles. Before he could, Miles reached out and caught him. Evan lifted his head towards his, and a long, eternal stare passed between them. Miles' eyes were smoky in the dim light, and Evan couldn't help but wonder if his own were darker. Intense. If everything he felt was reflected in them. The desperation. The desire. How hopeless he was against the two together; hopeless against Miles.

Evan could feel just how much Miles wanted him, hard against his stomach, pushing against the thin fabric covering his crotch, but Miles didn't move.

It was hard enough to take the first step here, it should feel easier to take the last. It wasn't. But nobody had ever considered Evan a coward, and he wouldn't act cowardly now.

Lifting his head, Evan fitted his mouth against Miles', and their lips moved against each other for a moment, uncoordinated and unsure, but then everything slid into place.

Evan had spent his entire life avoiding fantasy. He was practical and prosaic—all by necessity. But now, he had a sudden thought that this kiss wasn't just a physical manifestation of a deeply physical need, but that it was locking them together, two out-of-sync tumblers clicking uselessly, until one perfect moment when they clicked.

He almost wanted Miles to ask him if he was going to leave again, just so he could tell him that he wasn't, that he couldn't. But Miles seemed very uninterested in any more talking, hands moving down Evan's chest, only breaking apart to pull his shirt off, to pant unevenly into the damp skin of his neck.

It helped that Evan knew exactly where the bedroom was, and so exactly where to steer them, Evan shedding his shoes, then his sweatpants as they stumbled down the hallway, lips fused together.

When they reached the bed, Evan shoved Miles onto the edge, and placed a very possessive hand against the cock throbbing in his briefs.

Miles groaned into his mouth. Something insensible. Something very much like begging.

And Evan was perfectly happy to give him exactly what he wanted. He pulled the fabric down, watching as Miles' cock sprung from its confines, landing wetly against his abs.

Evan knew many people considered sucking cock to be a demeaning activity, like dropping to your knees somehow made you subservient, but he'd always gotten a power rush from it. Miles' shocked, pleased expression rushed through him as he lowered himself, flicking his tongue just briefly against the reddened head.

"Please," Miles said, and he sounded wrecked.

Probably Evan always felt a power rush because he liked making a big production out of a blowjob. Liked to tease. Liked to drive the man above him to barely wrung-out pleas. Some people wrote symphonies, some painted art, some sculpted out of clay and marble. Evan really liked to give a perfect blowjob.

He took his time about it now, wondering how far he could drive Miles with little teasing licks, fingers digging purposefully into the meat of his thighs, a counterpoint to the delicacy of what his mouth was doing to his cock.

Miles quickly fell to a litany of nonsense and moans. He seemed to understand that Evan didn't want his hands on him, and he kept them fisted in the comforter, knuckles white as he clenched the cotton.

But he must have gotten close before Evan even arrived, because it was too soon and he'd already reached a fevered point of begging. Evan tongued the slit, tasted the rush of salt, and knew he must be close, even though he'd barely given him anything to sink his teeth into.

As far as Evan was concerned, what made him really good at sucking cock wasn't a preplanned attack, but the ability to improvise in the middle. So he abandoned the delicate teasing abruptly, mouth sliding down Miles' cock, sucking with all the force he dared.

Miles' yelp was very rewarding and so was the flood of come on his tongue. He swallowed, taking his time about cleaning up every inch of Miles' prick as it softened in his mouth.

Finally Miles pushed him off, and there was only the sound of heavy breathing in the dim room. Evan suddenly was acutely aware of his own arousal, pressing against his thigh, sticky and hot.

"Give me a second," Miles breathed out, voice unsteady, "you might have killed me."

"But what a way to go," Evan said, feeling very satisfied—but not nearly as satisfied as he could be.

"If you'd believe it, you were doing the exact same thing in my head when you knocked on my door."

Evan raised an eyebrow. "Okay," Miles corrected with a silly little grin that shouldn't have made both Evan's heart and dick flex, but it did, anyway, "not quite the exact same thing. I don't have the same perverse imagination you apparently do."

"I'm about to get a lot more perverse," Evan threatened, the thrum of blood in his cock becoming more and more insistent.

"I've got you," Miles said, and the hand he extended to lift him up was gentle and so was his voice.

His hand however, was the right amount of rough friction that Evan didn't even know he needed as Miles fisted around his length and pumped him hard and reckless. Evan might have been ashamed at how quickly it ended, but then he had a feeling they both knew he hadn't only been teasing Miles.

Miles wiped his hand on the sheet and rolled over in the bed. Evan hesitated on the edge, not sure if he should stay or go. All of his hookups had always been only sex. Once orgasms were had, it was over, and Evan usually left, because he never liked letting strangers into his personal space. He'd spent too many years doing that.

But Miles was looking at him expectantly, like he expected Evan to roll over and go to sleep.

Evan almost said no. He almost said he was tired and he was going to walk the few yards back to his own place, and go to sleep in his own bed. But then he remembered the way their mouths had fit together, the eerie sensation of two people locking into each other, and though he wasn't sure he wanted to stay, he didn't really want to leave either.

So he lay on the bed in the warm spot Miles had vacated and watched as Miles reached over and flicked the light off. "Night," he said, and hated how uncertain he sounded.

"Night," Miles returned, all lazy satisfaction, like he'd gotten everything he'd wanted.

They both had; that much was clearly obvious from the way they'd both gone up in flames from the first moment they'd touched. Evan knew he should be feeling more resolved. But tomorrow's screen test still loomed over them, and there was too much ambiguity about the future for him to relax.

He rolled over and willed sleep to overtake him. It still didn't come. Even when Miles fell into a gentle patter of snores, too quiet to be annoying, and also too quiet to drown out his uneasy brain.

He told himself that he was making the right decision when he silently slid out of bed and locked Miles' door behind him with the key he still had on his ring. It was just a night of sleep, and in the grand scheme of things, it really shouldn't mean anything.

Was it fair of Miles to be pissed that he'd woken this morning and Evan had already been gone? Probably. Was it surprising that he'd opened his eyes to nothing but empty sheets? Not really.

Evan, even after admitting he wanted Miles and thoroughly acting on this desire, was still skittish. Still unsure. Never really convinced that Miles really wanted him, despite all the words and actions that proved otherwise.

A younger, more selfish Miles might have gotten frustrated with Evan before this, but Miles took pride in the fact that he wanted the other man *because* of how difficult he was to convince, not in spite of it. There was a careful hesitancy in Evan that Miles loved—because when he finally felt secure enough to let go, you knew you'd won him over, heart, body and soul.

And that was the end goal that Miles was really gunning for.

Now they only had to make it through this screen test and hope that it would be enough to convince Reed, because anything else they could fix later.

Miles just needed this *one* thing to fall their way.

They'd arrived on set to the expected chaos of a show that was just getting underway for the first day of filming. Reed was there, and his boyfriend, Jordan, who wrote the script for

Dream Team. Quentin Maxwell and Landon Patton, the talent, were running late, which didn't seem to surprise anyone.

"That's why they told us we could do our screen test today," Evan murmured into Miles' ear, and with the hot breath brushing his skin, he had to remind himself that Evan wasn't going to do that hot little nibbling thing he'd done last night.

"Because things are already chaotic?" Miles asked.

"Because they won't be likely to get much done today at all. Landon and Quen can be . . . tough to wrangle."

"So it's not just me, then?" Miles glanced over at Evan, grinning. Evan was not grinning. That was another thing Miles wanted desperately—for Evan to *relax*.

But asking Evan to relax in the middle of chaos, during one of the most important days of his career, was useless. It wasn't ever going to happen.

"That was never our problem. Or *your* problem," Evan said.

Maybe another day Miles would have asked Evan to detail exactly what his problem was, but the memories from last night—what could be if they could learn to work together instead of against each other—were too fresh. The last thing he wanted to do was dredge up all the shit from the previous weeks.

They hadn't really resolved it, and it still lay there, stagnant and sour, between them. Maybe Evan thought they could move on without dealing with it but Miles knew they couldn't.

Even if Miles cared about Evan enough to let it go—and despite how stupid it was, he was edging closer to that place—Evan would never let it go. Miles didn't think he even wanted to.

"Are you ready?" Evan asked, jerking Miles out of the melancholy fog that he'd felt from the moment he'd woken up and realized he was alone.

"I was born ready," he said, putting on a confident front that he didn't really feel anymore. Before he'd come here, *Pastry by Miles* always made him feel freer, an endless opportunity stretched out in front of him. Now thinking of what could happen to his show, all he felt was apprehension.

It was hard to face that at least half of that was his fault, but he forced himself to.

Without that email, Reed wouldn't have demanded a screen test, and he wouldn't have spent the last two days unsuccessfully recording himself baking peanut butter chocolate cookies.

The cookies had been fantastic; his performance had been anything but.

Before, it had only ever been him. Then it had been easy to think it was just him and Evan, for better and worse. And now there was a huge crowd of people, and even though Miles had never cared before, suddenly what they thought mattered.

He swallowed hard, and unsuccessfully ignored the sudden tightness in his chest.

"Just remember that it just needs to be good enough," Evan said.

The hardest part of the last two days was watching the hopeful light in Evan's eyes go out as he figured out that Miles couldn't perform on command. And hearing his words now only proved that even Evan wasn't sure he could do it.

"Okay," Miles said, shoving his suddenly damp hands into his pockets, wondering if anyone would notice if he ran away and hid in the bathroom.

He didn't even have a green room because this wasn't even his show.

"You're going to be fine," Evan said. He placed a reassuring hand on Miles' back, high enough to be professional. Stupidly, Miles wished that he'd move it lower, make what had happened last night official and public. But that wasn't Evan's style. It wasn't even Miles' style. At least it hadn't been before he'd met Evan. Evan made him want all sorts of things he'd always avoided, and the painful irony was that he was the least likely to get them because it *was* Evan.

"Fine," Miles parroted back, tongue thick and uncooperative. He couldn't remember the last time he'd even been nervous but he was undeniably nervous now.

Evan checked his smartwatch. "Time for makeup," he said, and with his hand still on Miles' back, steered him over to the makeup station.

Miles had never worn makeup for *Pastry by Miles* before, and he forced himself to remember that they were trying to up the production quality for the new version.

It didn't help.

He sat down in front of the mirror and watched as the nice lady put a new, strange face on him.

The bathroom had never looked more appealing. Miles didn't even think about his little dinky kitchen in Napa because if he did, he wasn't sure he could keep it together.

⁂

Would Miles be better if I had stayed?

The question echoed through Evan's brain for the hundredth time since they'd gotten to the *Dream Team* set.

Miles had been nervous and tense from the moment Evan had met him at the set, and instead of relaxing with Evan's hand on him, he'd only grown edgier.

Evan stood behind the central camera operator and crossed his arms over his chest, careful to keep the frown off his face, but feeling it reverberate through him.

Miles was standing in the kitchen, the place he always looked confident and sure, but he looked nothing like he usually did.

He looked like an apprehensive wreck, and it was taking every ounce of Evan's self-control to not walk up there and do something—*anything*—to calm him down.

Evan knew he should have stayed. He never should have left, never should have given Miles a reason to doubt that he liked him, that he cared about him, and Evan had been monumentally stupid enough to do it the day before the most important ten minutes of both their careers.

That was exactly why Evan almost never let himself do what he really craved. Because they were usually really bad ideas, and only made things worse, not better. Last night had been great. He couldn't even think about it without a little frisson of invisible pleasure, but it hadn't been worth throwing everything else away.

The director called for quiet. Miles forced out a painful little half smile, and then the worst ten minutes of Evan's life began.

He knew right away that Miles' performance this time was even worse than some of the recordings they'd done over the last two days. He'd worried about those, had been afraid that he was too stiff, so he'd pushed and pressed and hoped that they could make some improvements before this moment came.

Now Evan wished he'd just kept his fucking mouth shut, because he would have loved to have those performances be *this* performance.

"And now, uh, you put these in the oven for ten minutes," Miles said, and slid the cookie sheet into the oven. Wooden. Dry. None of the playful, laughing charm that had won over so many people who didn't care about pastry at all.

Evan had counted himself in that group, from the very beginning, and this hurt more than he ever could have imagined it would. Because it wasn't only his failure, it was the failure of a persona that Miles had believed in. A persona that he'd believed himself to be.

Evan wished he could take it all back, and leave Miles alone. Leave him to his bad production values, and poor lighting, and the single swipe of raspberry puree on one cheekbone. *Perfection.*

"Cut," the director yelled, and it blessedly, thankfully, ended.

"What just happened?"

Evan turned and Reed was standing there. Evan's stomach plummeted.

"He was nervous, uh, a little tense, I think," Evan said, and because there was nothing else he could do, pushed. "I have a lot of rehearsal footage that you should see. It's a lot better." Not by much, but it *was* better.

Reed raised an eyebrow. "You rehearsed? How much?"

"The last two days," Evan said, even though he was sure that Reed already knew the answer. Evan was unfailingly predictable.

"What I wanted to see," Reed said reluctantly, "was a meshing together of your two viewpoints. The organization and production value that you bring to the table, but the spontaneity and charm of who Miles is in the kitchen. Your point of view completely overwhelmed his. You rehearsed him way too much.

He knew what he was going to say before he even said it. There was nothing here from *Pastry by Miles*. It was more *Pastry by Evan*."

It was one thing to know it, it was another to have his boss pronounce it. Evan wanted to sink through the floor and die, especially when he saw Miles approaching behind Reed, clearly hearing every word he was saying. The worried crinkle between his dark brows told Evan everything he needed to know. Miles was half a step out the door, half a step away from going back to Napa and resuming a life that he'd already outgrown.

And Evan, for the first time in his life, confronted a problem that he didn't know how to fix.

"We can do better," Evan said, because he didn't know what else *to* say. He believed they could; he had no idea how to go about doing it, but they couldn't be so good together sometimes without some potential for success.

Reed just shook his head. "I don't want *better*. I want what you had." He turned and pinned Miles with a single look. "Just because you want in his pants doesn't mean you should just nod your head and smile whenever he tells you to do something. He's not infallible. And neither are you." He threw up his hands. "For the love of god, take a long weekend and figure out how to work together."

"Uh," Evan said. Because he couldn't take a long weekend and not know what that meant for his future. Was he fired? Was

Pastry by Miles as a *Five Points* property over before it had even begun?

"Get out of here," Reed said sternly, and his expression very clearly stated arguments wouldn't be tolerated. "I don't want to hear you did one minute of work. Go somewhere. Clear your heads. And come back here and we'll figure out this mess you two have made."

It was bad, but Evan supposed he was grateful it wasn't as bad as it could have been.

Miles looked like a thundercloud come to life as Reed walked off to supervise the finalization of the set for *Dream Team*.

"I'm sorry," Evan said, because everything else felt painfully inadequate.

"Yeah, you should be. The real question is what you're actually sorry for."

Evan swallowed hard. "I don't know what you mean."

"That's your whole damn problem," Miles said. "And we're going to fix it."

Which is how, two hours later, Evan found himself in another rental car, heading towards Northern California.

"You can't run away every time things get ugly," Evan said, because he didn't like where this was going. He knew what had happened the last time Miles had decided to go back to Napa, and they were on thin enough ice as it was.

"That," Miles pointed out, "is your other problem. You think I'm running away. I'm not. I'm blowing off steam. You've never blown off steam in your life. You're about to self-combust from all the steam building inside you. You put way too much pressure on yourself. Take too much on. We're going up to Napa to help you learn to let stuff go."

"Shouldn't we be working on how to fix the show?" Evan insisted. "We're half-fired at this moment in time. Blowing off work to drink and party doesn't seem like the best plan."

"Reed already told you that you're not working. And even if he didn't, I wouldn't let you. We've rehearsed enough. We need to learn to work together, and that's never going to happen if you can't fucking relax."

"So you're going to . . . teach me to relax?" Evan didn't know what to make of this plan. Actually, scratch that. He knew what he thought of it and it wasn't anything good. It was a terrible plan, probably going to result in them being totally, one hundred percent fired.

"Yes."

"I can relax," Evan insisted.

"And yet I have seen zero evidence of you actually relaxing," Miles said. "We tried things your way, and they failed spectacularly. You wound us both up so tight that I could barely breathe. I don't even know how you survive wound this tight. So we're going to do things my way."

"But . . ." Evan tried to point out, but Miles just interrupted him.

"No arguments. No circular logical shit. You're going to fucking relax if it kills me."

"It might, because I'll probably end up murdering you," Evan said, and he couldn't help how grumpy he sounded. He was *fine*. He didn't need to relax; relaxation never got anyone anywhere.

"Yeah," Miles drawled, his hand on the wheel relaxed as he smiled, skin crinkling near his eyes, "you can fuck me to death."

Evan harrumphed.

"Seriously, it might be fun. You might actually enjoy yourself for a minute."

"Are you going to keep bringing up sex just to remind me what happened last night?" Evan demanded. "Because trust me, I do not need a reminder."

Miles glanced over, and he was still smiling. Like the further north they drove, the further he unwound. Even Evan baiting the shit out of him didn't make a dent. "I don't know, I think *I* do. A little refresher, we could even say."

Evan snorted, because he just couldn't help himself. "Is that how you get guys in your bed? You never stop harassing them?" It wasn't hard to swallow the question of why Miles wouldn't stop harassing *him*. After all, he'd left Miles alone in bed, and fucked up his career.

He wasn't sure which Miles should be more pissed off about, but Evan knew he would never be big enough to let it go. But instead of biting his head off, Miles was driving them to Napa, relaxed and smiling, like last night had been perfect.

"When it's perfect, yeah, I'm not going to let that go. Let *you* go." Miles smirked.

And it sort of had been perfect, at least before Evan went and overthought everything. Before Evan remembered what the next morning would bring.

Somehow they'd both survived the morning, though Evan had a feeling that had more to do with Reed probably not wanting to deal with them than actually catching a break.

Still. They were still here. Still together. Evan felt the invisible belt holding him together loosen a single notch.

"It was pretty great," he admitted, and Miles' smile grew at least ten degrees brighter.

"See, that wasn't so hard, was it?" Miles teased.

"I don't know," Evan said, barely managing to keep a straight face. He was *not* going to grin at Miles like a lovesick loon. Except he sort of was. Miles was making him begin to believe in fate. "It might be pretty hard later."

Chapter Twelve

It was a long drive to Napa, almost six hours from the studio, but Evan felt like he spent most of it half-hard, blood simmering in anticipation of what they might do when they finally got to the hotel Miles had booked.

Miles seemed like he wanted it too, just as much as Evan did. The looks he'd been shooting Evan's direction were hardly subtle, and his comments were even less so. And every so often he'd put his hands on Evan, casually, in the middle of a conversation, like it didn't mean anything at all.

But it meant a lot. It meant that Miles worked him up and then carefully made sure he never really calmed down.

Instead of pulling into the hotel parking lot, they sailed right past, and Evan tried not to look too frantic as he opened his phone to verify the reservation. "This was the place," he said, trying to sound calm and not panicked. *Relaxed.*

He'd never considered himself particularly sex-obsessed before, but he craved Miles powerfully now that he'd actually allowed himself to.

"What?" Miles asked, as laid-back as ever. Evan wanted to strangle him and also shove his dick down his throat. He really hated how desperate Miles had made him—just by being himself.

"That was our hotel," Evan got out in a strangled voice. "We just passed it!"

"Oh yeah," Miles said. "It was. Good eye."

"What are you doing!" Evan didn't even recognize his own voice.

"Don't worry," Miles said, leaning over and resting a warm palm conveniently on Evan's thigh. Evan sucked in a breath. "We'll get there soon enough. I made us a wine tasting reservation first. A few of them, actually."

"A few?" Evan squeaked.

Miles shot him a soft, scorching smile. "A few, yeah. Is that a problem?"

If Miles thought Evan was going to be the first to break down and demand sex, he was crazy.

"No," Evan said, pulling himself back together only because he'd done it his whole life. "I'm good."

It was a complete and total lie, and Miles' expression made it clear he knew just how untruthful Evan was being.

"Yeah, you are," Miles said, and his voice was a slick caress across Evan's skin.

He was going to kill him by the time they made it back to the hotel. Or maybe he'd do as Miles had suggested and just fuck him to death.

"This," the sommelier said, "is our unoaked chardonnay." He poured a little of the golden liquid into each of their glasses. Evan shifted uncomfortably on his wooden stool.

He'd always believed wine tasting would be fun. Anything involving alcohol was *supposed* to be, right? But from the moment they'd driven up the winding road to the huge, imposing winery, with its expensive fixtures and obvious antiques, to being shown into the private tasting room, Evan had been on edge.

And not even the fun sort of edge that Miles had honed during the drive up.

This was the edge where Evan never knew what he was supposed to do, how he was supposed to act, what he was supposed to say. All accompanied by the fear and horror of choosing wrong and revealing himself as a fraud.

He might look the part of a young, successful adult, but it still felt like an act and like he might be exposed at any moment.

Reed had wondered once why Evan always made sure he was meticulously prepared and so extensively researched. *This* was why.

But Miles had dragged him up to these wineries before he could look into their dress codes, their wine lists, their tasting room etiquettes.

Evan didn't know how Miles could look so calm when he had no clue what he was supposed to say about the stupid wine.

Usually he looked up reviews, and formed an opinion before he even tasted it, because it helped create a good frame of reference. Evan knew he was wine-ignorant and even as he took a sip now, letting the liquid swell in his mouth, he was lost.

Miles didn't help at all, just tasted, expression thoughtful and frustratingly blank.

"What do you think?" the sommelier asked.

Miles had introduced him as Nate, one of his roommates' ex-boyfriends, and he looked the part of a professional sommelier—polished and urbane, his shoes probably costing more than Evan's whole outfit.

He'd only longingly glanced at the beautifully burnished cognac leather loafers a few times before they'd sat down.

The test had come and Evan had known there was no way he could pass. He didn't drink boxed wine, but he definitely bought wine under ten dollars. Sometimes even under seven dollars. He didn't have a rarified or educated palate.

Even though Miles claimed not to know much either, Miles still knew more because he'd worked at Terroir, and he'd lived in Napa.

"It's got a surprisingly buttery finish," Miles said, saving him even though he couldn't know how tense Evan had become at being asked to provide an opinion on the wine. "I thought you said it wasn't oaked."

"It's not," Nate sniffed.

"Could've fooled me," Miles said, downing the rest of the glass.

Nate scowled. "Amazing, you're still an asshole."

But Miles just smiled back, all charming congeniality. "And you're still a fucking snob. But you pour good wine, which is why we're here. So do your job, and pour us some more wine."

It shouldn't have been sexy hearing Miles tell off the sommelier, but it was an unexpected turn-on. Evan squirmed in his chair, torn between annoyance and fondness. He shouldn't want or like Miles as much as he did, but that ship had already sailed and there was absolutely nothing Evan could do about it now.

"This," Nate said, shooting a snooty glare from his brown eyes, "is an oaked chardonnay."

Evan glanced at the tasting card resting between them on the gleaming wood bar top. There was only one chardonnay listed—the one they'd just finished. He might not know anything about wine, but he did know how to read, so he spoke up.

"Which chardonnay is this one again? I don't see it listed."

Nate glared harder, but Miles' gaze met Evan's across their glasses, and they shared a conspiratorial, secret look that made Evan's stomach somersault.

"Costa, what would your old roommates say if they knew you were dating?" The sommelier lifted a glossy brown eyebrow, flawlessly groomed.

"We're not dating," Evan corrected frostily, and briefly considered explaining they were just fucking. But not enough for Evan's peace of mind.

"He's my producer," Miles said, completely breaking protocol by reaching over and pouring some more of the first chardonnay in his glass. "And that second chardonnay is disgusting. Don't pour that again."

He looked over at Evan, and the warmth in his expression made Evan wonder if he'd lied earlier. Were they dating? Was this a date? Was this whole weekend a date? Weren't you supposed to go on a lot of silly, short dates before you took someone on a weekend getaway?

It was stupid to even think it. They didn't even like each other, and they couldn't stop fighting for five minutes put together. But the times they weren't fighting? Evan lived for those moments. For the soft, sweet Miles who made him want to be soft and sweet too. Miles, who made him believe that he *could* be, even though he'd assumed for so long that he was hopeless. Too shut off, too closed, too much of a workaholic.

Miles made him want things he couldn't define.

"And to answer your question, we're going to a late dinner at the house tonight, so maybe you can call up Wyatt and ask him what he thinks."

Nate stiffened, and Evan would have had to be a lot more obtuse to miss the flash of hurt in his eyes. It was gone almost instantly, but it had been unmistakable.

"This," Nate said coldly after they'd drained their glasses, "is one of our library cabernet sauvignons. I hope your palate will appreciate it."

It was rich and complex, an enigmatic combination of the light and the dark. And Evan said so, out loud, before he could stop himself.

Nate merely looked constipated, but Miles smiled encouragingly. "It is good," he said. "Surprisingly dark, smooth finish, but light and drinkable. I like it." He downed the glass. "And you already know my palate won't appreciate it."

"True," Nate said. "But you," and he pointed to Evan, "actually have some potential, unlike that idiot sitting next to you."

Evan was almost stupid enough to protest, because of course he didn't have any potential. He drank cheap wine. He didn't really care too much what it tasted like—in fact, he ignored what it tasted like, because for so long, he couldn't afford anything better, and drinking wine at all had felt like a luxury, like he was better than he really was. But all that did was force him to remember who he was and where he'd come from. If Nate the snooty sommelier said his palate had potential, then it *did*.

Miles' smile was supportive. "Don't give him too many ideas, he'll be talking about cigar smoke and mahogany next." His hand reached out and rested on Evan's knee. It was big and warm and delicate and it made Evan shiver. He wanted to drag Miles away and damn the wine tasting to hell.

How Miles ever thought he was going to relax while winding him tighter than he'd ever been, Evan wasn't sure.

Nate poured a merlot next, which was apparently the winery's newest release. This time he looked to Evan for his impressions, barely glancing at Miles.

Emboldened by the compliment to his palate and the wine he'd already drunk, Evan felt marginally more comfortable offering his opinion. "It's spicy and burns a little, but a good burn," he said cautiously.

"You really shouldn't bring him over to that hellhole," Nate said as they were getting ready to go. They hadn't bought any wine, but when they were getting ready to go, Nate had pushed over a bottle in a brown paper bag. "For tonight," was all he said, and Miles had frowned. Evan was pretty sure the frown had something to do with Nate's ex-boyfriend, Wyatt. Miles' friend.

"It's not a hellhole. I lived there for two years," Miles said.

Evan figured he was allowed an opinion because he'd actually been there. "It's not even close to a hellhole," he defended. He didn't add that he'd seen actual hellholes growing up, and the run-down, worn house Miles had lived in couldn't even begin to compete.

Nate only shook his head. "You know where to find me if you get sick of them."

"What did he mean?" Evan asked as they walked to the car. He told himself he wasn't jealous, that Nate wasn't propositioning Miles if he got bored later. He was mostly lying.

"Nate works at a late-night wine bar too, pouring. Pays for his expensive shoes," was all Miles said as they got into the car.

"You don't like him," Evan stated, somewhat to his own surprise. "You really, really don't like him."

"Gee, what gave me away?" Miles asked with a lopsided grin in Evan's direction.

"I mean . . . you don't talk to me that way. I thought that's how you talked to people you didn't like." Evan had a fleeting thought that maybe this conversation shouldn't be happening now, after he'd had a few glasses of wine. Miles had pleaded required sobriety for driving, but Nate had poured most of the winery library for Evan.

At the time it had seemed like an excellent learning opportunity; a way to expand and refine his palate. Only now did Evan realize drinking so much wine had been a mistake. He was definitely tipsy, and even worse, he kept saying all sorts of things to Miles that he shouldn't.

Was this what being relaxed felt like? No. It was definitely what being drunk felt like. "That's because I don't dislike you."

"But, you definitely seem to. I mean, you *said* you did."

"I also said I thought you had a hot ass. Does that seem like something I'd say to someone I didn't like?"

"No." He *did* have a hot ass. It was hardly the first time he'd been informed of this fact, but none of those other times had made his face burn and his cock harden. In fact, all those other times, he'd varied between mildly and extremely creeped out.

"You're cute when you've been drinking," Miles announced.

"I'm not drunk," Evan said. Total lie. The way Miles grinned meant he knew just how drunk Evan was, and just how much he was lying.

"And yet you're still not relaxed."

Evan frowned. It seemed *very* obvious the best way to relax him. And because he'd apparently lost his brain-to-mouth filter, he said it. Out loud. "I know exactly how you can relax me."

Miles turned into a parking lot and pulled into a space. Evan glanced up at the sign above the rows of little wooden stalls. "What is this?" he bit off. This wasn't the sort of relaxing he wanted to sign up for. The wine tasting had actually been pretty fun; whatever this was, Evan already knew he wouldn't like it. Why? It was *cooking*.

"I thought you might want to come to the farmer's market with me," Miles said, so reasonably that Evan felt a tiny bit ashamed for snapping.

But only a tiny bit. After all, it felt like Miles had been pressing for weeks for them to have sex, so it shouldn't have been so difficult to get him to do it again. Especially when it had been so good the first time. Even better than he could have predicted.

"Is the farmer's market supposed to relax me?" Evan snapped.

"I thought watching me cook turned you on?" Miles glanced over, and there was so much heat in his gray eyes it was a miracle he didn't melt right onto the seat. Oh wait, that was Evan, who wasn't only feeling warm and loose from the wine he'd drunk.

"I don't think I remember saying that," Evan said. He should be a lot more ashamed at getting caught out, but this was *Miles,* and he'd probably read all the comments on his videos a few dozen times. And everyone thought Miles cooking was a turn-on, because it *was.*

It was those long fingers and the way he caressed every goddamn ingredient.

"Are you coming?" Miles said, eyes glittering with unrepentant amusement.

"*No.*" Evan gave a frustrated grunt. "Not even close."

"Come on," Miles persuaded, "it'll be fun."

"Fine, but if you fondle the raspberries again, I'm done," Evan said.

It was a hell of a lot sweeter than Miles had ever imagined it would be to see Evan so obviously needy for sex. And not just sex in general—sex with *Miles*.

Only part of it was that he'd never really had someone turn him down so many times and fight so hard against a mutual attraction. Most of it was that it was just Evan. Miles was beginning to realize he adored everything about him. From the way he'd stared enviously at Nate's stupidly expensive loafers, bought with too many long nights at the wine bar, to Evan's frustration that they hadn't immediately fallen into bed again, to his extraordinarily pleased expression when he'd been told he had a decent palate.

He was adorable, if you paid attention. Even if you didn't, Miles realized, but then he'd spent too long trying to ignore him. Even when Evan made himself difficult to ignore.

"Can you please explain what it is you're doing?" Evan asked, eyes obscured by a pair of aviator sunglasses he'd slipped on.

"As directed, I am not fondling the raspberries," Miles said.

Evan took a step closer, reaching up on his tiptoes to murmur into Miles' ear. "Then how come you're rolling them between your fingertips?"

Had he been? Given an inch, Miles was figuring out that he was desperate to go the mile. Consciously or even subconsciously. "Maybe because I want you as badly as you want me?"

"You're doing that annoying thing again, where you answer a question with a question," Evan hissed after Miles dropped the container of raspberries into the basket he was carrying.

"You love it when I do that," Miles insisted.

Evan sniffed. "No. I definitely do not."

"Sorry?" Miles asked, shooting Evan a lopsided smile. That smile had charmed legions during his single life, but all it did was emphasize Evan's frown.

"I don't get it," Evan said as they walked away from the fruit stand. "If you want me as much as I want you, how come we're not at the hotel right now?"

Miles shoved his own sunglasses on top of his head as he leaned down to examine some zucchini. Maybe he'd make a zucchini and squash ratatouille. Xander had a secret obsession with Italian food and would appreciate it. "Because," he said patiently, "we're at the farmer's market, buying supplies to make dinner. Also, because you're drunk and I don't want to do something you might regret."

A frustrated groan came out of Evan's mouth. "You're the one who took me wine tasting!"

Miles turned away from the zucchini, decided this needed his full attention. He couldn't get distracted by squash or Xander's *tendre* for rustic Italian. "I took you wine tasting because you like wine, and I thought you might have fun. Even though that jerk Nate was the sommelier."

"But . . ." Evan tried to say but Miles placed the produce basket on the ground, and wrapped his arms around Evan's narrow waist. Evan resisted a little, but eventually gave in, letting Miles pull him closer.

"No buts," Miles said seriously. "I do want you. I can't wait to take you back to the hotel, but this is also a break for you. A break you really need. And as far as I'm concerned, that's more important than getting a quickie at the hotel. *You're* more important than a quickie at the hotel."

Evan's eyes grew wide. Like he genuinely didn't believe he was more than a convenient fuck. Which, as far as Miles was concerned, was a bunch of bullshit. Yeah, he'd sent that email. Yeah, they fought and bickered like cats and dogs, but when had he ever made Evan feel like he didn't like him? Like he wasn't important? He'd been trying since he first realized to show Evan that he cared. Even more than he was ready to admit to.

"Oh." Evan seemed shocked and speechless. But maybe still not totally convinced.

So instead of letting Evan go and picking up the produce basket, ready to resume his shopping, Miles decided there was no time better than the present to do a little additional convincing.

It wasn't so easy for Miles to say the words yet—even in his own mind, he tripped uncoordinatedly over them—so he showed Evan just how much he was wanted. He kissed him, pouring in all the skill he'd learned and all the passion he felt for the other man, his tongue slipping between Evan's still-stiff lips, giving everyone at the farmer's market a nice show.

It took a long second for Evan to respond, but when he did, he threw himself into the kiss, tongue rasping against Miles', hands wandering down his back, landing pretty firmly on his own ass.

There were dim cheers somewhere over to his left, but all Miles could feel was Evan's mouth moving insistently against his own, his body pressed against his, his erection poking into his hip. And it hit him, like a ton of zucchini, that this was what he had really wanted, almost from the beginning.

Evan was what he had wanted. He had just been so slow—*way too fucking slow*—to see it.

Miles lifted his head and looked down into Evan's light brown sugar eyes. "You really . . . you really do want me," Evan breathed out unsteadily. Miles' own pulse was racing a hundred miles a second, and he didn't quite trust his own voice so he nodded.

And while Evan didn't say why he'd doubted, Miles thought as they resumed their casual stroll through the farmer's market that it weighed heavily between them. He ached for the young Evan, who had been convinced he wasn't worth anything, and that nothing had ever happened to change his mind.

Chapter Thirteen

"WHAT ARE YOU MAKING?" Evan asked, peering around Miles' shoulder as he sautéed the squash for the ratatouille he was making. "Something with a god-awful amount of zucchini, which I don't even like."

Miles glanced over at him, and even though he was still talking way too much and he'd taken his phone away from him twice now, Evan did seem a little more relaxed than he'd been in LA. Of course that might also be all the wine he'd drunk.

"You don't like zucchini?" He remembered Evan telling him he didn't like sweets, and then the way he'd devoured the peanut butter chocolate chunk cookie and then the *pain au chocolat*. Evan might think he didn't like something, but judgement should be held until he'd tried Miles' version.

He told Evan this, and his nose crinkled. "You're such an egotistical asshole," Evan said and Miles could only shrug.

"I'm a chef," he said, as an explanation. "And I'm making ratatouille, or a version of ratatouille. Xander loves rustic Italian, though he will almost never admit to it."

"Xander, huh?" Evan said, and he wasn't even the tiniest bit subtle about the green in his voice. "You've never asked me what I liked."

"You told me you didn't like sweets. I thought it was my duty first to change your mind on that score, and then we'd go from there."

"Your cookies were passable," Evan said, leaning against the opposite counter, sipping his wine. The wine that Nate had given him. Miles had already crumpled up the bag with its distinctive markings and buried it in the trash. Wyatt didn't need to backslide into that black hole of a relationship again, no matter how much wine Nate gave them. "The croissants weren't really yours, they were mine, so I can freely admit to loving those, even if they were a pain in the ass."

Miles pulled the zucchini off the stove. "So what do you like to eat then?"

"Pizza. Kung pao chicken. Tacos." Evan met Miles' surprised expression with a semi-belligerent glare. "What, I don't cook. So I order in or I go out."

"You need to learn how to cook," Miles said with a sad shake of his head.

"And I suppose you're just the guy to teach me?" Evan asked, leaning back into Miles' space. This time Evan kissed him, something quick and hot and almost brutal.

Miles pulled away, nearly gasping. "I'm a pastry chef. I know just enough about savory ingredients to get by. But," he added, dropping another quick kiss on Evan's cheek, "I'll be damned if anyone else teaches you."

"You two are disgusting."

Miles glanced up and Xander was standing in the doorway, holding a loaf of bread, the wrapper indicating their favorite bakery in Napa.

"And your heart is two sizes too small," Miles retorted. "I'll pick sappy and disgusting over lonely and miserable any day."

"I don't think we met before," Evan inserted, and though Miles couldn't figure out why, the casualness in his voice was replaced by a sharp edge. "I mean, we probably did, but I don't think we were properly introduced. I'm Evan Patterson."

Xander clearly had no qualms about looking Evan up and down because he did, freely. Miles ground his teeth and turned back to the tomato sauce he'd been simmering on the stove.

He didn't even put the bread down so he could shake Evan's outstretched hand. "And I'm Xander. Resident grinch."

Evan shoved the hand back in his pocket and took half a step closer to where Miles was starting to prep the ratatouille.

"What's this?" Xander said, sniffing appreciatively as he approached Miles' other side, resting a hand on his back. "You made ratatouille. For me?"

"Someday you're going to admit your obnoxiously refined palate loves Italian," Miles said.

"But not today," Xander said, sounding as smug as he ever had. Evan sniffed disapprovingly.

"I've never understood that," Evan said. "Someone makes you a meal, you should be grateful, not worried about how sophisticated it makes you look."

Miles felt Xander bristle next to him. "That's the difference going to culinary school makes," Miles said with a deprecating laugh. "It makes us all feel very important. Like we're culinary gods." He hoped that would be enough for Evan to let it go, and for Xander to back down and not engage. Because if Evan and Xander ever got into it, there probably wouldn't be anything left but rubble in his kitchen.

"I enjoy common food," Xander said, and Miles couldn't help but roll his eyes at his word choice.

"Yeah," he retorted, forgetting all about his vow to avert the fight and keep the kitchen intact, "'cause you're culinary royalty. I forgot."

"Like, In n' Out," Xander said defensively. "They use such fresh ingredients, and their cooking techniques aren't that shitty."

Evan glared at him. "Right, because McDonald's or Burger King is too basic for you."

"Yes, they are. If I want a burger, at least I want to eat a *good* burger, not some over-processed, greasy shit on a bun."

Miles could feel the waves of rage pouring off Evan, but even as he held a hand out to steady him—covered with tomato sauce and all—Evan snapped back. "Sometimes that's all people can *afford*."

And suddenly, Miles understood. People would never admit it, especially someone like Xander who had lived a solid middle-class life and had gone to culinary school right out of his parents' house, but good home cooking cost money. You needed equipment, you needed fresh produce and quality protein. None of that came cheap.

Miles had taken a class in culinary school on food sustainability, and he couldn't believe it when the instructor had informed them that eating out on cheap junk food was often much cheaper than cooking healthy meals at home.

And of course, Evan, living in a foster home and then living hand-to-mouth on his own, wouldn't have been able to afford to learn to cook. The guilt was sudden and sweeping, making him nearly nauseous.

"Xander, do me a favor," Miles said, words casual, his voice anything but, "shut the fuck up."

Evan knew he was supposed to be finding some magical well of relaxation in Napa, and up until now, even he could admit he was having a good time.

Separated from the antagonism that had dogged them from the first day, spending time with Miles was just as fantastic as Evan had hoped it might be, back at the beginning.

But spending time with Miles was not the same as spending time with Miles' old roommates, in particular the abrasive, argumentative one who was currently hanging off Miles like he wasn't going to let him go again.

The only romantic relationship Miles had ever described any of them having was Wyatt and his sommelier ex-boyfriend. He'd never said he'd been romantically or sexually involved with any of them, but it was hard not to believe this was lying by omission when Xander was putting his hands all over him.

Maybe that was why Xander was so bitter and unpleasant? Evan didn't want to think if things with him and Miles didn't turn out—which, he couldn't help but admit dispiritedly, was seeming more and more likely by the day—he would end up like Xander. Sad. Disillusioned. Resembling a rabid dog anytime someone talked to him.

"What?" Xander said, flinging his hands in the air, like he was innocent of all charges, which . . . had he *listened* to himself in the last five minutes? Evan didn't think so.

"You're an asshole," Miles said with a scowl.

This pronouncement didn't seem to phase Xander, who was probably called this on a daily basis. He sure deserved the title a lot more than Nate, Wyatt's ex, and *he* hadn't been particularly pleasant either.

Of course, Evan had partially incited the argument. He'd meant to keep his damn mouth shut, because he never brought up his old existence if he could help it, *especially* around people like Xander and Miles. But Xander had been so smug and obnoxious, Evan hadn't been able to help it.

"I'm going to go take a shower," Xander said. "I smell like lamb from all those chops I butchered during prep."

After he'd left the room, Evan busied himself with his wine glass, filling it again even though it had still been a quarter full. He couldn't look in Miles' direction. He'd been the one to insist he never wanted to talk about his childhood, and then he had blurted something like that out. The guilt on Miles' face had been unmistakable and the last thing Evan wanted was pity. Especially from Miles.

Evan had always imagined that falling in love felt wonderful, like rose petals and rainbows and kittens with balls of yarn. But all he felt was vaguely sick, like he might chuck up all the wine he'd drunk this afternoon.

"I'm sorry he's so . . ." Miles said helplessly. "So . . . Xander. I know he can be cruel, I should have warned you."

To Evan's horror, he felt sudden and unexpected tears in the corner of his eyes. Xander had been cruel, though it hadn't been premeditated. People said shitty things to Evan all the time and didn't realize just how shitty they were, because Evan avoided sharing any details of his past if he could help it.

Even Miles had only found out because Lucy liked to interfere.

It was stupid but Evan wished that he could have told him on his own, the way he wanted. He didn't know how long it would have taken him to finally tell the whole story, but Evan had a feeling it would have been good for him.

"You can't save me from everything," Evan said, trying to hide his sniff. "I'm plenty tough."

Miles' arms snaked around Evan's shoulders and pulled him close, his face tucking into Evan's neck. "I know, believe me I know. But that doesn't mean I like it when you get hurt. You deserve better. You've always deserved better."

"You didn't know me back then," Evan said because it was easier to argue petty details than it was to accept that statement. He kept waiting for Miles to force him to turn around and look him in the eye. To see the tear streaks on his cheeks. But Miles seemed to understand that this was a step too far, and to Evan's surprise, didn't push.

"I can't believe you've changed so much," Miles said softly. "I bet I would have loved the younger you just as much."

Evan's breath snagged. Had he just . . .? No, it wasn't possible. It was just a phrase. Miles didn't really mean it. He couldn't.

"Ha," Evan laughed unsteadily. "You know me well."

"I keep wanting to know you better," Miles said.

Somehow it was easier to say without having to look Miles in the eye. "Before you even came to LA, I wanted that." Miles' fingers tightened on Evan's shirt, the tips digging into his skin.

"How did we get so mixed up?" Miles asked, and Evan wasn't even sure he wanted an answer.

"We're both stubborn," seemed the most obvious answer. "But I think we're learning to compromise." He wanted to hope, out loud, that it wouldn't be too late, but they both knew better. They'd wasted their last chance, and the best hope they would have was for some part of the concept to be salvaged and for them both not to be fired.

It wasn't much of a hope, but it was something. Maybe they wouldn't end up separated by six hours on I-5. Maybe out of the disaster of the last few weeks, something good could still grow.

Evan turned and before Miles could say anything, kissed him hard. Saying everything he couldn't say out loud. It was incomprehensible that each kiss could be better than the last, but it was like they were slowing learning each other. They'd been so out of sync before, but that was changing.

It would be stupid and pointless to say that he wished it had happened sooner, but Evan still burned with it.

"Okay, you two are cute."

Miles broke away, and another one of the roommates was standing in the entrance of the kitchen. The young one, Evan thought with a resigned sigh. At least he'd been nicer than Xander. Not that that was particularly difficult.

"And I think your tomato sauce is burning," Kian added, crossing to the fridge and pulling out a bottle of water. He glanced over at the pot. "You're making Italian."

"Ratatouille," Miles said, returning to his pots and pans like Evan hadn't just almost poured his heart out. But if Evan looked close, he could see a tiny tremble in Miles' hands, and he couldn't remember ever seeing them anything but perfectly steady.

"So, you're dating now?" Kian asked, and Evan couldn't help but notice his casual look sharpened and also that he directed his question to Evan, not Miles.

He'd regretted telling Nate that they weren't dating from the moment the words had left his mouth, and the look in Miles' eyes when he'd said them.

"Yes," Evan said, and the world didn't stop spinning and the floor stayed shockingly level.

Miles turned around and the joy in his smile was worth how terrifying that had been.

"I guess we are," Miles said.

"I'm glad," Kian said. Evan had a feeling that Xander wouldn't be quite so glad.

"What's this?" the man in question said, entering the kitchen again, dark hair damp and eyes narrowed. "You're dating now?"

Evan lifted his chin. He really hoped Xander wouldn't continue being an asshole to him, but if he did, then he would deal with it. It wasn't like Xander was the first jerk he'd ever been confronted with. He wasn't entirely sure still what Miles had meant when he'd said he loved him, but suddenly he didn't care if Xander didn't like him.

It wouldn't mean that Miles liked him any less.

"We are," Evan said.

"That's stupid," Xander said, shaking his head. Like they were the first people to ever work together and date.

"It's sort of a tradition at *Five Points*. Unofficially of course. But you know about Quentin Maxwell and Landon Patton of course. And our boss, Reed, he's been dating Jordan Christensen for a few years now."

Xander's eyes darkened. "Aren't you all so fucking cute?" he sneered.

Evan realized with a jolt that Xander wasn't just an asshole; he was jealous.

Whether he was jealous of whoever Miles was with or just jealous in general, it was hard to say but if Evan had to guess, it was probably a combination. After all, he wasn't exactly going to find the love of his life walking around acting like a jerk.

Of course there were some guys who liked that, but Evan couldn't believe that would lead to a lasting, loving relationship.

"Yes, I'm sure it must be hard to hear about so many happy couples," Evan retorted.

Xander glared and he left the kitchen without a single word. Like Evan had just discovered his biggest secret. Or worst-kept secret, as far as he was concerned. Was it possible that Miles really didn't know how Xander felt?

Should Evan tell him? Or if he found out, would he drop Evan like a hot potato and run back to his ex-roommate? Evan squirmed internally; he didn't want to be selfish, but it had not been easy to get to this place. Was it wrong of him to not want to jeopardize it now that they'd figured some stuff out?

"Xander can be . . ."

"Xander," Kian piped up. He was cute and eager, like a golden retriever puppy. And thankfully, Evan got zero vibes from him that he was interested in Miles.

"I know it sounds hard to believe," Miles said, "but really, he does grow on you."

"Like a bad mold?" Evan said, raising an eyebrow. He glanced over to where Miles was meticulously arranging the squash and zucchini in an intricate swirling pattern over the bed of tomato sauce.

Kian laughed, and Miles huffed, fingers hesitating as he placed the last few vegetables into the dish. It didn't look like dinner, it looked like a work of art.

"Do you always make stuff that looks perfect?" Evan asked, which was a stupid question he already knew the answer to. He just didn't want to talk about Xander anymore, because his obvious feelings made Evan feel disloyal.

"I think he's incapable of making stuff that doesn't look flawless," Kian said. "But he almost never makes dinner. That's usually Wyatt or Xander."

"And Xander is still pissed at me for leaving, so we'd probably get paté foam or something equally odd, and Wyatt is . . ." Miles glanced up, questioning gaze directed at Kian. "Where is Wyatt?"

Kian shrugged. "He was right behind us. He came in with us. My guess is he's holed up in his room, skyping with his nana."

"They had to move her to a home last year," Miles explained as he slid the dish into the oven. "Wyatt is very close to her, and it's hard on him."

Evan wanted to ask who "they" were, because growing up with no family of his own had always made him morbidly curious about other people's. But before he could figure out how to politely phrase the question, Kian answered it.

"His dad left him and his brothers when they were very young, and then his mom died five years ago. Breast cancer complications. So it's just his two brothers and his nana."

"To be honest," Miles said, "I've never liked his brothers."

"They're weird jocks," Kian said. "I don't like them either."

"I don't think they contribute enough to help pay Nana's expenses," Miles said. "And they're weird jocks, besides."

Miles shot Evan a quick searching look, before returning to the stove, but Evan didn't volunteer anything. Maybe if he and Miles had been alone. Maybe if he had felt ready to share. But they weren't and he didn't. Not nearly. So he said nothing.

"Do I smell Italian?" Wyatt thankfully entered the kitchen a moment or two after they'd just finished talking about him. Not that he seemed like the sort of guy who would mind. He was tall, with wide linebacker shoulders, lots of tousled blond hair, and a laid-back, grounded attitude that Evan had immediately liked even though they'd only met briefly.

He was still trying to figure out why on earth these three great guys tolerated Xander's annoying attitude.

"Dinner will be ready in twenty," Miles said. "I'm gonna prep the bread, if you want to set the table?"

Wyatt raised an eyebrow at Kian, as he poured himself a glass of wine from the bottle on the counter. The bottle that happened to be the one Nate had given them. But he didn't turn an eyelash at the label, or ask where they'd gotten it.

Clearly, on Wyatt's side that relationship was over.

"Fine," Kian grumbled. Evan had a feeling that as the youngest, he ended up doing a lot of stuff that the others didn't want to.

"I saw Xander march out of here with a particularly virulent frown on his face. What is he bent out of shape about now?" Wyatt asked.

"That he's a miserable old man," Miles said.

"Well, that isn't new," Wyatt observed.

"I don't think he took the news that Miles and I are dating very well," Evan inserted, because he was curious to see how Wyatt would react to this. Would he guess that Xander was jealous? Was Evan really the first person to figure this out? That didn't seem possible, but Wyatt's expression still remained confused.

"Someday," Wyatt said, "he's going to meet someone he actually cares about, and it's going to hurt like a bitch when his heart grows a few sizes."

"Maybe it's permanently stunted," Kian answered cheerfully. "That wouldn't surprise me at all."

"But really, congrats. You seem like you'll be good for each other," Wyatt said, raising his glass. "It's high time Miles stopped playing it casual and breaking hearts right and left. I'll go get Xander, he shouldn't sit in his room and pout all night."

"He's going to if he wants to," Miles said.

"But he shouldn't," Wyatt replied firmly, setting his wine glass at one of the places of the big kitchen table Kian had set. And that convinced Evan once and for all that Wyatt was one of the good guys.

After he'd left the kitchen in search of Xander, Evan moved closer to Miles, bumping their shoulders together. "What happened with Nate and Wyatt?" he hissed under his breath. Curiosity was probably going to be the death of him.

Miles just shrugged though. "You met Nate, he's insufferable."

"But Wyatt dated him in the first place," Evan insisted.

"Yeah, I think Nate wasn't very happy he wouldn't get serious and introduce him to his family. To his brothers and his nana, rather."

"Yeah," Kian said, wandering over. "His brothers suspect he's gay, but his nana has no idea. She's sort of old-school Irish Catholic and I don't think he believes she'd understand."

The only nice thing about being a foster kid with no family of which to speak of was that when he'd come out, there hadn't really been anyone who cared or objected. Evan knew that it was definitely not that simple for everyone.

"I remember when I told my high school girlfriend I thought I was gay," Miles said, "and she just laughed and told me, 'of course you are.'"

"Yeah, not everyone is as understanding as your family, Miles," Kian said, and Evan, who wasn't the world's biggest toucher generally, surprisingly wanted to hug the apprehension out of his eyes.

"It's never easy," Evan said, even though it had been relatively cut and dried for him. He'd already been in a fairly open foster care situation with so many kids, the guardians hadn't really cared as long as you stayed out of trouble. Being gay hadn't ranked anywhere with getting arrested or burning the house down, so they'd just shrugged and moved on.

"What isn't easy?" Xander stood in the doorway, Wyatt following close behind him. "Dinner wasn't easy? If that was the case I could have helped you out, Costa."

Miles rolled his eyes. "Dinner was no big deal. Come sit down before I decide to punch you in the face."

But Xander did as he was told, and slumped into the seat at the head of the table, not surprising Evan at all.

The ratatouille was fragrant with oregano, basil and garlic; the zucchini and squash tender under the crusty lid of parmesan, the base soft with a zesty tomato sauce.

There was silence for a few minutes as everyone ate, sopping up the sauce with the garlic bread Miles had prepared.

"So where did you guys go today?" Kian asked.

Evan remembered how they'd crumpled the paper bag from the winery and buried it so Wyatt wouldn't see it.

"Uh," he said.

"A few wineries," Miles inserted and then very casually changed the subject. "I thought we'd do a picnic lunch up by the castle tomorrow. It's supposed to be a nice day. Wyatt, did you take care of that thing I asked you for?"

Wyatt nodded, mouth full of ratatouille. "It'll be under your name."

"Great, thanks." Miles smiled over at Evan, who was trying to decide if licking his plate clean would be rude.

"That was pretty good," Xander said. "Maybe if your video thing fails, you can go become a line cook at Olive Garden."

"Next time, I'm going to force you to make yourself Italian food. And it probably won't be as good as mine." Miles' voice still sounded kind, but he grimaced as he sipped his wine.

"What did you put in the sauce?" Wyatt asked. "There's an earthiness in it . . ."

"Evan," Miles said, leaning over, breath brushing his neck, which reminded him that it was only his stomach that was satisfied. "Wyatt's nose and taste buds are legendary. He can usually figure out what's in anything."

"But you asked?" Evan said, crinkling his own nose.

Wyatt shrugged. "People don't generally like it when I list their recipe out for them."

"You mean, *Xander* doesn't like it," Kian said, laughing.

"I think it's a wild mushroom, maybe? And red wine? A chianti?" Wyatt guessed.

"You're half right. Dried mushrooms reconstituted in some tempranillo."

"Damn it, that was the earthiness." Wyatt tipped his glass to Miles. "Well, kudos for fooling me."

Evan hadn't really realized how much Miles was giving up by leaving Terroir and his three roommates. Yeah, he'd taken a chance on a crossroads career move, but there had been reasons for him to stay in Napa. And a lot of those reasons were sitting at the table with them.

"How did you all meet?" Evan asked. He was sort of completely desperate to go to the hotel and remind Miles just who he was dating. And this time he'd only had half a glass of wine.

"Wyatt and Miles met in culinary school. Xander went to school in New York City and we met at Terroir. And I moved in last year, after I graduated, and got Chef Aquino's internship," Kian said.

"You mean, Chef Aquino's hard labor," Xander said.

"It's not that bad," Kian protested. "It's a really prestigious position."

Evan saw the concern Xander was voicing reflected in Miles' eyes. So Xander wasn't off-base or even overreacting.

"That's what they tell you to force you to take all the shit he dishes out," Wyatt pointed out quietly.

"I've got an early morning," Kian said, abruptly getting to his feet. "And I'm sure Evan and Miles have something important to do."

"You shouldn't push him," Xander said under his breath after Kian had left the room.

"Yeah, if I don't, then he keeps letting Aquino ride him. And I don't like that either," Wyatt said.

"It's gotten worse since I left," Miles stated rather than questioned.

"I swear to god, he's *obsessed* with him. Kian with Aquino, I mean. And, I don't know, maybe the other way around. It's weird. They're weirdly co-dependent on each other. I don't get it."

"I'll put out some feelers in LA," Miles said, getting to this feet. "Maybe we can convince him to leave. Take a job in LA."

"Kian ever leaving Terroir and Bastian Aquino? Yeah, good luck with that," Xander said bitterly.

CHAPTER FOURTEEN

Evan was quiet when they got into the car. Miles couldn't help but wonder if he'd pushed him too far, or if he was tired after such a long day. Maybe he should have given him what they both wanted, when they'd first gotten to Napa. He'd undoubtedly been eager then, and even though there'd been flashes of it through the day—some white hot in their intensity—Miles sensed now that he was deep in thought.

And not about Miles naked.

"You okay?" he asked.

Evan glanced up, his toffee eyes unexpectedly bright in the dim car. They slid down Miles' body, and Miles thought maybe he'd been overthinking earlier. Maybe nothing had changed.

"Xander really cares about Kian," was all Evan said, which really surprised Miles.

Evan wanted to talk about Xander?

Miles figured they'd been lucky to get out of the house without Evan punching Xander in the face. Why he wanted to discuss him now, Miles had no clue.

"Despite his best efforts tonight, he's not a jerk. I mean, he *is*, but not deep down. He's just . . . disgruntled. And yes, he cares about Kian. We all do. He's like our little brother."

Evan made a humming noise, clearly considering what Miles had said. They passed by a streetlight, illuminating Evan's flawless profile—elegant cheekbones, delicate nose, rosebud lips, proud chin—and Miles realized with a jolt that he had removed his bow tie sometime after they'd gotten into the car for the trip to the hotel.

"Eyes forward," Evan said, and he was clearly trying to pretend disinterest at the sudden, ravenous heat in Miles' face, but even he couldn't quite pull it off.

"No fair," Miles whined. Out of the corner of his eye, he saw Evan flick open one button of his shirt, and then another. And then another. Miles was pathetic and that was all it took to make him hard anymore—the chance to see Evan's bare skin.

"You made me wait all day," Evan said. "It's plenty fair."

"Cruel," Miles breathed out. Except that they both knew he liked it. Evan probably thought he'd get to control what happened when they got to the hotel, like he had the other two times they'd had sex, but Miles, while typically fairly laid-back and open in bed, was more than ready to assert himself.

And then Evan opened his mouth again. "I think Xander is in love with you."

Miles almost swerved off the road. "No. No way. That's just . . . that's not possible."

He took a quick, necessary peek to check the expression on Evan's face. He seemed concerned but not perturbed.

"Would it make a difference if he was?" Evan asked, and there was a raw honesty in his voice that Miles had never heard before. Sometimes it was tough for Miles to even figure out how much Evan contained and held back behind the wall he'd erected between himself and the world, but hearing him now, Miles realized just how much Evan cared about him.

How much he didn't want Miles to love Xander.

"No. Not a bit."

He chanced another glance over at Evan. He was smiling now, just a little one, around the corners of his mouth, but it was enough. "You really mean that."

"I mean, have you *met* Xander?" Miles asked.

"He's disgruntled and bitter and a little grumpy, but he's good-looking. And passionate. Those are two things I think you'd enjoy."

"*You're* what I enjoy," Miles vowed.

"I certainly hope so." The smug self-satisfaction in his voice was all Miles needed to hear to know Evan was okay.

"I can show you. Soon," Miles said, and saw Evan flick another button open. "Soon," he repeated, the word practically a vow.

Miles had never imagined that he would be making vows of any kind. He'd never imagined he was the sort of man who craved permanence that way, but Evan had changed everything.

"You'd better." Evan sounded just as impatient as Miles felt.

"Another mile," Miles said, pushing down harder on the gas. His driver's ed teacher would have been appalled at his driving. Probably also at his life choices, but Miles didn't really give a fuck anymore.

He whipped into the hotel parking lot. "I'll be back with the key," Miles said, reaching over, and leaving a brief but scorching kiss on Evan's mouth that promised everything he meant to do to him tonight.

Even though the desk clerk seemed to be efficient, he wasn't nearly fast enough for Miles. He pushed over his credit card across the counter and barely managed to refrain from tapping his foot on the marble floor.

Finally, he was given the room key, and he skidded out of the foyer to where he'd parked. Evan was already out of the car, leaning against the passenger side, impatient expression on his face.

And then, suddenly and unexpectedly, Evan let the ever-present wall fall and it was just the real Evan and him.

Usually he had to coax Evan out of his shell, and it felt so good to just press him against the car and not feel him hesitate before he kissed Miles back.

Instead Evan threw himself into it, and for Miles, it almost felt like the first kiss. Their first real kiss. The first time Evan kissed him and didn't think he was making a mistake, didn't wonder halfway through if it was the wrong thing to do.

He believed it was right and Miles was right, and Miles found that he had never believed more in the idea of the two of them against the world.

"Evan," Miles said, lips still hovering above Evan's. They were damp and shiny under the streetlamp and Miles almost gave in to the need coursing through him and said screw the words.

But Miles couldn't imagine that Evan had often gotten actions *or* words, so the words were important.

"Why are you stopping?" Evan said. Even with the emotional wall down, Evan was still completely himself. And Miles found himself enjoying the directness.

"Because we're still, unfortunately, outside. And I want to make love to you. Not against my car in a parking lot."

Evan's gaze was steady and warm. He didn't flinch, didn't cower, and didn't try to stop Miles. Didn't try to take control and make sure that Miles was too lost in pleasure to notice that Evan was still holding him at arm's length.

"Okay."

It was so hard to resist the urge to push, to rush, to devour Evan, but Miles held back by the skin of his teeth as they walked to the room. He'd even reached out and grasped Evan's hand, and Evan had let him.

Finally, they were in the room, the door was closing behind them, and Miles was free to do what he'd been longing to do all damn day.

He led Evan to the bed and kissed him, slow, but definitely not gentle. Miles poured every ounce of desire and love into the kiss, hands grasping Evan tightly around the waist, and then tugging out the shirt he'd tucked into his jeans.

"No khakis today, huh?" Miles murmured as his lips coasted down Evan's neck, pausing to nibble on his earlobe. "Taking a break in driving me insane?"

There was a definite catch in Evan's throat as Miles plucked open more buttons, his lips moving downwards across his exposed collarbones. They were so delicate, a delicious incongruity with his strength. Miles would be lying if he said that didn't really turn him on.

"I wasn't sure you could handle the khakis," Evan said.

"You're not wrong," Miles admitted ruefully.

"I almost wished I'd worn them," Evan admitted as Miles finished unbuttoning his shirt, and pushed it off his shoulders. Miles' mouth covered a firm pec muscle, then nibbled not very gently on his nipple. Evan gasped.

"Because I deserved it?"

"No," Evan said on another gasp as Miles' mouth moved to the other nipple. "Because I was jealous."

The idea was ludicrous but Miles didn't laugh because *one*, he had his tongue on Evan's glorious bare skin, pale and smooth and taut with the perfect amount of muscle, and *two*, this was Xander they were talking about. He couldn't even conceive of ditching Evan for Xander.

Miles' hands unbuckled Evan's belt. His cock was hard and there was an unmistakable wet patch on his boxer briefs. Just as Miles hoped, Evan gasped even louder, and suddenly he hoped, despite what he'd experienced so far, that Evan was loud and expressive in bed.

It was hard to imagine any interaction between them being devoid of a power struggle, but unlike the frustration that had dogged them before, Miles was definitely turned on by it.

"Maybe," he gasped himself, undone by Evan bucking firmly into his palm, "we just should have been fucking from the beginning."

Evan's look as Miles pushed him back onto the bed, and rid him of the rest of his clothes, was hot. Intimate. Everything

Miles had really wanted, even back then, and had never expected to get.

"Maybe we should just fuck now," Evan said, purring as he flipped over and pushed himself up, sending a spike of unrestrained lust through Miles.

Miles was still fully clothed and despite Evan's wandering hands, hadn't really been touched since they'd left the house. He was still suddenly in very grave danger of coming in his pants.

"I . . . I . . ." Miles stammered, undone by the sight in front of him. Evan was glorious naked, the most beautiful man Miles had ever seen. He couldn't have even fantasized about how good he would look like this. "I was going to take it slow."

Evan's glance over his shoulder was scorching. "Not after this whole day, you're not."

Some things, Miles realized, were inevitable and not worth fighting.

He grabbed the lube and a condom from his bag and shed his clothes so quickly, he was almost afraid he lost a few buttons.

But instead of immediately prepping Evan to take him, Miles leaned onto the bed and covered Evan's body with his own, skin to skin. Letting him feel how hard he was, how wet at the tip, just from touching Evan and seeing him naked.

"You're so gorgeous," he whispered into Evan's ear as he kissed his neck. "So fucking glorious."

"I know," Evan said, so smug that Miles couldn't help but love him even more. "Now stop fucking around and fuck me."

Miles would have been very stupid to argue at that point.

His hands smoothed over the curve of the ass he'd been watching and worshipping for so many weeks. Evan made a low groan as Miles carefully circled his hole with a wet finger.

"Stop teasing," Evan groaned as his body clutched around the digit Miles slid into him. "Goddamn it, Miles."

"If you're still talking," Miles said with a grin, "I'm not doing it right."

"Exactly," Evan wrenched out, as Miles pulled his finger out, only to slide two back in.

Evan felt so incredible, tight and hot, around his fingers, his body greedily clutching to them as Miles finger fucked him. He had a sudden, horrifying thought that he wouldn't be able to make it good. Make it last.

"Slow down a little," Miles panted, which was embarrassing because he wasn't even the one being fucked.

Evan pushed his body right back on Miles' fingers at that particular demand. "*No.*"

Taking a deep breath, Miles knew they'd waited long enough. He knew he could please his man. Felt it in his bones. It was time to show him just how much he cared about him.

He made short work of the condom, and slid his fingers around Evan's cock, circling it firmly as he began to push his dick into Evan. Pleasure short-circuited his brain, fierce and electric. He could only swear as he bottomed out, gripping Evan's hip and his cock.

"Move," Evan hissed and so Miles pushed back his own pleasure and focused on the man in front of him. The man he loved.

Maybe Evan couldn't accept the words yet, but he could accept this.

Miles set as powerful of a rhythm as he dared, his gasps echoing Evan's as he thrust. It was almost too much as Evan started to push back, to demand more, greedy and perfect, his cock thrusting into Evan's curled hand, his ass taking everything Miles was giving and demanding more.

Evan let out a long, drawn-out moan, louder than Miles had even dreamt, and came into his hand. Miles barely had a moment to enjoy the clench of his body before he fell off the cliff too, fingers digging into Evan's skin as he orgasmed.

For a half moment, Miles didn't move. It was impossible, but he still wanted to stay like this forever. He'd never felt closer to Evan.

"Here," Evan said in a small, hesitant voice, reaching over and handing his underwear to Miles, so he could clean up.

The very last thing Miles wanted was for Evan to decide this had also been a mistake. So he carefully pulled out, and smoothed a reassuring hand down Evan's back.

"I'll be right back," he promised.

Evan was sitting on the edge of the bed when he returned, and he wordlessly took the warm, damp cloth Miles handed him.

"Thank you," he said. "But I think I might just take a shower. Is that okay?"

Miles wasn't going to stop him. He might have wanted to join him, but he also wasn't sure he could keep standing another moment. The bed was calling to him. "Sure, of course. I'm just going to lie down."

"Yeah, it's been a long day," Evan echoed.

❧❧❧❧❧ ❧❧❧❧❧

The shower went on and on, and Miles lay in bed, wondering if everything really was okay. Was Evan going to come back to bed emotionally restrained again? Was he going to say, with his actions and not his words, that they'd made another mistake?

Miles squeezed his eyes shut and prayed that wouldn't happen. He'd never really been in love before, but he was pretty sure being in love alone sucked. He didn't want to know what that felt like.

Finally the shower shut off, and Miles watched as Evan came out of the bathroom, towel around his waist.

"This is a nice place," he said as he rummaged in his bag. "The water pressure is excellent."

Was this what they'd been reduced to? Talking about water pressure? Miles dreaded what subject Evan would bring up next; whatever it was probably making very clear to Miles that he needed space.

But instead, Evan climbed in bed after pulling on a pair of clean briefs, and to Miles' shock, laid his head on his bare chest.

They were quiet for a while, Miles trying to absorb what was happening, Evan probably trying not to freak out.

Finally Evan spoke, in a quiet voice, just as hesitant as he'd been after sex. "Is this okay?"

"More than okay. I love it," Miles said. *I love you.*

Evan took a deep, unsteady breath, and said, "I'm not good at this."

"It's okay. I'm not sure I am either," Miles confessed.

"You're better than you think," Evan said wryly.

"It matters to me that you know I care about you," Miles said carefully.

A sigh. "I know," Evan said.

"This is probably the wrong time," he continued. "But I should tell you, so I'm going to." He took another deep breath. "My parents died when I was two. I don't really remember them. I lived in ten foster homes. The last one, I was there for three years. I moved out when I turned eighteen. I didn't look back."

Miles' fingers gripped Evan's damp skin. "I'm glad you told me."

"I'm not good at letting other people control me," Evan said, and the unspoken end of that sentence was, *because too many people controlled me before.*

"I'm not going to control you," Miles promised. "And if I ever do, feel free to slap me."

"I'm going to hold you to that," Evan said, his voice was growing drowsy. Miles realized that this was all part of letting down his emotional guard, and that staying the night was part of it. That trusting Miles enough to touch him like this was another. They had come so far from those first distrustful days, and Miles could only hope that when they returned to LA, he could convince Reed of that.

Chapter Fifteen

Miles had never understood why people committed themselves and their hearts by falling in love. It had always seemed like a very risky proposition with a lot to lose and very little to gain.

But somehow, the morning was better when he and Evan woke up together, both smiling bashfully, and the sun brighter as they sat on the hill by the *Castello di Amorosa* and nibbled at meat and cheese that Miles had spent too much money for at Dean & Deluca.

Even the champagne was more effervescent on his tongue as they did a tasting at Domaine Carneros.

He'd gone to bed almost certain that Evan would wake up and the emotional wall blocking Miles out would be back in place, but to his own surprise, he'd watched the whole day as Evan worked to keep it down.

Miles could tell that it didn't come naturally, but his heart was nearly bursting at how hard Evan was trying to make things work between them. They would probably never be able to avoid a power struggle—even for a laid-back guy, Miles had difficulty relinquishing control, which he knew was a bad habit he'd picked up in the restaurant kitchens he'd worked in—but there could be spice in a little day-to-day friction.

The most important thing was that Evan understood that Miles was in this for the duration. He was done cutting and running; he was done pretending anything other than this partnership had been life-altering.

But even through the great afternoon, Miles had wondered in the back of his mind about what Evan had insisted last night.

There was no way that Xander felt that way about him and he'd somehow missed it. Miles knew he wasn't the most observant person in the world, especially about relationships, but surely Xander couldn't have liked him *that* way without Miles realizing. They'd lived and worked together for years.

It was impossible.

And yet Miles couldn't dismiss it completely. Not because he was at all tempted to ditch Evan for Xander—but because it didn't feel right to come up here and flaunt his new relationship, all while his friend was hurting.

He needed to know. So he kissed Evan goodbye at the hotel, told him to take a long soak in the tub, said he'd be back before they needed to leave for dinner, and headed to Terroir to confront Xander before the dinner service started.

❧☙

"What are you doing here? Aren't you supposed to be blinding the whole Valley with your annoying PDA?" Xander sneered as he added finishing touches to the sauces at his station.

He had a magic touch with sauces that even Bastian Aquino didn't have—not that the head chef ever would have admitted that. But Xander had been doing the sauces very early on in his tenure at Terroir and that only could mean one thing.

"Come in the dining room in a few hours, and I'm sure we could oblige you," Miles said. He wasn't technically supposed to be in the kitchens since he didn't work here anymore, but he'd left on good terms, and he didn't think anyone would kick him out. Maybe.

He shoved his hands in his black pants. "Why are you so angry?" he asked Xander point blank, because he needed to make this quick before anyone saw him, and also because he was sick of fucking around. Love had definitely shown him how vital it was to value what was really important.

"Nature? Habit? Preference?" Xander paused. "Take your pick, and then get out of this kitchen. You don't work here anymore."

"Here's the thing, Xander, you're not mad at everyone like you're mad at me. And it's new, since I left. So what's the deal? You're angry I moved on and left Napa? Left Terroir?"

Xander's aborted, angry hand movements told Miles only part of the story. He needed to know *why* Xander was so pissed.

"You've always been free to do whatever the fuck you wanted," Xander said.

"It was all me, you know that right? I was bored as fuck here, you know that, I know you do." Miles didn't like how defensive he sounded but maybe he was feeling guiltier than he liked over Xander's anger.

Xander's feelings weren't entirely his problem, but maybe they were a little his fault.

"Not everything is about you." Xander's knife flew over a bundle of chives. Then basil. Then Italian parsley. He was just about finished with the sauces, and then the dinner service would begin. Xander was an asshole, but he was a punctual asshole.

In five minutes, the line would be crowded with chefs. Miles tried not to panic and threw his Hail Mary pass. "Evan said that you were in love with me, and that's why you were angry I left."

Xander's eyes flew to his, shocked and belligerent. But he didn't deny it. "Evan is a nosy bastard. That might seem cute now, but you'll get sick of it. You can't take high maintenance and he's the King of High Maintenance Land."

"Are you?"

Xander slapped his knife down on his cutting board, sifting tiny circles of chives onto the floor. "Why does it matter?"

Miles was torn between strangling him and hugging him. "It matters."

"I wasn't in love with you, you egotistical bastard. Did I think . . . maybe? Maybe once or twice? Sure." Xander furiously stirred the mustard sauce he'd made his own since starting at Terroir. Miles had seen him make it a thousand times since they'd met, and it occurred to him suddenly that he wouldn't ever see him make it again.

And even though leaving this place had felt easy and like the right thing to do, emotion suddenly strangled him.

"Life is about change, Xander," Miles said softly, when he thought he could speak without embarrassing himself. "And we would have been a flaming disaster. You know that too."

"And?" Xander snapped. "It's not like you and Prince Charming have had an easy go of it so far."

"No, but we're getting there." He paused. "Xander, please. Don't hate me. In six months or six years, you're going to realize that you're done here too, and you'll leave."

"Maybe." Xander's testy tone had faded a little. Not much, but enough to give Miles hope.

"I know you're not going to be happy making Bastian Aquino's sauces for him your entire career. You're too talented for that, and you know it."

"I do." Xander stirred basil into another saucepan, and Miles realized with a pang that he didn't even know this sauce. It had been invented since he'd been gone. And that hurt more than he could have dreamt.

"Moving on is hard, but it's worth it. There's a whole life you can experience when you open your eyes."

"Don't worry, I'm not going to be up here, pining after your sorry ass." But Xander flashed a bright, quicksilver smile and it was enough that Miles knew he'd done the right thing coming here and talking to him.

"I wouldn't expect you to," Miles retorted fondly. "It's not that good of an ass."

Xander chuckled. "Get out of here before Aquino sees you and does something terrible."

"Throws me out?" Miles asked.

"No, forces you back into an apron."

⚜

"Did you go talk to Xander?" Evan asked, forcing his voice to remain light and casual. He shouldn't care if Miles had gone to talk to his friend; it had been the right thing to do to clear the air. It had just been impossible for Evan to think of the conversation without the very slightest waver of concern.

Miles and Xander had known each other for years. Xander was a great chef, talented and intense, probably the sort of person that Miles had always imagined he'd end up with.

He definitely couldn't have foretold that he'd end up falling for someone like Evan.

Even Evan, who'd secretly been harboring a little crush after spending so many hours watching *Pastry by Miles*, couldn't have predicted it. It still felt very new and like a significant bump could derail it.

Of course, if the last three weeks hadn't stopped it from happening, then he should consider their relationship inevitable.

"I talked to him, yeah. Everything's good," Miles said, sitting on the bed next to Evan, resting a hand on his knee casually like it didn't still cause fireworks to explode under Evan's skin. He was never going to get used to touching so casually; each touch still felt momentous and important.

Evan told himself that it was in Miles' nature to share less and his own to be inquisitive. He still couldn't help himself from asking, "Did he admit to it?"

"Not exactly. But I think he'll be okay."

Evan felt like a terrible person for not caring if Xander would be okay. Of course Miles did; Evan still felt too threatened to be so selfless.

"What are we doing for dinner?" Evan asked brightly, changing the subject. The last thing Miles needed was to find out that he felt unsure still, *especially* unsure about Xander. Especially because Miles himself had given Evan zero reasons to be concerned.

It wasn't Miles' fault that Evan was, and would probably be for some time to come, a neurotic, insecure mess.

"I want to take you somewhere special," Miles said, his soulful gaze making Evan's heartbeat skip.

"You know," he giggled a little self-consciously, "I never imagined you were such a romantic."

Miles smiled. "Oh, yeah, you did. You dreamed about it."

This was so completely accurate Evan blushed.

"Does that mean you're going to let me spoil you?" Miles asked.

"Spoiled how?" Evan told himself firmly not to be apprehensive because wasn't that what every lonely, miserable boy of twelve that nobody gave two shits about dreamed about? Someone making an effort? Someone trying to impress them even if it wasn't particularly hard?

Why then was it so hard for Evan to accept?

If Evan had ever been able to open up to a therapist—and he had *tried* but therapists wanted you to talk about yourself and he never could—he was sure they would have been able to tell him why. As it was, Evan had his suspicions.

"I'm going to take you to the best restaurant in Napa," Miles said.

Evan had a sudden, horrified thought that he knew exactly what Miles meant. "You're taking me to Terroir."

Miles blushed. "I did say the best restaurant in Napa."

"I'm not sure your ego is going to fit through the doorway," Evan teased. It was easier to poke fun than to face what Miles was trying to do.

He couldn't think about it without his hand trembling, so he reached over and gripped Miles' hand hard.

"You're gonna love it," Miles promised, eyes soft, like he knew exactly what had Evan reaching for him like a lifeline.

It would have been so natural for Evan to just say back, "I love *you*," because he was pretty damn sure he did. Miles had hardly made a secret of his own feelings, but they still felt so inexplicable to Evan.

Evan kissed him instead, hard and hot, both a promise for later and as a replacement for everything he couldn't say. *Yet*, he swore to himself, but even Evan didn't have a clue when he'd be able to.

If Evan had imagined that they might be treated any differently because Miles had worked at Terroir, he was incredibly wrong.

From what he could see, the same excruciatingly perfect service was given to every guest as they checked in at the gracious patio that served as the open-air waiting room. Vines dripping with grapes wrapped around the wood beams, arcing over their heads as they waited for their table to be ready.

"Would you like a glass of wine?" Miles asked.

If going to wine tastings had been intimidating, it was nothing compared to standing at the entrance to the throne room of American dining. Did he want a glass of wine? Evan thought he *needed* one if he was going to make it through without breaking into a sweat or declaring loudly that he wasn't worthy.

"Sure," Evan said.

Miles was only at the bar for a second, and of course, he got the best service, because the bartender's eyes lit up when they spotted him. He returned with two flutes of sparkling wine.

"Cheers," he said, tapping Evan's glass with his own. "To the best weekend I've ever spent."

"You mean, the part where we weren't being insulted by your old roommates?" Evan teased, enjoying the light that heated in Miles' eyes. He knew exactly which parts those were. Making love in the hotel room. Feeding each other bits of fresh bread in the meadow this morning, making out in the grass and not feeling the tiniest bit ashamed if anyone saw.

"I mean the part where I got to meet the relaxed you," Miles said.

Evan froze. How could he have forgotten Reed's admonishment as they left?

"Though," Miles continued thoughtfully, "I really like all the parts of you. Even the part that shoots daggers out of his eyes at me."

"You like that part?" Evan asked incredulously.

Miles' gaze took on a conspiratorial glint. "I love that part. It's sexy as hell knowing you want to kick my ass and that you will if I take a step out of line."

Something unwound in Evan at Miles' words. There had been a tiny kernel of doubt that had wondered if he would have to be on his best behavior from now on. If he would have to be the sweet, relaxed Evan all the time. Because there was no chance in hell of that happening.

"Don't worry," Miles said casually, "you know I love you."

Evan was torn between the eye-dagger-shooting thing or just dumping his champagne all over Miles' sharp black button-down, but then the designer-clad hostess approached, telling them their table was ready.

Their table wasn't on the patio, which from the reading Evan had done was considered a prime spot, but it was still near a huge bank of windows that overlooked the valley.

"I couldn't get the patio," Miles apologized after they sat down. "It was too late of notice. And even I don't have that sort of power."

"I'm impressed you got a table at all," Evan said. He wasn't disappointed they weren't on the patio. How could he be when he was here at all? The most any of his pseudo-dates had ever done was bring over Chinese or pizza before a hookup.

Miles had brought him to Terroir. The place he'd once described as the finest restaurant in America. The only Michelin-starred restaurant in California.

"Can you blame me for trying to impress you?" Miles said, reaching over and brushing his hand over Evan's knuckles.

Evan hid behind the menu, most of which was incomprehensible to him. He didn't know what half the words meant, and he didn't think he could really get away with googling them on his phone.

"Uh, yes," Evan said. "I was impressed by you before we even met."

"But then I made a shitty impression," Miles grinned charmingly, "so I'm just making up for lost time."

"Well, if that's the way you're going to play it, then figure out what I should be trying," Evan said, smiling back and feeling lighter than he had in forever. Maybe ever.

This must be what relaxing felt like. Or maybe it was love. It was fabulous either way, and he felt as light as the bubbles in his champagne flute. If anyone, especially Xander, tried to take this away from him, they were going to find out just how hardcore Evan Patterson could be.

"Yes, sir," Miles said smartly, and Evan couldn't help it, he burst into laughter.

Suddenly he was very sure it was going to be one of the greatest meals of his life, and that had nothing to do with the food.

❧❧❧❧❧ ❧❧❧❧❧

Evan was really damn sure it wasn't just the food when Bastian Aquino showed up at the table between the main course and dessert.

"Miles Costa," Chef Aquino said, a self-satisfied edge to his voice, like he'd believed that Miles really couldn't stay away and that belief was now justified.

He was a powerful man, with short dark hair just beginning to silver at the edges, intensely dark eyes, and a pair of serious biceps bulging under his immaculate black chef's jacket.

Evan was struck a little dumb. It wasn't his finest moment, but pictures didn't do Bastian Aquino justice. He looked like he could snap his neck just as easily as he could a chicken's. Evan swallowed hard when Aquino turned his attention to Miles' dining companion.

Him.

"You're the individual who lured Miles away from my kitchen with promises he'd be famous," Aquino said, a crease forming between his brows.

Evan decided he might as well own it; if Aquino killed him in the middle of his restaurant, then at least he'd die a happy man. "Yes, I did."

Miles blustered across from him, a frown on his face. "That's not exactly true," he said.

Evan smiled. "Maybe next season when Miles is on the Cooking Channel, we can invite you to guest star with him."

Aquino clearly didn't like that at all. "Food doesn't need fame," he said. "Was the food up to the standard?" he questioned, directing it to Miles.

Evan supposed he should be a little offended, but then Miles was the professional between them. What would Evan know, besides that everything had been delectable and incredible?

"Your lamb was a little overcooked," Miles said, laughing. Evan thought that if Aquino killed both of them, Miles would go out happy too. A month ago, that might not have meant much to Evan, but it meant everything tonight.

Bastian Aquino practically growled. "I forgot, you're just a pastry chef." Then he smiled, and it was like the sunrise over the desert. Evan was surprised at how handsome he was when he wasn't wordlessly threatening people's lives.

"Dessert is still to come," Miles said with a lot of satisfaction. "Tell René that he'd better send his best."

Aquino gave a sharp nod. He turned to Evan. "He is happy. Thank you for giving him what he needed."

When Bastian Aquino left, just as abruptly as he'd arrived, Miles giggled. It might have more to do with the thrill of love than the wine they'd drunk tonight or even the fantastic food—no matter what Miles said about the lamb.

"What exactly is it you're giving me that I need?" Miles asked with a quiet snort, probably thinking Evan was going to say something dirty and inappropriate. And ninety-nine percent of the time, Evan probably would have. It wasn't like his wall was coming down; instead, it felt like he was welcoming Miles inside.

Evan hoped the truth of it was in his eyes when he replied, "Everything I can."

Later that night, lying in bed with Evan drowsing against his chest, the TV turned on low, a text came through on his phone.

Leaning over, he must have shifted Evan too much when he reached over to grab it, because he made a sleepy, annoyed noise.

"Sorry," Miles said. "It's Gina."

"Gina?" Evan asked, and Miles felt like a shitty brother, or maybe just a shitty person. How had he not texted her lately? How had he not told Evan about Gina?

"Gina is my younger sister," he said. "We're close. Well, we used to be, I mean we still are, she's just in her freshman year of college in Berkeley and we've both been a little busy."

Evan propped himself up on an elbow, hair mussed, eyes glowing in the dim light of the room. He stopped Miles' heart, because only in his wildest dreams had he imagined he'd get to see the other man like this.

"Is she okay?" he asked.

Miles didn't know what had given it away. The late hour, maybe? Or his own worried expression?

The text had said: **You're in Napa and no text?**

Miles had felt guilty enough that he hadn't told Evan about Gina; now he was feeling doubly guilty.

A second text came in before Miles could even reply to the first. **If I keep guilt-tripping you, will you let me meet him? Brunch. Noon.**

"Xander," Miles growled. He was *really* regretting introducing Gina to Xander. There was always another shoe to drop with him. He'd assumed things were good between them after their conversation today, but then he'd gone and texted Gina and told her all about Evan.

"What did he do now?" Evan didn't seem particularly concerned, which was good, because he had nothing to be jealous of.

"Interfered," Miles said reluctantly. Was he ready for Gina to meet Evan? Was *Evan* ready to meet Gina?

"Isn't that what he's best at?" Evan wondered.

"My sister wants us to stop by Berkeley so she can meet you tomorrow," Miles said. "I'm guessing she got a whole series of texts from Xander after he got off work."

Evan's arm was still across Miles' bare chest, so he couldn't help but feel him tense.

"Is that okay?" Miles asked gently. It seemed so unfair that he could have this whole incredible, infuriating, *real* relationship with his sister, and Evan had nobody.

"Are you asking if I'm ready to meet your sister or if I'm okay that I don't have a sister?" Evan questioned.

Miles flushed. It was a good thing that they'd both been lowering their shields, but he hadn't realized he was so easy for Evan to read.

"It's okay," Evan continued with a little smile. "Lots of people don't have sisters, I just happened to be one of them. I'd love to meet her, if you're good with it."

They'd acknowledged to each other and to several others that they were dating now, but it was definitely something more for Evan to meet his family. Miles' heart had made the commitment already, there was no going back from that, but now he had to make sure his head was on the same page.

"I'm good with it," he decided. As if there had been any other decision he could make. Evan would torture him slowly and Gina would help Evan finish him off.

He was in this now, and the truth was, he *wanted* to be.

"Then I guess we're going to lunch with your sister," Evan said. He seemed calm enough. "I'm glad I brought another bow tie."

"Someday," Miles said, cradling him in his arms, and then suddenly rolling him underneath his body, hovering above him. He let his hips drop, flush and hard, against Evan's. "I'm going to tie you up with those fucking bow ties."

Evan's gaze was bright and challenging. Miles couldn't get enough of it. "I'd love to see you try," he said.

And how was Miles supposed to ignore a dare like that?

⁕⁕⁕⁕⁕⁕ ⁕⁕⁕⁕⁕⁕

Evan didn't think he was nervous—at least not precisely nervous. Apprehensive was probably the better term. It wasn't like he could do research to help him feel more comfortable; Gina was a person, not a location or a task or an activity. Any research he did should be restricted to brunch, conducted by actually *talking to* her.

He'd never had to go to brunch with a sibling of a boyfriend before. He wasn't sure he'd ever really had a boyfriend before, definitely not in the sense that he and the other guy had actually agreed that's what they were. He'd had half-assed relationships, he guessed, if that was what it meant when you drifted together, spent time together, slept together sometimes, and eventually drifted apart.

But nobody had ever wanted him to meet their family before. And it wasn't like Evan had any family for them to meet. None of the handful of guys in college had even known he was a foster kid; it definitely wasn't something he'd ever talked about.

But Miles knew, and he didn't care. It certainly seemed like he more worried about Evan's feelings than if Gina approved.

"She's going to love you," Miles said as they pulled into the restaurant parking lot. His smile was sweet and reassuring.

"I'm not worried about that. People usually like me." Evan shot Miles a coolly sardonic look. "You're the only one who didn't, and that turned out okay."

Miles laughed. "I did too like you."

"You had a very strange way of showing it," Evan retorted as they got out of the car.

Miles caught Evan's arm as they walked towards the entrance. "You should . . . um . . . definitely stay quiet about that part of it," he murmured. "Especially to Gina."

Evan might not have had any blood-related siblings, but he knew exactly how this worked. "So she can't give you any shit about it, right?" He grinned. "I don't think so."

"You're so cruel," Miles groaned in exaggeration. "I'm not sure this was a good idea."

But then a high-pitched voice yelped Miles' name, and Evan had the luck to see Miles' face the moment a tall, slender girl with long, curly dark hair piled on top of her head, came into view.

Evan had already figured out that Gina meant a lot to Miles, but seeing the joy on his face, then watching them wrap each other up in a tight, prolonged hug, made it crystal clear.

The first thing Gina did when Miles released her was turn towards Evan.

"Hello," she said in a friendly, conspiring voice. "You must be Evan." She extended a hand and Evan shook it immediately. She turned to her brother. "You didn't tell me how *cute* he is!"

Miles flushed, and Evan was greatly amused at his discomfort. "But," Gina continued with a quick, clever grin, "I shouldn't be surprised at all. I know what this one is like. But you, you I'm definitely looking forward to getting to know better."

Gina tucked her arm in his without prompting, and the stacked turquoise bracelets on her arm rattled.

"I'm hoping so," Evan said, and to his own complete surprise, he really meant it.

Miles threw his hands up in the air and made noises about going to get them a table.

"First, you need to tell me if he ever apologized to you," Gina said.

Evan was more than a little shocked that she knew so much. "No. Yes. Not exactly precisely when he should have."

Gina's expression was grave, belying the flushed excitement on her cheeks. "He's sort of an oblivious asshole, sometimes. But I guess I don't need to tell you that."

Evan laughed. "No, no, you don't. I know what I'm getting with him."

"Good." She leaned closer, bracelets clanking again. "Xander told me he took you to Terroir last night. Was it amazing?"

"It was terrifying, intimidating and incredible," Evan said.

"Miles tried to take me there once and I told him, over his dead body," Gina said. "I'm much more comfortable grabbing a burger."

"Don't worry," Miles said dryly, "I'm sure you can get a burger here."

"It's breakfast, Miles," Gina replied, all deadpan voice and sparkling eyes, "that means bacon and eggs and something sinful, like a cinnamon roll or a Danish as big as my head."

Miles ruffled her hair affectionately. "I'll have to send you a box of goodies. We've got tons of extras in my freezer. Some of them actually edible."

"Don't believe him," Evan inserted. "All of the ones he saved are definitely edible. More than."

"Oh, I like you," Gina said. "A lot, I think. You're going to be *great* for him."

Evan looked steadily over at Miles, who was still beaming at his sister. "I'm sure as hell going to try."

Reaching over, Gina squeezed his hand. "I wouldn't expect anything less."

Evan was sort of glad when this was the moment the hostess called Miles' name to let them know their table was ready. He was a little mistier in the eyes than he felt comfortable being, especially with someone he didn't know, even if that someone was Miles' sister.

❧ ❧

"And I'll have the pineapple upside down pancakes," Evan said to the waitress who was taking their order. "And a side of bacon. Extra crispy, please."

"I'll have all this right out," the waitress said, stuffing her pad back in her apron, and moving on to the next table.

Evan only knew something was wrong by the strangled, stifled noise Miles made.

It hit him all at once. So long, being so careful, so cautious, never visibly enjoying any of the cookies he'd been making, or the *macarons*, or even the incredible dessert last night at Terroir.

No, all it took to screw him up was Gina beaming at him like an idiot, casually accepting, like he was going to be around for a long time. Like he was going to be a member of their family.

Miles made the sound again.

"What's wrong with him?" Gina asked, taking a sip of coffee.

"I think he just discovered that I like sweets," Evan said evenly.

Gina looked confused. Miles looked murderous.

"Explain," Gina said, looking rapidly more interested by the second.

But before Evan could open his mouth, Miles had cut in. And he sounded pretty pissed, but not cruel, or cold, or truly angry, which was better than Evan could have hoped for. After all, there had only been a limited amount of time he could keep this secret while dating an extremely talented pastry chef.

"The second day Evan and I worked together, he told me that he did not like sweet things. No desserts. No cookies. No pastries. Nothing. And he," Miles said, mouth twitching, like it was difficult for him to keep a straight, annoyed face, "kept up this charade until this moment."

"I was a little distracted today," Evan added, by way of explanation.

"You didn't even break over the dessert course last night at Terroir," Miles said incredulously. And that *had* been difficult, but truthfully, the toughest times had always been whenever he was eating something that Miles had made. There was something about taking what Miles had made with his own two hands and then putting it into his mouth that always made the taste even more exquisite.

Even the batches of peanut butter chocolate chunk cookies that hadn't quite turned out had nearly made Evan moan once or twice.

"You were right," was all Evan said. "They should have used thyme, not rosemary, in the white chocolate lemon mousse pyramids. But you *were* right about the gold; they certainly looked impressive enough."

Gina was giggling so hard she nearly choked.

"You guys . . . you are . . . *perfect* . . . for each other," she managed to get out in between hysterical chuckles.

"You're not mad?" Evan asked, lifting an eyebrow.

Miles just shrugged. "If I remember correctly, that was the morning after I filmed myself baking Ding Dongs. Anything you said that day is just payback for the video. Besides," he lowered his voice, "I definitely plan to get you back, at the soonest possible opportunity."

"Gross," Gina exclaimed, but she was smiling so big, her smile took over her face. And Evan couldn't help but smile right along with her.

Chapter Sixteen

As shitty as leaving LA had been, it was worse going back.

It was like the fury of a rainstorm after the weatherman warned you to bring your umbrella. Expected, completely inevitable, and very shitty.

"I can't believe you're not worried," Evan said to Miles as they walked into the lobby of *Five Points*. They weren't holding hands, but Miles liked to think just about everyone could see the growing attachment between them.

"It's pointless," Miles said. "Has anyone ever convinced Reed Ryan to do something he doesn't want to do?" Besides—and he wasn't quite ready for Evan to find out about this yet—he'd played the last card he could think of, and if that didn't work, maybe it was right for *Pastry by Miles* to die off.

"When I was really lonely last year, sometimes I pictured Jordan doing lots of stuff he didn't want . . . at least initially," Evan said.

Miles burst out laughing. "Of course you did."

"Have you seen them?" Evan demanded, laughing with Miles. "I mean, that's a lot of hotness to contain in one relationship."

Of course, that was the moment they ran into Reed, in the corridor outside their adjoining cubicles.

He raised an eyebrow. Reed was one of those men who could say a speech and never open his mouth. He definitely looked like he was talking now, even though he hadn't said a single word.

"Who's a lot of hotness to contain in one relationship?"

Miles thought Evan was pretty damn brave, but it seemed telling his maybe soon-to-be ex-boss he'd fantasized about him and his boyfriend was where he drew the line. If that was the case, then Evan was even smarter than he'd imagined.

"Miles and me," Evan said, chin jutting out, like he was half-expecting his boss to disapprove.

But Reed's frown rearranged into a big smile. "Then the long weekend was good for you," he said. His eyes took on a darker, amused glint. "You certainly seem more relaxed, Evan."

"We're working on it," Miles inserted, because he could see this conversation going all sorts of inappropriate places. And Evan, who had seemed so formal and wedded to professionalism when they'd first met, could be shockingly dirty when he was in a good mood. And thanks to Miles, he was definitely in a very good mood.

"I'm glad to hear it," Reed said, sounding genuinely pleased. Miles found himself praying to whatever god was looking down on them that maybe that was enough to save *Pastry by Miles* and Evan's job. They could manage if Miles at least saved his show, and Evan saved his job. They had each other. Miles felt certain of that, even if the rest of the world felt unpleasantly uncertain right now.

"Miles," Reed said, turning to him, thoughtful look on his face. "Come see me after you get settled in. I think we need to talk."

The moment Reed was out of earshot, Evan shoved Miles into his cubicle, excitement and terror warring on his face. "Is this it?" he whisper-yelled. Which, for Evan, was mostly yelling and very little whispering. "Is he going to cancel your contract?"

Miles had a very good idea what Reed wanted to talk about, and it was only tangential to his contract. "No clue," he said. He didn't like lying to Evan, even if it was a lie of omission, but he wasn't entirely sure Evan would be happy about this development. Even if it meant his job was saved.

Evan was one of those sticklers who he imagined might care more about how his job was saved, not just that it had been saved. Miles really hoped that he was wrong in this scenario, but they were still getting to know each other, now that Evan had actually started to let him in.

Reed was leaning back in his big leather chair when Miles walked in.

"Close the door," Reed said, and he still sounded thoughtful but not angry. Not angry was good.

Miles shut the door, sure that Evan had just gone into a paroxysm of curiosity and tension as he hid around the corner, desperately hoping that he'd be able to overhear their conversation.

Reed knew Evan better than he realized.

"You sent me this video," Reed said, rotating his gigantic monitor so Miles could see the screen. Not that Miles needed to; he knew exactly which video Reed was talking about.

"I thought you might want to see that our rehearsals provided some great footage," Miles said.

Reed chuckled. "You making a Ding Dong *was* solid gold footage. But," and he paused, that thoughtful look returning, "I don't think you made this during rehearsals. And not with Evan."

It had been a long shot for Miles to convince Reed that they had made this video together. It was funny and clever and a little subversive, which was everything that Miles was, and everything Evan mostly wasn't. At least the side of Evan that he tended to present at work. Miles had discovered in the last few days that he could definitely unbend if he wanted, if his mood was right, and he was surrounded by people he trusted.

But Reed probably didn't know that.

Reed frowned. And Miles realized that he *didn't* know that. Evan had never trusted Reed—his beloved boss, the person Miles might have guessed he was closest to in his whole life—enough to show that side of himself. He'd trusted only Miles. That revelation only made Miles more determined to convince Reed that they'd made this clip together.

"Evan was there. We made it together," he said. He'd heard once that the most effective lies were the simplest. He didn't know if that was even true, but he was willing to give just about anything a shot at this point.

Reed made a frustrated sound, but he still didn't look angry. "I know you're not telling me the truth." He hesitated. "The question is why. Are you worried I'm going to tear up your contract? Are you worried I'm going to send you back to Napa?"

"No," Miles said, and realized, belatedly, that he meant it. Suddenly the worst thing wasn't that *Pastry by Miles* might end, or that he'd be forced to beg for his old job back.

He'd known he loved Evan, he just hadn't realized how incredibly necessary he was to his life. It wasn't a great time to have this realization, but it certainly provided him a hell of a lot of motivation to pull this off.

"Then what is it?" Reed demanded. A meaty fist landed on the solid wood desk with a heavy thump. Reed's cooking had always been considered bold, bombastic and straightforward. Sort of like the man. Miles just hadn't seen a lot of evidence of it until now.

"Of course I don't want to get fired. Of course I want to convince you to green light a season of *Pastry by Miles*. Of course I want you to keep the team intact."

"I know you're trying to save him," Reed said. "And you're not alone in that. I've been trying to help him since I first met him, years ago. He's come a long way from that skinny, terrified, overly proud college kid. But that doesn't mean he's right for this show."

"I do love him. But that isn't why I'm doing this. I'm doing this because he's the best fit for the show. For me."

"What if I told you that it was either the show or him?" Reed asked, and that thoughtful look that had reassured Miles at first now only terrified him. He didn't know what it meant, and the unknown could be a bad place.

"Then I'd say it was an honor to meet you, I'd pack up my cubicle and I'd drive back to Napa today," Miles said.

"You really would," Reed observed, clearly a little mystified.

"I won't do this without Evan. Period."

"What if I promised he wasn't fired, that he'd be reassigned to a different department? Would that make a difference?" Reed asked.

Miles wiped his sweaty, trembling hands on his jeans. "No."

Reed tilted his head, intense eyes cataloging Miles minutely. Then, suddenly he nodded sharply. "Okay, then. Go get Evan. He's probably loitering in the break room, hoping that he can hear some of this conversation. It doesn't feel fair to leave him out of it."

Sure enough, Evan was there, pacing with a cup of coffee in his hand. "What's going on?" he hissed.

"Reed wants to talk to both of us," Miles said, and gestured towards Reed's office. "Let's go."

This time Reed didn't ask him to close the door.

"Here's your official shooting schedule," Reed said, almost before their butts were in chairs. He slid a piece of paper across the desk. "But only if you promise me the Ding Dong video stays. It's too funny to cut."

Miles could feel Evan's happy confusion radiating out of him, even as he said all the right things: about how they wouldn't let him down, about how they'd commit themselves to making the best show possible, how happy he was that Reed had reconsidered.

It was inevitable that as soon as Reed dismissed them, Evan would drag him into the break room. It was probably inevitable that Reed had popped his head out of his office and was listening to the whole conversation. It was definitely inevitable that the entire office had tuned in and was listening to their conversation.

"What is Reed talking about, Miles?" Evan demanded. "Did you really send him that stupid Ding Dong video?"

"Yes," Miles said. It was hard to meet Evan's disbelieving eyes, but he did it. He'd sent it; he had to own up to it. "I told him that we'd recorded it during rehearsals last week. He needed to know that we could do this. Together."

"You lied," Evan stated, and started to pace again.

"Technically," Miles said. "But I know we can produce content like this together. High production value, that's what you bring to the table. And I can bring the creative flair. I know everything we've done for *Pastry by Miles* has been a hot mess so far, but all each disaster has convinced me of is that we're meant to do this together. I don't *want* to do it without you."

"You sent it to Reed without telling me," Evan said, whirling around, voice and face unbearably hard. Miles could sense the wall going back up, and he wanted to beg, to plead, to fall to his knees. But with Evan, those things would fall on deaf ears. That much he'd discovered about the man in front of him.

"I saved the show. I saved your job. I saved our future, working together. Why are you mad?" Miles asked in exasperation. "Because I didn't tell you ahead of time? Because I lied to your precious Reed? Don't worry, he knows I lied. He knows and he doesn't care."

"I'm mad because you felt you needed to charge in to save me. I can save myself. I don't need your help with that," Evan said coldly.

"That's what people in love do," Miles said, leashing in his temper as close as possible. He needed Evan to realize what he'd been trying to do, not escalate this argument until both of them were so mad neither of them were listening. That was the mistake he'd always made before. He wasn't going to do it again.

Evan looked incredulous.

Miles retrenched and tried to explain again. "I want to be by your side for a long time. Long enough that there's going to be times when I need you. And times you need me. Nobody can be strong and perfect all the time. This time, maybe I helped you. Next time, I'm gonna expect you to be there for me. Hell, that's something you've already done. I sent that incredibly stupid drunk email, and you didn't instantly forward it to Reed. You had my back. The way I had yours today."

"Reed might have fired you for lying to him," Evan said.

"He might have. I was willing to take that risk."

"Why?" Evan asked, even though he had to know why. Reed had instantly known why.

"Because I love you," Miles said, rolling his eyes. "And you know that's why I did it. You know I love you. And you love me too."

"I . . . I . . . I don't know about that," Evan said, sounding unsure for the first time since he'd dragged Miles into the break room.

"Bullshit. You love me, and I love you." Miles reached and pulled Evan to him. The tension in his body cut like a cord, dissipating almost instantly.

"I might love you a little," Evan admitted into Miles' shoulder.

"What? What was that again?" Miles said loudly, teasingly.

Evan's head lifted from his shoulder, looking at him straight on. "I love you, you jerk." And he kissed him.

EPILOGUE

"Today, we're going to be making one of my favorite things," Miles said, leaning on the counter, staring at the camera like they were best friends and not a man and a machine, "a dong."

There was a ripple of laughter through the assembled staff. Wyatt Blake found himself joining in even though the line wasn't new to him. It might have been Miles' delivery or it might have been who he was delivering it to—regardless, the opening line was just as funny and just as effective as it had been the first time Wyatt had heard it.

Evan leaned against the end of the counter, hip popped, white shirt immaculate, bow tie flawlessly tied. He grimaced comically at his boyfriend's words, and Wyatt would never have guessed that this whole exchange was scripted, except that he'd seen it developed and then rehearsed.

"A *Ding* Dong," Evan corrected crisply. "It's a pastry, which is something I would guess you know about. A chocolate cake to be precise, filled with cream. Don't tell me you need *me* to educate you about a dessert."

Miles raised an eyebrow at the last part, and another round of laughter circulated through the crowd.

"You like cream-filled desserts, huh?" Miles asked Evan, who rolled his eyes.

"Bake, you idiot," Evan retorted. There was a thread of annoyance in his tone, and the ever-present eye rolls, but he still looked enamored. Probably because he was. Wyatt might have doubted it—couldn't help but doubt after what the two of them had done to each other—but he couldn't anymore. Not after Miles insisted he come to the first few days of filming for moral support, and Wyatt had seen firsthand how much they cared about each other.

Wyatt was still surprised that Miles had asked him and not Xander, but then he'd been so angry lately, he probably would have been shitty moral support. And Bastian Aquino never would have given Kian the day off.

That was probably why Miles had sent him a ticket and asked—more like pleaded—for Wyatt to fly down to LA. Wyatt had been happy to do it, because Miles was a friend, and selfishly because Wyatt needed a break of his own.

Miles followed Evan's command, with a single amused glance shot over to the other side of the kitchen, and started to assemble the dry ingredients for the chocolate cake portion of the recipe. The original concept of *Pastry by Miles* had always been Miles baking, and Miles still did bake, but now he was also peppered with questions by his producer, who instead of standing behind the camera, stood in front of it.

The concept was new and fresh and it worked like gangbusters. Miles had told Wyatt that they'd initially come up with the idea in a meeting where Reed Ryan had slammed his hand down on the table, interrupting one of Miles and Evan's many debates, and said, "You're going to think I'm crazy, but you have to film this. You two are *insane*."

It definitely wasn't like other cooking shows, but it also worked.

Because Miles was Miles, and he could sift flour in his sleep, he kept talking.

"Right now we're sifting because we don't want lumps in our dry ingredients. Or stuff that doesn't belong."

Evan was still watching, eyes narrowed, from the other end of the counter. He had a bunch of papers spread out in front of him, and it was clear he was still in charge of the episode. He was just doing it in full view of the camera, as ballsy as he'd ever been.

"I don't believe you've ever actually *found* something that didn't belong in the flour," Evan drawled. Wyatt didn't remember this particular dialogue, but Miles didn't miss a beat.

"Sand, grit, a marble, I think I even found a condom once," Miles said, flashing a charming smile to the camera, like *can you believe this guy?* "Don't worry though, it wasn't used."

"I'd be a lot more worried if you were finding used condoms in your flour," Evan said.

"Jealous?" The smile Miles shot down the length of the counter could have impregnated anyone within a few paces, regardless of gender.

Evan just laughed. "Of the guys who stuck their condoms in your flour, hoping to get your attention? No. Not even a little."

Wyatt realized with a bright, blinding flash why Miles hadn't invited Xander. How had he found out? Wyatt had been so certain that Miles hadn't realized Xander had that impossible crush.

But he must have, and that was why he hadn't invited Xander. On the other hand, Wyatt thought a little bitterly, he was safe because he didn't have a crush on anyone.

After the way his relationship with Nate had ended, Wyatt had been happy enough for awhile to stay unattached and single, but watching Miles and Evan flirt with each other would make anyone long for even a fraction of what they'd found together.

It wasn't just that he was sick of cleaning artichokes and prepping lamb chops and being held to a painfully exacting standard every second he was at work, he was bored and lonely. He'd thought that getting away for a few days and going down to LA to see Miles would help, but all being here did was throw into sharp focus what was missing in his own life.

"They're hilarious, aren't they?" Wyatt looked up, and Reed Ryan was standing there, grinning like a loon. Or like someone who'd just won the lottery. And he probably had, from an online cooking show perspective.

Miles had just begun to slowly whisk in the wet ingredients to the dry, and he was waggling his eyebrows, making more and more outrageous comments, aiming for some unknown reaction from Evan.

"It shouldn't work, but it does," Wyatt admitted.

"I knew they could work it out," Reed said. "I had a few dark moments. Once or twice I thought they might kill each other before working it out, but I was happy to be wrong about that."

Wyatt had no interest in such a combative relationship, but there was an invisible, undefinable thread between them, shining with love and respect and affection. It shouldn't hurt to see it, it should be something to admire, not something to be envious of, but Wyatt found he couldn't really help himself. Nate had been his only serious boyfriend, and they definitely hadn't had that.

"Now, I have the Cooking Channel sniffing around my set," Reed said, voice smug with satisfaction. "And the sort of buzz about our new show that I couldn't manufacture no matter what draw our marketing team comes up with."

Wyatt reminded himself firmly that he had come here to be a support to Miles, not to eat his heart out with jealousy over what he'd found, professionally and personally. He *wasn't* Xander.

"They're both very lucky," Wyatt said, and no matter how much he tried to regulate his voice, it still came out sadly wry.

Reed put a reassuring hand on his shoulder—Wyatt thought that next time he saw Xander, there was now something else he could lord over him—and said, "I know how talented you are. The possibilities are endless. Maybe it's time to leave the nest and explore them."

"With you?" Wyatt wondered if maybe this invite had also been a way to get him down to LA for a job interview. With Reed Ryan. Xander was going to *die*.

"Not necessarily," Reed said. "But I know about a few open positions in the area. I like to keep my ear to the ground. Would you be interested?"

Would he be interested? Wyatt didn't even know. All he knew was that he was suddenly and inexplicably sick of his own life. He was tired of trying to make ends meet, of struggling to keep his nana in the home, and having nothing left over for anything else. Sick of being told what to do.

"I'd be willing to listen," Wyatt said.

"Then we'll be in touch," Reed said, squeezing his shoulder again, then disappearing, merging into a group of people who all seemed to want to ask him a dozen questions.

Back on set, Miles was carefully pouring his cake batter into molds.

"Now," he said, "we can finally get onto the cream-filling part of the dessert."

"Your favorite part," Evan inserted.

Miles' expression turned hot and sweet. "Yeah, you don't enjoy it at all," he retorted, but his voice was so intimate it was impossible not to picture them pressed up together, instead of being separated by six feet of countertop.

"Cut," Alex, the director, called.

"What?" Miles asked, and Evan shot him a darker look.

"Dressing room," Evan said briskly, and Miles let himself be led off to their green room.

❧ ☙

"What did we talk about before I agreed to do this?" Evan asked as soon as the door was firmly closed behind them. It was bad enough they were airing out their personal shit for the world to see; he was not willing to do it with three-quarters of their co-workers listening in.

"That there was a line," Miles said, expression growing concerned. "Did I cross the line?"

Evan honestly wasn't sure if Miles had crossed the line or if he'd crossed it on his own, but suddenly, he'd felt hot and cold all over, freaked out by how public this all was. Their relationship, and how they'd learned to make it work, completely exposed to everyone.

It was weird that throwing the doors open would make him feel closed-in, but it was happening anyway and he couldn't help it.

"I'm not sure. Maybe I did, without thinking. However it happened, it happened. I freaked out. And Alex must have noticed."

"You did have a weird expression on your face," Miles said. He reached out and pulled Evan close to him. Evan rested his head on Miles' shoulder. He shouldn't feel less exposed now, with Miles wrapped around him, but he inexplicably always did. "I'm sorry," he continued, his voice a warm murmur.

"This isn't easy for me," Evan murmured back. "I'm the one who's sorry for freaking out all the time."

"You didn't get into this expecting to be in front of the camera," Miles soothed, "I don't blame you for freaking out about it."

"But I agreed to it," Evan argued. "I agreed, and I knew exactly what I was agreeing to."

"You agreed because you were thinking with your producer hat," Miles said, a tiny bit amused.

"I knew it would be great TV," Evan admitted.

"You're amazing, you know," Miles whispered into his temple. "I love you so much. Even when you freak out. Especially when you freak out."

"At least you didn't come over and start kissing me," Evan said prosaically.

"I wanted to," Miles said.

Evan closed his eyes. "I wanted you to." He hesitated. "This is harder than I thought it would be."

"We can always stop," Miles insisted. "I told Reed this might not work out, and he's okay with whatever. You know that. You probably know that better than me."

"I don't mean . . . being in front of the camera is too hard. I mean not crossing the line is harder than I thought it would be. I look over at you, and I want to say what I would usually say, I want to do what I would usually do. And it sucks to hold back."

Miles' fingers flinched; Evan felt it through the cotton of his button-up, all the way to his skin. He shivered in response.

"How about you do whatever you feel comfortable with, and we'll just figure out the rest," Miles suggested.

Their relationship was so new, Evan was still figuring out how Miles knew the perfect thing to say to make him feel better.

"How do you do that?" Evan asked.

"Do what?" Miles ran a reassuring hand down Evan's back.

"Always say what I need to hear."

"I know you," Miles said seriously. "I love you. I expect the two are somewhat related."

Evan rolled his eyes, even though Miles couldn't see them. "I can't believe I didn't know right away what a sap you are. I love it. I love *you*."

"It's only you that brings it out," Miles admitted. "You know that."

"Thank you for being patient and you know . . . generally amazing," Evan said, waving a hand, shockingly unable to verbalize everything Miles was for him. Which did make sense because he'd discovered that love could be very difficult to pin down specifically.

"I told you once, we're going to be what each other needs. A strong relationship doesn't always have two strong people in it. I'm good taking my turn now, and you can take yours later." He paused. "Like during all the marketing and publicity."

Evan laughed damply. "I'll keep that in mind."

"You do that," Miles said, sounding very content, like he never wanted to move.

Someone rapped on the door. Evan was pretty sure it was Reed. "Time's up," the voice said. Yes, it was definitely Reed.

"You ready to go back?" Miles asked.

Evan knew they didn't have much of a choice, because he was both the producer and the star. He knew they had a strict schedule to keep. "As long as you're next to me. As long as we do this together."

"Always," Miles said.

Read **Catch Me**, the next *Kitchen Gods* book, about Wyatt, and his unexpected journey to love when he becomes a personal chef for out and proud baseball player Ryan Flores.

Want to listen to Evan & Miles' story on audio? Check it out here!

INTERESTED IN READING MORE OF
BETH'S BOOKS?

CHECK OUT A FULL LIST OF TILES
BY SCANNING THE QR CODE
OR VISITING HER WEBSITE

WWW.BETHBOLDEN.COM/BOOKLIST

WANT TO FOLLOW BETH?

MAKE SURE YOU NEVER
MISS A RELEASE?

SCAN THE QR CODE BELOW
OR VISIT HER WEBSITE
FOR A SOCIAL MEDIA LIST,
NEWSLETTER SIGNUP,
AND SO MUCH MORE!

WWW.BETHBOLDEN.COM/ABOUT